Sara Shepard

# Agatha Harkness

## Fall of the Coven

Random House New York

Random House Books for Young Readers
An imprint of Random House Children's Books
A division of Penguin Random House LLC
1745 Broadway, New York, NY 10019
penguinrandomhouse.com
rhcbooks.com/disney

MARVEL



Jacket art by Evangeline Gallagher
Jacket design by Emily Fisher and Kurt Hartman



Library of Congress Cataloging-in-Publication Data is available upon request.
ISBN 978-1-368-11469-1 (trade)—ISBN 978-0-7364-4788-1 (ebook)

The text of this book is set in Mrs Eaves/Emigre.

Manufactured in the United States of America
1st Printing

The authorized representative in the EU for product safety and compliance is Penguin Random House Ireland, Morrison Chambers, 32 Nassau Street, Dublin D02 YH68, Ireland, https://eu-contact.penguin.ie.

Random House Children's Books supports the First Amendment and celebrates the right to read.

To my Readers
Here's to finding your coven.
—Sara

## *Salem, Massachusetts*
## *October 1691*

This probably comes as no surprise, but October is a witch's favorite month of the year.

It's not just because of Halloween, either. Besides, in my time period, most people are kind of puritanical about Halloween—*literally*. I am living among Puritans, after all. Only a superstitious few leave carved turnips outside their homes to ward away bad spirits, and absolutely no one would dream of dressing up or making merry. No, it's more that October has a foreboding vibe *in general*. There are so many shadows for a witch to lurk and conspire in. Feet make such a satisfying *crunch* on the fallen leaves—like grinding your toes on dry bones. And the sound of the icy wind as it screams around every corner, rattles through the skeletal trees, and sends such a tingling chill down every spine on every silly little villager is so delightful. Who doesn't love watching people shudder?

So I've been trying to relish this October, too. Trying not to feel nostalgic about all the Octobers from my past. Some of them I remember quite clearly . . . others not so much. It's a side effect of living hundreds of years, in countless places, and amassing great depths of knowledge and power from dangerous underlords. You wouldn't get it.

But it's been hard to enjoy myself because where I'm living—Salem, in the New World, in the year 1691—leaves a lot to be desired. It's a better spot than others, I guess—less grim than when I traveled back to the foothills of Wundagore Mountain, and let's not even talk about when I got stuck in the past in the frigid Himalayas with Scrier and the Silver Surfer. But it's only *barely* better, and not by much.

And don't even get me started on my coven here. Thank goodness I'll be leaving them soon.

"Miss Harkness?"

I jerk to attention. Elizabeth Good, the coven's head witch, stands at the front of a half-moon of petrified logs in the middle of the forest just outside Salem. Elizabeth is a haggard fifty-five-year-old with the weathered, wrinkled skin of a hairless cat and a snarl of long gray hair that's the consistency of seaweed. I'm technically hundreds of years older than she is, but because of a powerful aging spell, I've kept my youthful looks. My dark hair is long and shiny, there aren't spiderwebs of wrinkles around my eyes, and my skin is as dewy and plump as a ripe peach. I even feel young emotionally. In fact, the only thing that's grown as I've aged is my powers. Technically, *I* should be the head witch here, but this coven doesn't work that way. Elizabeth has *seniority*—meaning what she says goes. Including attending coven meetings. *All* coven meetings. Even if a witch has more important things to do.

"I *said* are you paying attention, Miss Harkness?" Elizabeth calls.

The other members of the coven give me the side-eye. I'm sitting at the very back of the group—I've made it clear that I sit *alone*, no exceptions. (It doesn't help that a few of the witches have lice, and that's one type of bug I want nothing to do with.)

Then Martha Pennywell rises and points a finger like she's ready to cast me down to Hades.

"She hasn't been, Sister Elizabeth! She's been looking at the trees!"

"So now it's a crime to look at the trees?" I mutter.

Elizabeth sighs. "What we're discussing is very important, Agatha. I suggest you try to be part of things."

"I *was* listening," I protest. "I heard every word you said."

"Oh? Then what did she say?" Martha challenges in a singsong voice.

I groan. When I first came to Salem, arriving through a portal on a hunch that the relic I've been searching for was here, Martha wouldn't leave me alone. She showered me with questions about how I got into witchcraft, offered to show me how to make some of her specialty tinctures, and nosily demanded details about my upbringing. But because I'm me, I didn't take Martha's let's-be-friends bait. Friendly people and I don't generally mix. It wasn't like I could tell her about my past anyway.

Martha didn't take the rejection well, though. She went from all warmth and sunshine to looking for any way to throw me into a boiling cauldron.

I try to shift my toes inside my tight leather buckle shoes, but in 1691, shoemakers can't manage to make shoes that fit actual human feet. The truth is, I wasn't paying attention to Elizabeth's speech. Not a word. There's no way I'm going to give Martha the satisfaction of being right, though. So I close my eyes and quietly recite a short-term memory spell. Within moments, Elizabeth's words flutter through the air and dart straight into my ears. The whole conversation comes back to me in a rush.

I smile triumphantly. "Elizabeth was talking about the strange weather shifts. She was asking if anyone had an incantation to appease the gods and calm down the atmosphere, but so far, no one has any suggestions." *No kidding,* I think. Of course no one has a handy spell. None of these witches have any talent for actual magic.

The weather swings *are* concerning, though. Since I've arrived, Salem has had a brutally hot summer and a winter that started mid-September, killing off all the crops prematurely. There have been some bizarre short-term weather changes, too—heat waves turning to violent rainstorms turning to snow squalls in one twenty-four-hour period, tornadoes and hurricanes and walnut-size hail, which everyone thought was a curse from God. It's made everyone very jumpy—and this place is full of uptight people already. The townsfolk are also starting to give the members of my coven damning looks, like they think the weather shifts are our fault. Like perhaps we've been colluding with the devil.

"What else did Elizabeth say?" Martha quizzes me. "Because she brought up something *more.*"

I groan, consulting my spell again. Soon enough, I get the answer. "She also mentioned that Prudence hasn't been seen in a while." And then a lump forms in my throat. Wait. Prudence is missing? *Since when?*

Prudence Jones is thirteen years old. Her parents died of scarlet fever or some other dreadful colony disease last year, and then she ran away from her cruel relatives from another village, and *then* a wolf chased her but she got away in the nick of time. It's a wonder she didn't stumble upon an enchanted gingerbread house in the forest. Instead, she found our coven.

Prudence showed up at our little encampment and begged for us to take her in. She's small for her age and pale, too, like she's never seen the sun, and she wears her hair in two neat braids on the sides of her head. There's something so innocent about her, like she might burst into tears if you look at her the wrong way—which made it all the more curious that she wanted to commune with witches. Probably for this same reason, most of the coven didn't want her to stay, but she was stubborn and wouldn't leave. In exchange, they make her do their most hated chores—fetching water from the stream, cleaning up after our animals, and collecting money from the townspeople for the tinctures we sometimes sell. I was the only one who didn't force her into indentured servitude. I may not be a nice person, but I'm not going to make someone else do my dirty work, especially not a kid. I guess because of that, though, Prudence deemed me "the friendly one."

Which is completely laughable. And also a first.

Now Elizabeth clears her throat. "Well, Agatha, some money from our coven's collective coffers is missing. We suspect Prudence may have stolen it when she left. So when did you last see her, exactly?"

I think back. "Three, four days ago?" Prudence had brought me a wounded rat she'd found on the path, blubbering about how it was suffering. I just wanted her to stop crying—histrionics always set my teeth on edge—so I taught her a teeny, tiny little spell that would heal the creature's broken leg.

Prudence was *thrilled*, naturally, which goes to show you how much real magic is actually practiced in this coven. (Hint: zero.) But then she said I shouldn't be keeping this talent to myself—I should show everyone how to heal living creatures. I caught her arm and said we couldn't tell *anyone*—not even the other witches.

But I didn't see her after that, come to think of it.

"I heard she was spotted in the village," another witch, named Sarah, says, breaking me from my thoughts. "She has a friend there, Betty Parris. I've inquired with her family, but they swear they haven't seen her."

"Well, we need to recover that money," Elizabeth says sternly. "Perhaps we ask around again."

"Prudence didn't steal any money," I blurt out. "It must have been someone else."

Elizabeth narrows her eyes. "What makes you say that?"

Intuition? Common sense? Prudence doesn't *care*

about money. She doesn't want to leave this coven and strike out on her own. These other coven witches, though—I could see any of them as the thief. I don't trust a single one.

On the other hand, I really, *really* hope that Prudence didn't do something as foolish as show Betty Parris how to heal animals with magic. See, I've been keeping an eye on Betty's family anyway, since I received information that the relic I had been searching for used to be hidden in their cellar; the Parrises are the quintessential intolerant, hysterical, devil-fearing Puritans everyone dreads. Not long ago, I overheard Mr. Parris saying that women should be locked up for laughing. Mrs. Parris fainted at the sight of another woman's bare ankle. If the Parris family saw Prudence use real magic to fix one of their horses' sore hooves or one of their chickens' broken toes, they'd think she was Beelzebub.

Suddenly, I feel a burst of clairvoyance . . . and a pull of dread. "Betty's family lied about not knowing where Prudence is, actually. They *do* know. They're doing something bad to her."

The rest of the coven falls silent. I can feel them staring at me in the darkness. Elizabeth sighs. "Now, now. I've lived in this village much longer than you, Agatha. We keep our distance from the townspeople, and they keep their distance from us. It's always been that way, and it's been peaceful. Let's not make trouble."

Here's the thing about the witches in this coven: They practice basic witchcraft, yes, like fortune-telling, tincture-making, and a few healing spells. They're outcasts in the community, yes. But they don't have powers like I do. They're nothing like I am, actually. They don't even know the significance of *who* I am, which is why I was able to go by my true identity here instead of going by another name, like I sometimes have in other times, places, and dimensions. But because they don't have powers, they also don't have any foresight—in other words, Elizabeth Good can't even see the warty nose plain on her face. Prudence practicing magic around Betty Parris and her God-fearing parents could be the straw that breaks the camel's back in this town. Elizabeth might have lived in Salem longer than I have, but I've endured way more people suspicious of witches.

So I win.

"But I'm certain of it," I say emphatically. "That family wants nothing to do with anyone who doesn't think exactly the way they do. Prudence is in danger."

Martha snorts. "You barely participate in the coven's fellowship, and all of a sudden you're issuing warnings and expecting us to believe you?" Then she focuses her beady little eyes on me. "Why are you defending Prudence? And why are you so certain she didn't take the money? Did *you* take it?"

I squeeze my eyes shut. *"No."*

"Are you lying?" Martha sounds excited. "You're hiding something. You have a secret."

I grit my teeth. "I do not."

But I *do* have a secret. A big one. Something I found in the Parris home just this morning, as a matter of fact. But it's not like the coven can know.

I picture creeping down to the Parris cellar. It was challenging to sneak into the house—I did so only when the entire family was at church. Once there, I followed the instructions about where my sources foretold the relic would be. *It's in the form of a bat*, my sources said. *Do not be fooled.*

And sure enough, there was a bat in the cellar sleeping upside down in the rafters. It put up quite a fight when I woke it, but I prevailed—and now I've stashed it in a locked box so it can't escape. To anyone else, it looks like an ordinary, if slightly grotesque, nocturnal creature, but it's not an *actual* bat at all. Its wings and fangs are just a diversion. No one in her right mind is going to handle a bat for fear of getting bitten—unless, of course, she knows what the bat unlocks when enchanted back into its original form.

And what is that? *The Darkhold*. The most powerful book of spells in the world, a book I've craved all my life. Call me curious. Call me power-hungry. Call me confident that I'm the only person who'd know how to *handle* the

Darkhold. It's not like I'm one of those sketchy witches out there who might be more than happy to destroy the universe. I intend to use it wisely—judiciously—without losing my head. I'd use it to protect witches, not tear them apart. And, okay, I'd get to learn a lot of incredible spells that could let me do, well, *anything*.

But I thought it was lost to the ages. I've been searching for the Darkhold for centuries, popping into this country and that era, this planet and that dimension, knowing it's out there but never quite tracking it down, the need inside me to find it as involuntary as hunger or thirst. Searching is what I've been doing instead of keeping tabs on Prudence, actually—but that's not fair. It isn't my *job* to look after Prudence. And what was I going to do, bring her on my search? That could have put her in danger.

Only, what if she's in *worse* danger now? I try to intuit where the Parrises could be hiding her. Not their cellar—I was just there. I would have heard her cry out. Somewhere else, then?

It certainly doesn't seem like the coven particularly cares. I guess I'll have to look for Prudence on my own. It will be my one last task before leaving this place, I figure.

A mouse skitters across my shoe, and I gently nudge it away. Elizabeth's attention has moved on to something else; she's talking now about gathering more herbs in the woods for tinctures and supplies. I zone out again, daydreaming of the moment I can return to the enchanted Darkhold—the only reason I came to this meeting, besides the fact that Elizabeth mandates it, is because if I didn't, I feared the coven would be suspicious about my actions. But once I transform the bat back to its book form, I'll be able to use its spells to enhance my magic tenfold. Finally, I'll be the most powerful witch in the world.

But then I look up. Something is off. It takes me a moment to realize what: The log in front of me is missing a witch. Where has Martha gone all of a sudden?

I survey the line of cloaked bodies, short and tall and thin and wide, many with cats winding around their ankles. The moonlight is just bright enough to make out their faces; they're all staring at Elizabeth reverently, a few sipping tea, a few clacking their knitting needles, one of them shuffling a deck of cards. Martha isn't among them.

A sour feeling wells in my gut. I think of how Martha was staring at me. Accusing me of keeping secrets. And then I spring up from the log, grabbing the lantern by my side.

"Agatha?" Elizabeth sounds aggravated. "Where are you going?"

I ignore her, weaving around the logs and toward

the wooded path. I hold my lantern out in front of me and forge through the woods, praying that my paranoia about Martha is wrong.

Soon enough, our coven's community swims into view—it's a group of ramshackle cottages made with materials the rest of the community didn't want. They're rather poorly built, with gaps in the siding and holes in the roofs, because construction isn't usually something on a witch's résumé, and we certainly didn't have the help of any of the town's respected builders, though admittedly a few kindhearted men pitched in here and there. Faint candlelight shines through the door of the last cottage on the left—*mine*. I'm certain I blew my candle out before I came to the meeting, though.

I burst into the cabin, the door making a loud bang as it slams against the wall. Martha stands in the middle of the room with her back to me. By the high-pitched screeches and the way Martha's wrenching this way and that, I can tell she has unleashed the enchanted bat from its box. She cackles, her shoulders shaking with glee.

"Enough with the spying, Martha," I growl.

Martha spins around . . . but there's something different about her. Her eyes, normally dim and vapid, sparkle with intelligence. Energy snaps from her limbs. She doesn't just look excited at this strange, unfamiliar treasure—she looks *satisfied*.

Like she knows exactly what the bat actually is.

"Martha," I repeat, feeling a little unsteady, "put that down. Walk away."

A sneaky smile plays on Martha's lips. "Can't do that, *Agatha*."

My limbs turn to stone. As I said, I use my real name among the Salem coven because these witches are too daft to know how important I am. But the way Martha says it now—it's with *meaning*. Like she knows what my name signifies. But the only way *that's* possible is . . .

A fierce wind kicks up inside the little cottage. I whirl around as my meager possessions start to spin, tornado-like, into the air. One of my hats whips like a kite. The wind lifts a teacup high only to slam it hard into a wall, shattering it to pieces.

"What the—?" I whisper just as another gust of wind shoves me against the wall and pins me there. I struggle to break free, but it's like the wind has two monstrous invisible hands that are pressing against my chest and restraining me. In the middle of the room, untouched by the wind completely, Martha stands with her head tipped back. Her laugh is loud and throaty.

That's when I understand. This isn't about getting me in trouble with the coven. This isn't about figuring out if I stole the coven's money. I've underestimated Martha. She's not like the other witches here. The strange, volatile weather in Salem—it's been *her* doing.

She's a *Tempestarii*. A weather witch. These sorts of witches have the power to create atmospheric conditions of their choosing—sometimes to disrupt, sometimes to benefit, but more often than not, the violent storms are manifestations of their wild swings of emotions. I can't tell if she's just really moody right now or has created this tornado in my house to throw me off guard—it's probably a little bit of both. There's one thing I *do* know, though.

She wants the Darkhold, like I do.

Power surges through my fingers. I shrug my shoulders, break free of the wind's hold, and fight my way through the hurricane to get back to her. Then I raise my hands toward her, lightning zapping on my palms.

Martha just chuckles. "I'm not scared of you."

Before I can strike her, she sends the wind blowing so hard that the walls of my cottage start to buckle and snap. Then she whirls around and points her finger at a spot in the corner. An eerie circle of blue light appears, its energy force field sending off a big wave of heat.

I blink hard, amazed at what I'm seeing. Martha has just opened a portal.

The ghastly blue glows against Martha's features, making her skin look corpse gray. Her hair whips around with every gale of wind. She steps toward the glowing gate, but I lunge and grab the end of Martha's long cloak before she can get too far.

"That's my bat," I say through clenched teeth. "If you wanted it, you should have found it yourself." Except then I remember: Weather witches usually have no power of clairvoyance. She needed *me* to find the Darkhold—that's why she's been watching me so carefully. It's been her plan to steal it from me all along.

I need to stop her.

I step back so I can get a good aim and send a bolt of energy at Martha's shoulder, but she ducks out of the way just in time. Flames hit the cottage's thatched wall instead, and the whole thing ignites. The fire leaps up the walls and to the ceiling. Smoke billows into the room. I can't deal with that now, though. I wheel around—Martha has moved again. The bat is shoved under her arm, and she's just feet away from the shining gate that leads to another place and time. *No.*

I'm about to scream but stop myself. Out the window, faint voices ring out. It's men from the village. They probably see the smoke, the cabin buckling from within.

I point at the portal. "Shut that down. They're going to see—they'll think it's the devil. They'll go after the coven."

Martha narrows her eyes. "Oh, like *you* care about the coven?"

She sends another gust of wind my way. It hits me

square in the chest, and I fly backward against the far wall and sink to the floor. By the time I've scrambled up, Martha is stepping through the glowing door, the struggling, flailing bat in her hands.

"No!" I scream, but it's too late. She disappears into the shimmering, breathing circle.

As soon as she's gone, the gale-force wind inside my little cabin dies down. All my floating possessions drop to the floor with thuds or earsplitting shatters. But the fire is still raging. The room is filled with smoke so thick it makes my eyes water and my lungs burn. It won't be long before my entire cottage is gone and the fire leaps to the other homes. The men's voices grow closer. There are gruff, angry shouts. Someone yells, "This way!" As I peer out the window, I spy torches on the path.

They're going to see this. All of this.

I turn back to the glowing portal. It's surprising that it's still here—usually, after someone dives through one of these, the passage to another time seals up immediately. I feel like I need to make a choice. I must either close the portal or dive through it before the villagers see. It could lead anywhere, though. Somewhere far worse than this. Somewhere far more dangerous. It will take me away from Prudence, leaving her completely alone. But wherever the portal leads, the Darkhold might be there. And there's no way I'm letting Martha run away with it.

Besides, if I can get the Darkhold back, I'll be able to save Prudence. I'll be able to fix everything.

And so, with bits of my cloak sparking with fire, I leap for the portal door, praying I haven't made a terrible mistake.

# *One*

My head pounds.

*I'm falling . . . falling . . . and then swooping.*

A flash appears before my eyes.

*I'm flying over rooftops. In a bigger city. A* huge *city, actually, surrounded by water. An island. Is this . . . Manhattan?*

I fight against the vision, but it's like I'm trapped inside it. It's like I've transmogrified into another creature. A bat, even. Have *I* become the Darkhold?

*I swoop lower, down to a set of windows near the harbor.*

I try to moan, but no sound comes out.

*There's someone at the window. An old woman. She has gnarled, arthritic hands. Stooped posture. Silver hair. And her eyes . . . Wait. Her eyes. I know them. It's . . .*

"It's me," I whisper, watching the vision unfold. "Only I'm . . . old?" Then I shudder. *"Ew."*

The vision . . . *dream?* . . . is so haunting and real, except the details are impossible. I'm not an old lady. I'll never be an old lady. I'm on a strict anti-aging spell regimen!

But it's my face staring back at me. Pretty much the worst dream ever.

My eyes flutter open for real. I wince and moan, all of my senses rushing in at once. It feels like someone has taken a giant log and cracked it across my temple. When I try to breathe, my lungs feel filled with broken glass. *The fire,* I remember. My shabby little cottage in Salem is definitely ash. How am I going to explain to the coven how the fire started, anyway? *Oh, you know, I was just throwing some flames around, no big deal. . . .*

Yet, am I even still *in* Salem? I remember diving through the strange portal. I did *that* because I was following . . .

*Martha.*

Her name comes back to me like a dreadful smell. I suck in a ragged, scraping breath and then look around.

I'm lying on a floor. This must be a palace, though, because the ground is flat and clean and . . . *smooth,* not pebbly or dirty or scratchy with straw or animal droppings like the floor in my cottage. The room has windows made of thin, remarkably clear glass and walls that look clean and stark, made of flat white panels instead of stone or mud. It *smells* good in here, too—like blooming flowers instead of rot. There are two small beds on either side of the room, fresh-looking and fluffy. I spy a table with some kind of strange box on it; the box has an attachment that sort of looks like an odd writing device. Beyond the desk is another door, slightly ajar; inside hangs a line of garments on a rod . . . except I've never seen garments like this. They aren't gray or blue or brown, like what most women, even witches, wear in Salem. Some are the color of the sun, or water, or orchids. Some seem to be made out of dandelion fluff. There's a coat that looks like it's made out of animal hide, except the hide is smooth and glossy and beautiful, possibly made from some sort of animal I've never seen before.

I peer out the window and spy a familiar stone church and some farmland beyond. The fields of grazing sheep and cows look a lot like some pastures on the edges of Salem's village . . . except something isn't right. I just can't believe this lavish room would exist in the village with its gloom and suspicion and murky little corners. Even the wealthiest people in Salem don't live like *this*. The Puritans value modesty over everything. You dare to have something nice in your possession, and they strike you down.

I rake my hand through my hair. Then I pull my

hand back and stare at it hard, realizing it's different, too. My fingers aren't gnarled like the old-lady Agatha. *So I'm not old, then.* That's a relief, anyway.

But it's still disarming. My skin is creamier and smoother than I remember my skin looking in Salem. When I touch my hair, it feels longer, flowing down to the middle of my back. It's silky to the touch, too, and bouncier, like a child's. When I stand, my muscles don't ache and my joints don't hurt like they sometimes do when getting out of bed in my little Salem cottage.

There's a mirror on the wall across from me—once again, the glass impossibly shiny, not half broken or rusted like the few mirrors are in Salem. When I see the reflected version of myself, I stare, goggle-eyed. My face is fuller. My eyes are brighter. I look . . . I look like a *teenager.*

Well. That's an interesting little bonus.

My gaze flits to something taped to the wall above one of the beds. It's a calendar, and there's another very realistic painting of the view of the church right outside the window. At the top are the words *Salem Conant Academy*. They mean nothing to me. I notice the date. *October.* The same month, then. Next I look at the year. 2025.

I move closer, certain this is wrong—but it's not. *2025.* Has Martha's portal shot me forward 334 years? This is . . . *new.* Sure, I've bounced around through time before, but I've always traveled *backward.* But here I am, *forward* in time . . . hundreds of years.

My legs feel unstable. I rush to the window and fling it open, relieved that the air outside seems like the same consistency as the air in 1691—crisp, cool, breezy.

Then a crow flutters past, and I get an idea. *Perfect.* A crow will give it to me straight.

I conjure my magic and pull the crow to me like a magnet. We make eye contact, and it lands begrudgingly on the windowsill—I can tell it doesn't feel like chatting, but that's why I like crows. They remind me of me.

*Yes?* go its thoughts.

*Where is this?* I ask it. *Where am I? What part of the world?*

The crow's head jerks. *What's in it for me?*

Typical. Crows always want to bargain. Gritting my teeth, I glance around the room and find two small objects sitting on the writing desk. It's a pair of earrings, delicate little silver drops. Crows love things that sparkle.

I bring a single earring to the crow. The bird looks at it, tilting its head this way and that. *My goodness, you don't have to be picky*, I tell it. *It's the best I can do.*

Finally, the crow snatches it up in its beak. *This is Conant Academy*, it thinks.

*What's that?* I ask.

*A school.*

I gaze around, confused. *A school for children?*

*Large children. Young men and women, like you.*

Like me? That's funny. But before I can ask the crow

what it means, something screeches in the distance, and the bird startles, secures the earring, and flutters away.

I groan. *Some help* you *are! You didn't even answer all my questions!*

I spin around the quiet room. A school, eh? I know what school is, obviously—there was a schoolhouse in Salem village, and if Prudence had lived with anyone other than us witches, she likely would have gone there. But *I* don't belong in school. As I quickly search my knowledge and past, I'm pretty sure I never attended school in my life—and I don't want to start now. It's got to be a mistake that I've landed here. But maybe lots of mistakes were made in traveling through the portal. Maybe Martha—and the Darkhold—landed here, too.

Time to play hide-and-seek.

With a flick of my hand, I conjure the door to the little room holding the garments to open wide, enchanting all the clothes to move aside so I can inspect the nooks and crannies at the back . . . but there's nothing.

"Come out, come out," I murmur.

I will the lids off boxes, I levitate some sort of soft carrying case and turn it upside down, but the only thing that falls out is a flat object with bristles on the end. Frustrated, I enchant another door to swing open . . . except inside this door is an exceptionally clean room containing a basin, a tub for bathing, and an indoor privy. I draw in a breath. I can't even believe what I'm looking at. I've had to suffer way too many centuries using outdoor bathroom facilities. Oh, the spells I've tried to cast to fix the problem—but nothing's worked. This? It's . . . *magnificent*.

I turn back to the room and, just by narrowing my eyes, enchant the covers off both beds, whip open the drawers of the desk, even pull down the grate built into the wall, sucking everything out from inside in hopes of finding the ancient book. There's dust, some stray socks, some kind of writing utensil. I whip open a drawer to an end table—one drawer is stuffed with things, but another is bare. There's writing on the wood on the inside of the drawer, however—someone has scrawled something in black ink. I move closer to check it out.

***Darkness is among us.***

What does *that* mean?

A *clink* sounds behind me, and I freeze. Another door at the far end of the room creaks open. I swing back to the messy room and, with a blink, return everything to order. Then I brace myself, expecting to see Martha with the fluttering enchanted bat clutched to her chest. I flick through my catalog of spells I can cast on her to make sure she hands it over immediately. I could turn her into a piece of furniture. I could melt away her hands. I could enchant her into telling me exactly who she is and why she's done this. I'll overpower her for sure. She isn't stronger than I am. I refuse to believe that.

Only, the young woman who walks through the door doesn't have Martha's long icy-blond hair but reddish-brown curls to her shoulders. Her eyes are brown, her skin is pink and rosy instead of pale, and she doesn't look wild, hungry, and conniving but contented and pretty much the healthiest-looking human I've ever seen.

She stops short when she sees me, and I'm at a crossroads. Do I use my powers to zap her to the ground? Do I *run*?

But then she speaks.

"Oh, hey!" she cries. "You must be my new roommate!"

# *Two*

This girl stands upright and proud, unashamed to be taking up space in the world. Her teeth are so white and straight, not like any teeth *I've* ever seen. In Salem, people are lucky to even *have* teeth.

What she's just said sinks in, too. *Roommate?*

"Pardon?" I sputter.

She searches my face. "I figured they'd pair me up with someone new eventually. I'm Ursula Greenwood." She sticks out her hand. "What's your name?"

I blink. It's a simple question, but I don't know how to answer. And yet, if I *don't* answer, this girl is going to think there's something wrong with me. There have been other instances when I've time-traveled where people seem to know who I am before I know them, and I just have to . . . go with it. If I act too confused, people will misinterpret it for madness, and the last thing I need is to be sent to some doctor. When I lived through the Roman times, doctors used urine to whiten people's teeth. During a plague in England, doctors tried to cure sick people by making them chew on weeds, sniff sponges soaked in vinegar, and breathe in smoke-filled air. Who knows what sorts of rituals they've come up with in this future land.

I can't give my real name, though, either. It's still possible Martha is lurking nearby and will hear me.

"Alice Harvey," I blurt out. It's the fake name I use sometimes when I don't want to be recognized by my enemies as Agatha Harkness.

"Well! Welcome, Alice!" Ursula sweeps over to the spare, plain bed—which, I realize, must be mine. Her smile drops. "I guess your things haven't come yet?"

"Uh . . ." Judging by all the books and papers and pillows and wall adornments and everything else in this girl's possession, I'm guessing that in this century, it's perfectly normal to own way too much stuff. It seems awfully excessive, though. Does one actually use *five* pillows for sleeping?

I just shrug. "I don't need much."

Ursula nods sagely. "A minimalist. That's cool. So where are you from?"

"Uh, here," I say dazedly, waving to the window. "Out . . . there."

Ursula frowns. "Salem? In the town?"

I come to my senses. "*Near* Salem." Saying I'm from *right* here, possibly this very plot of land, would sound ridiculous. "Not so far."

"Ah." Ursula nods slowly. "Well, you will need *some* things for school—a uniform, toiletries, books and supplies." She points to the empty, plain bed. "And that's your side. I took Sylvie's side. Sorry it's not by the window."

"Who's Sylvie?"

"My old roommate, Sylvie O'Toole." She searches my face. "You didn't hear the news?"

I shake my head. Ursula pulls in her bottom lip and looks like she wants to say something, but then gently lifts a small painting in a frame from her desk.

"This was her," she says.

I study the picture. The brushstrokes are immaculate. Absolutely invisible. The future must have very sophisticated art tools. I recognize Ursula's freckles and curly hair. The girl next to her is smaller and slighter, her dark hair in two braids. I draw in a breath—the resemblance is striking. The pale skin, the short stature, the sweet smile—she looks so much like Prudence. The only difference is that she's leaning against Ursula happily, her mouth open in a laugh. I've definitely never seen Prudence that boisterous. I have to forget I'm not in 1691 Salem, where that kind of emotion would get your knuckles slapped.

"Where is she now?" I ask.

"I . . . don't know," Ursula says in a small voice, placing the picture back down. "She's been . . . missing."

"Missing?" I frown, and swallow. "I've got a friend who's missing, too."

Ursula looks up. "Really?"

I have no idea why that just slipped out of my mouth—what am I trying to do, *empathize* with this person? Yet I see Prudence's irritatingly earnest face in my cottage doorway. How her eyes lit up when I healed that rat. *Oh, Agatha, I knew you were the real deal.*

And it's true—she *is* missing. Well. Three-hundred-some years ago she was. Is time moving forward in Salem the same as it is here?

I wave my hand, my head hurting from the mental gymnastics. "Never mind. But I hope your friend is okay." I think of the message I saw on the inside of the dresser drawer. *Darkness is among us.* The handwriting was shaky, like it had been written quickly . . . or under duress.

Ursula steps back and looks at me as though she has just actually noticed something. One eyebrow lifts. "Whoa. That's . . . quite an outfit. Are you into witchy stuff?"

I look down. Even though my face and body have become magically more youthful, I'm still wearing the long wool dress, stockings, and buckle shoes I had on before I dove through the portal. My scratchy cloak is wrapped around my shoulders. My buckle shoes look worn and tight. These garments seemed perfectly normal to me in 1691, but now I can tell, instinctively, that this is *not* what people wear in 2025.

Not only that, but around Salem, *only* witches wore cloaks. For a while, we were proud to stand out, proud that the people of Salem knew we were different . . . but I could tell the tide was turning. I think of the distrust I sensed from the townspeople in Salem. The premonition I felt that the rift would grow wider between us.

What do people think of witches three hundred years later? What if it's gotten even worse? What if people aren't just wary of us, they think we're killers?

But then my blood boils. Why should this girl judge me? Why should anyone?

Before I can answer, though, Ursula breaks into a grin, showing off those dazzling teeth again. "This is going to work perfectly. I'm into witchy stuff, too!"

I stare at her. "What?"

"I mean, I'm not an *actual* witch." She laughs. "But it's all so cool—and also, we're in Salem, so it only feels natural! A group of us at school are all really into it together. We read each other's charts, and I love tarot cards, and a few of us are growing herbs to make, like, tinctures. Do you do that as well?"

It takes me a moment to respond. "Uh, yes. From time to time." I probably shouldn't mention that I'm into the *magical* version of tarot, where you turn over the Knight of Swords, say, and an actual knight appears and chops your enemy's head off.

Then I realize something else. So we *are* still in Salem, but likely a very different Salem I'm used to. And now . . . Salem is *famous* for witches? When did *that* happen?

"Whew, what a relief!" Ursula flops down on her bed. "I was *so* afraid they were going to pair me with a cheerleader." Then she sits up again. "And you obviously love Wanda Maximoff, right?"

"Who?"

"Uh, only the most powerful witch *ever.* You've never heard of the Scarlet Witch?" Ursula reaches for another framed picture. This time, it's of a petite woman with olive skin and reddish-brown hair. The woman has a devilish smile, which annoys me infinitely.

*You're not so great*, I say to the image. This Wanda person doesn't even look scary.

"Wanda's incredible," Ursula says. Then she touches my witch's cloak. "This is so gorgeous—is it vintage?"

"Uh, yes?" I say, because this seems like the right answer.

"I have to say, it smells sort of . . . musty." Ursula wrinkles her nose. "How about we have it cleaned?"

"Won't that take forever?" It's a pain to clean my cloak. The wool takes days to dry, and afterward, it still smells like a wet sheep for weeks.

"Nah, I can send it to the dry cleaner—on me. We'll get it back tomorrow. You can borrow something of mine until then."

I think of the strange, fluffy things in her closet. Admittedly, I *am* sort of curious about wearing 2025 clothes. "Well, okay. . . ."

"And you'll join the coven, right? It's top secret—the school is really strange about covert gatherings that aren't school-approved—but it's a lot of fun, and we could always use new blood." Then she shuts her eyes, looking embarrassed. "Look at me. You just got here! I'm always like this—I instantly thought I was Sylvie's friend, too. I can't help myself!"

She loops an elbow around mine, and my head is spinning with the whirlwind that is Ursula. I'm relieved, of course—and kind of impressed. Ursula is certainly the opposite of an intolerant Salem townsperson. And my mind catches on something else—*friend*.

But I push that thought away. I don't need friends. That's not my style.

"So have you gotten your schedule yet?" Ursula asks.

I blink. "Schedule?"

She has that smile again like I'm joking around. "For classes? Wait, you haven't met Peabody? And where's your uniform?"

I have no idea how to answer.

Her eyebrows shoot up. "Headmistress Peabody runs this school. Surely you met with her when you came."

"I . . . did . . ." I babble, thinking that maybe this is the correct answer. "But, um, I didn't get a schedule. . . ."

"Oh, we can fix that." Ursula walks toward the door. "I'll walk you over to her office. I'm sure she has it for you, and she'll show you how to log in to your student portal online, too. Maybe we'll have classes together!"

I feel lightheaded. The last thing I want is to go see some headmistress to get a schedule of classes I don't even want to take. Pretending that I'm a student is one thing; actually going to school is another.

I need to get out of here.

I glance at the little door to the area with the basin and toilet. I think I saw a small window in there. "Do you mind if I . . . ?"

Ursula looks amused. "Uh, it's our bathroom. You don't have to ask my permission."

I step into the little "bathroom," close the door, and sink against the wall. I always get a rush of exhaustion when teleporting to a new place, but traveling this far forward in time has really taken it out of me. I don't feel like I should be here. I don't want to be a student. I need some control.

I squeeze my eyes shut and conjure the spell to create a new portal. Wherever Martha is in this weird future time, I need to drag her into the netherverse so we can hash this out as the powerful witches we truly are. Enough playing around. Enough talk about uniforms and the Scarlet Witch and cheerleaders.

I can feel energy snapping within me, but I can't summon my usual powers. It happens, sometimes, especially after traveling through portals. I'm too depleted. I try and try to conjure my powers, but I just can't do it. I'm so frustrated that I take a little bottle of something on the sink and throw it down hard on the floor. It bounces into the corner.

"Alice?" Ursula calls from the other side of the bathroom door. "Everything all right?"

"Sorry!" I eke out. "Fine!"

I close my eyes again. And then, unexpectedly, I feel the familiar sucking feeling of being pulled into another dimension . . . *finally*. In a blink, I'm floating in darkness.

I hover around the endless space. "Martha?" I call out, my voice echoing. "Where are you?"

A figure slowly emerges through mist. I squint, taking in the smaller frame, the meek smile. Then my heart sinks.

*"Prudence?"* I whisper.

The girl is wearing her usual dress and apron, a cap on her head and her hands folded at her waist. Her eyes are big and sad, her mouth is pursed, and she looks pale and starved. Prudence was always skinny, but now she looks downright . . . *ill.*

"What happened to you?"

Prudence gazes at me pitifully. Her mouth opens, but no sound comes out.

"Come on," I beg her. "Talk to me!"

But it seems that Prudence *can't* talk. Sometimes, mere mortals can't communicate in these strange alternate dimensions. Then I hear flapping to my left. When I turn, I spy a pair of dark wings, a beak. It's a crow with a familiar silver earring hooked around its foot—an earring, I realize, that must be Ursula's. It's the crow I was talking to before. How did *it* get dragged into this space?

The crow looks at me with his beady eyes. *She's in a bad way*, he says—because he, apparently, can communicate just fine. *You need to help her.*

I shut my eyes. Perfect. I was *right*, then, about the Parris family keeping Prudence hostage. I *knew* it.

"I'm trying to come back." I reach out and touch Prudence, but my hand goes straight through. "Are you all right? Are you in danger?"

She just stares at me, her eyes large and scared. I look at the crow. It rustles its feathers.

"Did the Parrises do something?" I ask Prudence. "Where are they keeping you?"

She looks down. Her shoulders start to tremble. Maybe it's *worse* than I thought. Again, the crow doesn't answer.

"I chased Martha here. You know how we didn't like her? Well, now I *really* don't like her. But I'll make a portal to come get you as soon as I get my strength back." Normally, I wouldn't be telling Prudence this—it's not as if she understands true witch magic. But here, in this parallel world, it seems like I can tell her everything.

Prudence shakes her head vehemently. The crow lets out a squawk. *She says you can't come back yet. You need to find Martha first. And the Darkhold. Before it's too late.*

*Huh.* Prudence knows about the Darkhold? I look from Prudence to the crow. "But do you know where Martha is?" I ask. "Here? At this school?"

*She's not in the form you expect, so you need to be careful*, the crow tells me. *She doesn't know who you are, either.*

"She doesn't? Are you sure?"

*Yes. But watch for magic—that's how you'll find her. And be careful. She's looking for you, too. You're a great threat to her, and she wants to destroy you.*

*Great.* I bite down hard on my lip. "And the Darkhold? Does Martha still have it?"

The crow says that, no, Martha doesn't have it anymore—it flapped away when hurtling through the portal. *It's close, though. Use your abilities to track it down.*

"I don't *have* any abilities at the moment," I snap. "In fact, I feel more exhausted than I usually do when I fly through a portal. Any idea what that's all about?"

*You know what it's about.*

"Uh, sorry. I don't."

*You do. You know how to reverse the loss of magic.*

I glare at the crow. "Stop talking in riddles and just tell me how already!"

But the crow ignores me. *You must find the Darkhold. If it falls into Martha's hands, she'll destroy you and much, much more. And you must help Prudence. A storm is coming to Salem, but not of wind and rain. Something different—something worse.*

I'm losing patience. "What do you mean? What's worse?"

But Prudence and the crow are already turning translucent. The young girl stares down at herself, a terrified look settling over her features. She's scared to go back.

"Prudence!" I reach out for her. "Prudence, why do I need to help you? Are you imprisoned? And what do you mean *before it's too late*?"

She's still staring at me imploringly. Spots form in front of my eyes. "Please tell me," I say, but then I feel myself fading. "I'm sorry. I'll try my hardest—and I'll make it up to you. I'll be back."

Then my head hits something hard on the ground. When I open my eyes again, I'm on the floor of the bathroom at Conant Academy. Someone is pounding on the door.

"Alice!" Ursula cries. "Alice, are you okay? I heard a thud!"

I push myself to sitting. "I'm okay. Just, um, dropped something."

The vision swims in my head. Prudence's frightened face. Her warning that I need to help *before it's too late*. And a sick realization settles over me, too.

I'm stuck here. Until I find Martha and the Darkhold.

Before she finds me . . . and destroys me for good.

# Three

Once I pick myself up off the bathroom floor, splash some clean water on my face, and sample a few of the scrubs, cleansers, and creams—I've never felt anything so luxurious, and surely Ursula won't notice a little is missing—I open the bathroom door to find her sitting on the bed. I follow her out of the dormitory, down some steps, and out to a public green to meet with the headmistress.

It's not like I want to. Being a student is about as desirable as someone putting stones in my pockets and forcing me to walk into a deep, cold lake. But Prudence's desperate plea, told to me through that strange, nosy bird, rings in my ears. She's in trouble. She looked *terrified*. The coven won't help her—they think she's a thief. I'm her only hope, then.

But I can't leave until I find the Darkhold . . . *and* avoid Martha finding and destroying me. But who *is* Martha? Apparently she isn't in her expected form, meaning she isn't hiding in the academy looking like herself. Most likely, she took over someone else's body. It's not something witches do often, only in dire circumstances, but it can work sometimes. So is she another student, a teacher? Is she an *animal*?

It also makes me wonder if I should be selective with my magic—the magic I can still perform, anyway—and use it only when absolutely necessary. Witches can sometimes sense when magic is afoot; performing powerful spells might put a big target on my back. Then again, if I can't practice a little magic, how am I going to get through the day? Because you'd better believe I'm not going to go to school like a normal person.

My mind returns to another part of the crow's conversation—the part about my magic. The crow insinuated that the reason I don't have my normal powers isn't just because I'm tired from transporting. It's because of something else. I hope it isn't what I'm thinking of. Though it's never happened to me, I've heard that sometimes, when a witch experiences great energy shifts, her powers become blocked. And apparently, the only way to unblock the powers, say the ancient scrolls, is to *look within thyself. Look within one's truthfulness*.

But it seems like a load of nonsense. Be true to yourself, and *poof*, all of a sudden you're strong again? I *am* true to myself—and nothing's working. I'm probably just tired.

Soon enough, I'll feel like myself again.

We step out of the dorm and onto the green, a wide square surrounded by brick school buildings. The weather is crisp and cool, and the leaves on the trees have all changed to red, gold, and orange. Autumn, it seems, still looks the same three hundred years later. All these little reminders that 2025 is at least somewhat like 1691 Salem are a relief.

Suddenly, I look up and scream. There, just past the path, stands Samhain, the ancient god of Halloween. He has long, sharp, curly goat horns and stands eight feet tall. In his giant hand is a sharpened scythe, and his eyes glow red.

Electricity snaps at my fingertips. Forget the no-magic plan. Blurry memories flood back—it's been a long time since I've seen this demon. Last I heard, he'd been imprisoned in an ancient book not unlike the Darkhold in ancient Celtic times. How did he get out?

This is Martha's true form. It must be.

I set my jaw as I make eye contact with the ugly creature—which, for some strange reason, hasn't noticed me yet. Maybe that's because I'm no longer wearing my witch's cloak but a curiously soft tunic the color of daffodils of Ursula's and a pair of tight-fitting bottoms Ursula called "leggings." I'm about to tackle him around his middle, but then Ursula grabs my arm.

"Isn't he funny? They went all out for Halloween this year!"

I turn and stare at her, astonished she hasn't fainted at the sight of this beast. "You need to hide. *Now.*"

"Huh?" she asks. And then, to my horror, she walks right up to Samhain and *touches his arm*. The ghoulish goat springs to life, and I grab her arm.

"Stop!" I scream. "He'll turn you to stone!"

She looks down at my arm on hers and laughs. "He's just a decoration! Satan, maybe? Though I always thought Satan was red and held a pitchfork." Then she smiles. "Wait, you thought he was real?"

I blink and look at the goat again. His movements are jerky and restrained, not like the real version. A *decoration*. An imposter. A fake.

"Of course not," I say. "I was making a joke."

"He totally fooled me the first time I saw him, too." She points around the quad. "Some of the teachers pooled their cash to buy a bunch of animatronics for

Halloween. You should see the creepy clown near the fitness center! Definitely already giving me nightmares."

I follow her gaze. Beyond Samhain—or this fake version of him—there are other scary statues around the green moving in the same jerky ways. Nosferatu. Cerberus the three-headed dog. A ghoul lurking by a gravestone. There are some other creatures I don't recognize: a pale-faced, greenish-haired man in a black-and-white-striped suit, a pumpkin-headed man with a pitchfork, a delightfully terrifying inside-out sort of man where all of his bones are visible for everyone to see.

I'm actually impressed. I can only imagine what the Puritans would have done had these things been plunked down in their town square. They'd probably paddle back to England.

Ursula points across the green to a large stone building. "The headmistress's office is in there." Then she holds up my cloak. "I'm going to take this to the dry cleaner. Meet you back at the room in an hour? Then we can go to the dining hall."

I look around. The green isn't very busy with students. I thought it would be, since it's a school. "Wait, why aren't you in class?"

Ursula grins bemusedly. "Because it's Sunday?"

Sunday. Right. "And we're sure this headmistress is going to be in her office?"

Ursula chuckles. "She's always working. In fact, since you just arrived, she's probably expecting you." She pats my arm. "Good luck. Don't let her talk you into playing field hockey, okay? But definitely join the Historical Society!"

Ursula traipses off. I stare at her receding form for a moment; she's heading toward a pair of tall iron gates. Beyond it is an eerily familiar house. Looking around to make sure no one is watching, I conjure a spell of long-distance sight. All of a sudden, the words on the small placard in front of the home are clear. *House of the Seven Gables*, it reads. *The inspiration for the famous Nathaniel Hawthorne novel.* I have no idea who that is. *Established 1668.*

I passed this house whenever I wanted to walk by the water when I was living in Salem three hundred years ago. Martha yanked us forward in time, but she's practically plunked us directly on top of where our coven's community once was. I look down at the spot where I'm standing—if I'm judging this correctly, it was once the deep, dark woods where we had to sit through those exhausting coven meetings. A few paces away, near a Halloween statue of a floating ghost, was the old path back to the cottages.

But I don't see the cottages anywhere. How long ago did they vanish? I think of those men with their torches coming through the woods during my last moments in Salem. Did they put out the fire, or did they let all our cottages burn? I shudder. Like I told Martha, I don't really *care* about the coven, but I'd feel slightly bad if they had nowhere to live.

I start down a brick path decorated with pumpkins, gourds, stacks of hay, and little signs that read things like *Welcome, Fall* and *Harvest Time*, not that I see any harvest. A few students pass, and I keep my eyes peeled for Martha's blond hair, but I don't see her anywhere. I peer into hollow parts of trees and under bushes, but there's no wily little bat to be found. If only it were that easy.

When I get to the building where the headmistress's office is, there's a sign on the front door: *Halloween Dance, October 31! Wear your costumes, witches and warlocks!*

I smirk. *That* won't be hard. But then I realize what I'm thinking. Obviously, I won't *be* here by Halloween.

The inside of the headmistress's building is as clean and shiny as Ursula's bedroom, with polished windows, beautifully lush couches and rugs, and floors that gleam so brightly I can nearly see my reflection in them. The lobby is empty—I guess because it's Sunday—and all the doors are shut. I have no idea where I'm supposed to go.

I glance around once more, then quickly conjure a spell. Instantaneously, a tiny, glowing arrow appears on the ground, pointing me toward a staircase. Once I'm up it, another arrow appears, directing me to the left.

Upstairs, Headmistress Peabody's name is on a plaque outside the closed door—*success.*

With a wave of my hand, I make the arrows vanish. Then I put my ear to the door. Sure enough, I hear voices inside. But I hesitate, not sure what to do.

*Bam.* The door swings open, startling me. A stout, pie-faced woman with springy curls and wearing a checked shirt that reminds of a tablecloth steps back in surprise.

"Oh!" she cries.

I wheel back too, my cheeks burning. "S-sorry." Great. Now it looks like I was spying. Which I kind of was, but I don't want her to know that.

She frowns at me. "Who are you?"

I straighten up. "I'm, um, a new student. Alice Harvey."

She looks even more confused. "I wasn't informed of a new student."

*Of course you weren't,* I almost say. Yet I have to think quickly. I want to use magic, but I consult my Martha radar. Headmistress Peabody seems wholesome, but sometimes wholesomeness is deceiving, and I can't be too careful.

"I received a letter that I could attend," I say, hoping I don't sound too foolish.

"But where are your transcripts?" the headmistress

asks, leafing through a stack of papers on her desk. "And what about the school fees, and the entrance exam?"

"Perhaps the transcripts were lost in transit," says a voice. "You know how finicky the mail can be sometimes."

A man stands up from a chair on the other side of a large desk. He's lanky, with prominent cheekbones, a long nose, graying temples, and an intelligent-looking face. Of all the people I've met in this century, he looks the most like he could fit back in Salem times. That's likely because of what he's wearing: a wool vest and a long blazer almost like I've seen some of the Puritan men wear. I get a strange feeling about him, like I don't want to stop looking at his face. Like maybe I've . . . *seen* him before.

The headmistress turns to him. "Alice, this is Dr. Novis. He's a new teacher."

Dr. Novis reaches out his hand for me to shake, which is quite a change from my Salem days—men didn't bother shaking most women's hands back then. "Pleasure," he says. When our palms touch, I get another little jolt of familiarity, but when I rack my brain, I can't place him. Maybe he just has one of those familiar auras.

"Dr. Novis teaches quite a few of our science classes: Advanced Physics, Chemistry . . . a few of our teachers shifted around after Mr. Haverford unexpectedly left us," the headmistress goes on. But then she gives her head a little shake. "I can't let you attend here simply because you want to, Alice. This isn't a public school. It costs money."

Dr. Novis clears his throat. "Yes, but you were just telling me there are a few scholarship spots available, Miss Peabody."

"Only for those who excelled on their entrance exam," the headmistress argues hastily. "And she hasn't even taken them!"

"Couldn't that be arranged?"

The headmistress looks at me again. "How did you even get on campus? The gates are locked."

I clear my throat. As much as I sympathize with her confusion, I need to stand my ground. "I was told I could move into the dorms. My roommate is Ursula Greenwood."

Her eyebrows shoot up. "Ursula. Oh my."

"Ah, Ursula." Dr. Novis looks thoughtful, like he already knows of her, too.

"Such a sweet girl. It's a real shame about her previous roommate, Sylvie," the headmistress murmurs. "A strange, terrible thing . . . We're all still reeling from it."

"What happened, exactly?" I ask. "Did Sylvie run away? Did someone kidnap her?" I keep thinking about the inscription on the inside of that drawer. *Darkness is among us.*

"We're not sure, but it's certainly not something for you to worry about," Peabody says. She looks down at her desk again. "I just don't understand how this could have happened without me knowing . . . but I suppose I did take a leave of absence for a few weeks after all of the ruckus last month. Maybe one of my colleagues approved your application?" She pauses a moment to think this over, then shrugs. "You'll have to take the entrance exam. And I don't even know where to place you. Which school were you at before this?"

I look away. "I, um, was self-taught." Quite a few of the witches in Salem learned to read and write on their own. I learned all those things so long ago that I don't even remember how, they just seem second nature.

"Homeschooled?" Headmistress Peabody purses her lips. "Interesting that you'd make the jump from a homeschool environment to here. What sciences have you taken? Math courses?"

Half the words she said don't even make any sense. *Math?* What is that? And only great thinkers and scholars study science in the end of the seventeenth century—certainly not young women.

But I make a guess. "I know everything there is to know about plants, if that helps."

Dr. Novis looks surprised. "Botany is advanced for someone your age. Usually, new students have just taken basic cell biology."

I shrug. "Ask me anything about a plant, and I'll tell you how to use it, where it grows, and if it's poison."

Dr. Novis's eyebrows shoot up. He glances curiously at Headmistress Peabody. "My, my!" she finally says. "Maybe we'll put you down for Chemistry, then, though perhaps you'd like to take the AP Biology exam. And what about the humanities? Did you take American History, or were you more studying ancient histories, like the Romans and the Greeks?"

"The latter," I answer—again with confidence. I *lived* through ancient Roman and Greek times. That's got to count for something.

"All students are also required to take Agriculture as well," the headmistress continues. "We have a working farm on campus, and every student helps care for the animals and the crops. Your first class—should you pass your exam—will be tomorrow. I should also add that the academy is *quite* structured. We expect students to come to every class and complete the rigorous syllabi requirements. And we don't tolerate misbehavior. We have strict curfews, and we forbid any gatherings or clubs that aren't school-sanctioned. It seems that a few have popped up here and there, and believe me—we work hard to shut them down." She points at Dr. Novis. "Dr. Novis here is on the committee that investigates underground student groups. So if you hear of one, report it to him."

I shift in my seat. There's no way I'm going to betray

anyone. I think of the coven I was part of in Transia—it was long before Salem. The other witches and I endured quite a bit of anti-witch persecution and even witch hunts, where the townspeople killed many of our kind. We all tried to put a stop to it. In fact, to fend off a new threat of attackers, one of my fellow witches, Jacquette, invoked a demon lord named Valtorr from the underworld—she wanted to borrow his impressive powers.

But Valtorr required a sacrifice as part of the bargain: one of our own. I argued that the price was too high—we couldn't let go of one of our witches as a bargaining chip! That made us as ruthless as the witch hunters! But Jacquette didn't see it that way. *Only the strong survive* was her rationale. So, behind my back, she offered Valtorr Corina, the weakest in our group. Valtorr accepted the sacrifice and dragged Corina, screaming, into the underworld.

There was nothing I could do. For years, I tried to undo the spell that was over Corina and rescue her from imprisonment, but I never could. Jacquette's easy betrayal left a terrible taste in my mouth. I left the coven after that. Dealing with people's callousness and all the ways they could disappoint me—it was just too much. I'm much better off alone.

Peabody's voice breaks me out of my thoughts. "And

every student needs to join the Historical Society. Salem is very famous, and it's our duty as the oldest school in town to teach tourists about our past. We also mandate that students participate in one organized sport each semester, no excuses."

"Sport?" I think of racing horses or dogs, or stool ball. The Puritans hated such games because they relied on luck.

"Now, now, don't act like you've never heard of exercise," Peabody teases. "The fall sports are girls' soccer, field hockey, and cross country. Do you like to run?"

"When I'm running from something, sure." Which isn't even true. If I truly have the need to escape, I'll just fly.

"Well, you'll have to change your mindset. We'll put you down for field hockey. Dr. Novis is coaching that, aren't you, Dr. Novis?"

But then we both look around, and he isn't in the room anymore.

"Where did he run off to?" the headmistress asks, then waves her hand. "No matter." She writes something in a book with some kind of apparatus that makes ink without a little inkpot. "I'll arrange for you to take the entrance exam right away." She reaches for a device on her desk, lifting one end of it to her ear and talking into the other. "Bethany? We have a student here who needs to take the entrance exam. Can you set her up in a library study room?"

This is a bizarre situation, even for me. I'm sitting in this funny little room with more books than I've ever seen in my life, trying to remember what Ursula told me about Peabody and field hockey and feeling completely clueless about whatever she means about a Historical Society. And now I'm being forced into taking a three-hour test that I'm surely going to fail?

"Maybe this *is* a mistake," I blurt.

Headmistress Peabody moves the device she was speaking into away from her ear. "What do you mean?"

I smooth my hands over Ursula's strange stretchy pants. "Perhaps you're right. Maybe this isn't the place for me."

She speaks into the device again. "Let me call you back." She sets it in its cradle, and her expression softens. "Oh, my dear. I didn't mean to sound harsh when I spoke about you being homeschooled. There is a diverse group at Conant Academy. I'm sure you'll find your community. There are plenty of other students on scholarship, too—students from other countries, and as much as I talked about the rules, we have a lot of fun, too. Why, there's a Halloween dance in a few weeks! With a costume contest!"

"Yes, but I have more important things to do."

The door opens then, and Dr. Novis returns. "Apologies," he says. "I needed the restroom. Where were we?"

"Alice is having second thoughts."

Dr. Novis settles back into his chair. "And why is that?"

*Because I'm not a student!* I want to scream. And then I just blurt it out. "Has anything strange happened here lately? Unexpected?"

Dr. Novis frowns and leans forward. "How so?"

"Like . . ." How to get through to them that someone evil is lurking without sounding suspicious?

Just then, a loud *boom* fills the air. The room goes dark. Seconds later, a siren blares loudly. The floor starts to jump and shiver.

"Oh, heavens." Headmistress Peabody leaps up. Both she and Novis get down on all fours and crawl under an open space under the desk as books tumble off the shelves.

Peabody sticks her head out from under the desk to look at me. "Get down here with us, will you, dear?"

"What?" I cry.

More books plop to the floor. A carved bust of some grumpy-looking man falls. I peek outside. The wind is swirling. The sky grows dark, too—but only over the school. All the strange Halloween decorations, some of which are made of flimsy, sail-like fabric, blow wildly in the wind, a few even breaking free from their tethers. The statue of Samhain lifts into the air, turns, and faces the window I'm looking out of. It's like he's seeing right into me.

"Alice!" Peabody cries. "Get under here, please, before something lands on you!"

Suddenly, as though a window has been left open, the wind gusts inside the office as well. I duck under the desk as the wind knocks a picture off the wall. It shatters on top of the chair where I was just sitting.

The area under the desk is tight and narrow. It's strange being so close to other people—I can't even think of the last time I let anyone get this near. I feel Novis's gaze on me, but I pointedly look away. I can also feel magic literally crackling through the air. The tornado twister spirals through the door like an unwanted guest, whipping up everything in its path. The wind is so strong that it makes the paint curl off the walls.

"Is this *normal*?" I yell over the gales.

"It will be over soon," Peabody assures me. "Just brace yourself."

And she's right: The tornado vanishes as quickly as it arrived. The air goes still. The sirens stop. The sound of shattering glass finally ceases.

"*Very* curious," Dr. Novis whispers.

I scramble out from under the desk before Headmistress Peabody says it's okay, but I'm really not a fan of being in tight spaces with people. Books are all over the floor, furniture is knocked over, there's a big crack on the wall, and some of the glass in the windows has shattered, but at least the air is calm again. Then I look out the windows. Fluffy clouds drift over the school. The Halloween statues have settled neatly back to the grass. The candle in the ceiling flickers on again.

Dr. Novis and Headmistress Peabody climb out from under the desk as well, seating themselves back in their chairs and adjusting their rumpled clothes.

"Sorry, dear." Peabody's smile wavers. "Salem has had some strange weather patterns recently. Must be climate change, eh, Dr. Novis?"

But I don't think this is simple weather. I think it's a witch. A witch I know well.

The headmistress fumbles around for the folder she was holding—it's shifted around on her desk with all the rumbling. "Anyway. As you were saying, Miss Harvey, if you'd rather not take your entrance exam, then you'd best go and pack up your things. Plenty of others would—"

"Actually," I interrupt, "I will take the exam." I can cast a spell to find the right answers. "I want to attend Conant Academy after all."

Peabody looks a little harried. "Ah! Well, then." She reaches for the talking device again. "I'll set you up right now."

Dr. Novis smiles at me. "If you pass your exam—and

I think you will—I'll be your Chemistry professor." There's a knowing expression on his face. "Chemistry is full of magic. If you're into that kind of thing."

I flinch at his words. Novis seems to notice, and there's now an even more mysterious glint in his eye. "I hope you find what you're looking for at Conant Academy, Alice."

A chill goes through me, but I hold his gaze, suddenly full of confidence. Martha isn't so sly. She's just showed her hand with that little weather trick. She *is* here. And I'm going to find her.

"Don't worry," I tell him. "I will."

# *Four*

I startle awake. For a moment, I don't know where I am or even *who* I am. Then the unsettling realization comes: This strange school. This strange future time. This strange young me who's now a student. Just like Novis predicted, I aced the entrance exam. Thanks to my pen writing in the answers all on its own, of course.

Moonlight spills across my blanket. I sit up in bed and check on Ursula sleeping peacefully on the other side of the room. Outside, the air is still, and not a soul crosses the empty green. It must be the dead of night.

Which means I can go hunting.

I slide out of bed and place my feet on the cold floor. Ursula hasn't brought my cloak back from the cleaner's yet, so I pull the sweater she loaned me around my shoulders and grab my worn buckle shoes. I hold them in my hands as I pad across the room, not wanting to wake Ursula up.

The hall is quiet and very dark. I wish I'd brought a candle—or that I could create a little fire of light with my palms—but it will probably be better to remain in the shadows as much as possible. I feel along the sides of the wall until I see moonlight through a window a few paces ahead.

I have a feeling that the strange tornado earlier today was Martha trying to unearth the Darkhold. I'm kicking myself at the missed opportunity—had I not been hiding under a desk with the headmistress, perhaps I could have caught Martha in the act. She got lucky this time, but I'm not going to make the same mistake with her. I need to stay subtle in my Darkhold search so Martha doesn't detect who I am. But it doesn't mean I'm not going to look.

Then again, randomly ransacking this enormous school for the Darkhold will take too long; what I really need, I've decided, is a crystal ball. They're invaluable tools for witches, not only showing future events but also handy at locating items that have gone missing. Where to find one, though? Earlier this evening, Ursula took me to this glorious place called "the dining hall," a giant room where people could choose *any type of food they wanted,* including delicacies I'd never seen before: warm breads topped with cheeses and a juicy piece of meat between a soft bun, and something called *French fries,* which were so delicious I burst out laughing. While we ate, I asked Ursula if this coven she was part of ever used a crystal ball. She said no, but sometimes they consulted a Ouija board—whatever that is.

But there's got to be one *somewhere.*

The floor creaks as I turn a corner. I'm going the right way—ahead of me, I see the dorm's big lobby and front door. I finally reach it, and my fingers clutch the cold, heavy knob. I twist it open, and the latch gives.

And then a terrible screeching noise wails in my ears.

I stumble backward. The alarm is so loud it makes my eyeballs ache. Behind me, doors fly open. "What's that?" someone shouts.

I spin around and look at the front door again, thinking that maybe I can escape into the darkness without being caught, but to my horror, it has slammed shut on its own. I try the knob. It doesn't even twist.

"Hey!" comes another voice from down the hall. "Who's out there?"

I whirl back around, trying to make sense of the darkness. In seconds, whoever it is will find me . . . and they'll have questions. Headmistress Peabody already warned me about this place's strict rules. If I get in trouble, it might mean I won't be able to move freely around the campus and search for the Darkhold.

I spy a utility closet next to the front door and dive in, tripping clumsily against jugs and brooms lined up across the floor. I press myself against the back wall and plug my ears as the alarm continues to wail.

"Come on," the same angry voice protests. "I know someone's here. Just come out, okay? It'll be worse if you hide."

I hear her footsteps as she races to find me. Wood scrapes against wood as she moves furniture to peek in dark corners. Soon enough, she'll get to this closet—and then what?

I peek out a tiny crack. A girl searches the room, hands over her ears to muffle the alarm. She's wearing pajama pants, a T-shirt, and flip-flops, and her dark hair is in a tangle. It's Jenna, the dorm's RA; she introduced herself to me earlier today. She was friendly but kind of bossy, like she was just looking to get students in trouble. I highly doubt I'll be able to talk her out of turning me in . . . and she's only a few feet away from opening the utility closet door.

I grit my teeth. As much as I don't want to use magic, I'm not sure I have a choice.

It's easy to enter Jenna's mind, slipping in between her ears. I start to play with her thoughts. *Turn around*, I whisper to her telepathically. I pray *she* isn't Martha—she'll figure me out immediately. I'm also relieved I can do small spells like this one. Thankfully not all my magic is hindered.

Jenna stops and draws in a breath. I bet she's wondering where that voice came from.

*There's no one here. No one tried to sneak out.*

She frowns. Pulls her bottom lip into her mouth. My voice is inside her, but the brilliance of the spell is that she thinks it's her own intuition.

*The alarm tripped on its own. You know it does that sometimes.*

Trance-like, she walks over to some buttons on the wall and presses a few numbers. I watch carefully, memorizing the pattern, filing away the information for later. Blessedly, the screeching stops.

Jenna presses another button and speaks into a box. "Think it's a false alarm, Mr. Haines. I'm going to do a bed count now to make sure."

"Okay," crackles a voice through the box. "Let me know if you want me to come by."

She steps back from the alarm then. After looking around the room one more time, she shuffles down the hall, whispering to a few girls who have poked their heads out of their doors that everything's fine and they should go back to sleep.

I want to sigh with relief, but I'm not off the hook yet. *Bed count.* I need to get back upstairs before Jenna notices that I'm missing. Luckily, she's starting her check with the first floor's rooms, and there's a second stairway in the other direction.

I take the stairs two at a time, my only focus on diving under my covers. But at the big window at the landing, something makes me pause. There's a strange glowing where the grass meets the woods. It doesn't seem like a light.

I squint. The glowing shape moves and shimmers. If I look hard enough, I can make out long hair, two arms and legs, and blurriness where a face should be. Is that . . . *a girl*? Why is she just . . . standing there? Why is she radiating?

A door bangs, and my spine straightens. I hurry up the rest of the stairs, down the hall, and push into my room, shutting the door softly behind me. Ursula is still sound asleep in her bed, thankfully unfazed by the blaring alarm.

I climb under the covers and close my eyes, too. A few minutes later, when Jenna opens our door to make sure we're both here, I'm tucked in and feigning sleep.

My heart is pounding hard, though. I'm still trying to wrap my mind around the figure I saw in the darkness. Whatever it was, it was floating.

Is she . . . a ghost?

Is she *Martha*?

"So," Ursula says to me the next morning, her mouth filled with foam. "What's your first class?"

I'm too entranced to answer. Not only does water flow from a spigot and down a drain instead of from a dirty bucket, Ursula and I are standing at the basin brushing some kind of minty mixture onto our teeth with a clean bristled apparatus and *not* an old rag, like we used in Salem.

*Toothbrush*, I remind myself. Last night, when I was too wired to sleep after my foiled escape attempt, I stood under the shower and was able to gather enough magical power to perform a crash-course spell to catch up with all the slang and modern marvels of 2025. It's a spell I've normally used when teleporting to a country where I don't know the language, but it worked pretty well in this case, too. It was a risk, of course—Martha could have sensed the energy disturbance—but I've found that spells involved with thinking and knowledge tend to attract much less attention than, say, levitating, or shooting fire from my fingers.

I now know what a computer does, how a cell phone works, that it's perfectly normal for girls to ask boys on dates (and what dates *are*), and that life in 2025 in Salem, Massachusetts, is not filled with backbreaking work, misery, and constant fear of starvation, attack, and terrible diseases like it once was. In fact, most of the diseases we worried about aren't even an issue for people in 2025. There are vaccines for them. Medications. *Cures.* On the other hand, there are things in 2025 that are much more terrifying. Weapons have become devastatingly sophisticated. There are still wars all over the world. My mind is now filled with the knowledge that people walk into crowded spaces and open fire on innocent civilians, and that governments are still corrupt, and people are still persecuted for all kinds of reasons, and in many places, living conditions are still intolerable and wretched. But the school seems like a little bubble of cleanliness, safety, and privilege. Or it was . . . until Martha came along.

The spell hasn't filled in all the blanks—Ursula has made references to music groups and TV shows that mean nothing to me, and she's referred to a popular "meme" that I can't wrap my head around, and I'm astonished that our country is now called America and not *the colonies* and I want to know *why* . . . but I figure it will all come in time. At least I feel like I have a handle on things here, finally. At least I don't feel completely blank whenever anyone talks to me.

I spit out the toothpaste and, remembering that Ursula has asked me a question, pause to look at the printed schedule Headmistress Peabody handed me yesterday in her office. "Let me see. . . ."

"Cheese!" Ursula cries suddenly.

I look up. She's holding up a square object I now know is an iPad. Phones aren't allowed on campus, but tablet devices are, as long as people don't load social media onto them.

I frown. "Cheese . . . *what*?"

"Cheese, like smile!" She turns the device around to show me. "We need a picture of your first day at the academy, see?"

I stare at the image of myself on the screen. I look stunned as I stand at the mirror with the schedule in my hands. Half of Ursula is reflected in the mirror, too, her face obscured by the camera device.

I consult my schedule. "Um, I have Chemistry first. With Dr. Novis. I met him yesterday—he was in that meeting with the headmistress."

Ursula makes a face. "He's weird, huh?"

I shrug. "He did seem a little . . ."

"Awkward? Creepy? Does he always look at you funny, like he thinks you're doing something bad?" Ursula looks guilty. "Sorry. My mom says it isn't nice to gossip. But we used to have this really nice teacher, Mr. Haverford. Dr. Novis took over his classes, and it's just not the same. I don't trust him at all."

Then I think of something else. "What was with that weird . . . *disturbance* yesterday? Those tornadoes?" I didn't mention it to her last night at the dining hall because, well, I was so enamored and amazed with the quality of the food. I'm curious to see what the students think about it.

Ursula's eyes widen. "It's happened a few times."

"How many?"

Ursula places her toothbrush back in a little cloth bag that also holds a hairbrush and some makeup. I don't have one, so I wrap my toothbrush in a piece of toilet paper. Amazing that I even have a toothbrush. This morning, there was a little basket with my name on it in our bathroom containing all kinds of useful toiletry items.

"Three times? Four?" Ursula says. "It never lasts long. Don't be scared. The teachers have assured us that we're safe here."

I find it interesting that the teachers think everyone is safe if they don't even know how or why the disturbances are happening—if they *did* know, they'd be terrified.

I turn to my uniform on the hanger. Just like my fairy godmother toiletry kit, I found several identical Conant Academy uniforms in my closet this morning. The skirts seem indecently short, the sweaters are soft but unnaturally constricting, and the knee socks don't seem to provide any warmth. At least the loafer-style shoes don't cut off the circulation of my toes.

"Has anything else weird happened?" I ask Ursula, my back turned. "Like . . . eerie?" I can't stop thinking about whatever it was I saw at the edge of the trees—that strange spectral girl. "Weird . . . apparitions, maybe? Ghosts on campus?"

Ursula cocks her head. "You mean the Halloween animatronics?"

Oh. Maybe *that's* what I saw through the window last night.

"I know being in a boarding school is an adjustment, but you'll get used to it," Ursula assures me. "Besides the tornadoes . . . and besides what happened with Sylvie . . . the year's been pretty calm."

*Sylvie.* The haunted look on Ursula's face appears again. My antisocial side is telling me not to get involved, but my nosy side wins.

"So you really have no idea what happened to her?" I ask as I walk over to the bed and sit down. "Maybe she just ran away?"

Ursula shrugs.

"How can you be so sure she isn't with her family?" I press.

"Because I called them."

"Where do her parents live?"

"Um, Connecticut." She turns up her palms. "They don't know where she is, either."

Her shoulders heave up and down. It looks like she wants to say more, but then she seems to swallow the words. "Is that the way you feel about your friend, too?" she asks after a moment. "You, um, said, you'd been in my same situation."

"Oh. Sort of." I pull my pillow onto my lap, thinking of Prudence. "I kind of looked out for her. I wish I could find her."

Ursula frowns. "She's still missing?"

The words have flown out of my mouth before I realize I've said them. I wish I could spool them back in. "Well . . . no. Not now. It's sort of . . . complicated." Isn't *that* the truth. "By *now*, I'm sure she has been found. But *I* still don't know what happened."

"And you haven't looked her up on Instagram? TikTok?"

Thank goodness my spell explained those apps. "She's, um, not on any of those."

"What was her name? Was her disappearance public—like, on the news?"

"Nothing like that." Salem didn't have a newspaper. The only people even aware she was gone were the coven . . . and we all know how much they cared. "Her name was Prudence. Prudence Charity Jones." It's weird to say her name out loud.

Ursula narrows her eyes. "Huh. I feel like I *know* that name. But . . . maybe not. Anyway, I'm really sorry."

"Thanks," I say, uncomfortably touched. "I'm sorry about Sylvie, too."

Ursula smiles at me shyly. "Well, here's to a *new* friendship."

I resist the urge to burst out laughing. Agatha Harkness does *not* make cheesy friendship promises. But Ursula meets my gaze, and her smile is pure. Hopeful.

"Cheers," I mutter. I don't want to hurt her feelings.

I poke my arms through the holes of my sweater, eager to change the subject. "So where did you grow up, anyway? Before coming to Conant Academy, I mean."

"New York City. Which isn't nearly as glamorous as everyone thinks. I'd rather never go back there, honestly." She shudders. "Too many buildings. Too many crowds. And it's so *dirty*. All the rats—it's disgusting."

Her words send me down a long tunnel of memory. *New York City*. All at once, I'm back in that vision I had when I went through the portal—swooping, bat-like, around a city, looking at the buildings from above. But they were old buildings, small and meager, bigger than the ones in Salem but barely. I knew I was flying around New York City even though I've never been there.

I remember arcing down to the window . . . and seeing an old version of myself inside. What *was* that? The memory shivers before me, threatening to vanish, but I fight hard to keep it in my mind. I gotta say, Old Agatha looks really irritated to be an old woman. She glowers out the window of her little shack. And then I hear footsteps. Someone is coming.

A woman appears on the path. It's a fiery-haired being I've never seen before—not in 2025, and not in my past. I knew instantly what she was and that we were different—mutant and witch—but also the same in so many ways. She floats instead of walks, and there's an eerie yellow aura around her body. After checking the address, she drifts to Old Agatha's door and knocks. Nothing happens. She knocks again.

*I know you're in there, Agatha,* she calls. *We need to talk.*

Finally, Old Agatha whips the door open and glares at the redheaded witch. *Firestar,* she grumbles. *Why have you darkened my doorway?*

*Firestar?* I think. Who is *that*?

"Alice?"

I jump. Ursula is staring at me.

I look down at myself. I'm sitting on my bed. I have

on one knee sock and haven't even fully pulled on my sweater. I have no idea how much time has passed.

"Are you . . . okay?" she asks. "You sort of . . . disappeared for a minute."

I nod and try to smile. "S-sure. Just, um, remembering a dream." I wish it were only that.

Then Ursula turns to her desk. "I meant to ask you, have you seen my earring?"

I blink at her.

She holds a glint of silver in her hand. "One of them is missing. I swear they were here just yesterday. You haven't seen it on the ground?"

I open my mouth, but no sounds come out. She knows I handed it over to a crow. This is the moment she decides not to be my ally and sees me for who I truly am.

I shake my head and shrug, feeling guilty, but to my surprise, Ursula shrugs, too. "Oh well. It probably fell off while I was walking to class. C'est la vie. Now, you ready?"

She opens the door for us to pass through, and I duck my head, not wanting her to see my guilty expression. I'm relieved she didn't figure it out, but on the other hand, I can't believe she's so trusting. *No one* should trust me. Ever.

The Conant Academy Green on a Monday morning is shockingly different than it was on a lazy Sunday afternoon. The paths teem with students in uniforms rushing here and there, some with noses in books, others in shoving clumps, and still others walking slowly like they'd rather take as long as possible to get to class. But one thing's for sure: Everyone knows Ursula.

"Hey, Urs!" a group of girls crow, pausing so they can all hug. Then they turn to me. "Is this your new roomie?"

"This is her!" Ursula trills. "Alice Harvey."

"Hi!" The girls lunge at me for a hug. "Welcome, Alice!"

I back away from their outstretched arms. "Whoa, whoa, not really into touching."

They introduce themselves regardless, their names flying at me quickly like enchanted butterflies. Samara. Bethany. Jasmine. Yumiko. They fawn over Ursula, saying how happy she seems these days, how great it is that she has someone new as her roommate, how they knew she'd be feeling better. Some of them even exchange cautious, worried smiles. I wonder if they're being delicate around Ursula because of Sylvie's disappearance, trying to bolster her up because she's been so sad and traumatized.

Once those girls move on, another group hurries up with more encouraging words for Ursula. More introductions, too: Lila. Polly. Maria-Therese. They're a mix of ethnicities and nationalities, but they all share a common language: public affection. My excuses not to touch anyone become more and more bizarre: "I have sensitive skin." "I'm getting over smallpox." "I haven't showered in three hundred thirty-four years."

"Do you know *everyone* at this school?" I ask Ursula wearily as we extract ourselves from yet another adoring throng.

"It's not a very big place," Ursula says, laughing. "You'll know everyone soon, too."

But then her expression sours. I follow her gaze to a girl with dirty-blond hair across the green. Instead of rushing toward Ursula like the rest of the world, this girl stands at a distance, smirking. A few others are with her, too, whispering and pointing.

"What's going on over there?" I ask.

"That's Campbell Sweeney," Ursula says. "She's also new."

"Why's she looking at us like that?"

Ursula's shoulders droop. "It's kind of become a thing with her."

Campbell and her posse walk right up to us, which is a little unnerving. Up close, she's quite tall and has the clearest skin and the longest eyelashes I've ever seen.

"Who are you?" she asks me.

I straighten. "Alice. Just got here."

"What's with your face?"

I blink. What kind of question is *that*?

But before I can ask, Campbell and her group burst into peals of laughter and skip away. "Party in my room Friday night," Campbell tells her group in a loud voice like she wants us to hear. "Everyone's invited. Well"—and now she glances at us pointedly—"everyone on my *list*."

They laugh again. I feel my fingers forming a fist. "*She's* a delight," I mutter to Ursula. "I'm guessing we're not on her list?" Not that I'd attend her party anyway.

"I don't know what I've done to upset her." Ursula looks distressed. "She has something against our whole coven, in fact. You'll meet them soon enough."

"Come on," I say, grabbing Ursula's hand and dragging her away from the group. "We don't need her anyway."

We continue walking. A bunch of lively boys barrel through, shoving and bumping into each other, playing some sort of game on the green. They almost run us over, but I step out of the way just in time.

"You're beasts!" I call after them.

The boys wave like this is a compliment. It's been a long time since I've had much interaction with the opposite sex—covens are mostly women, and in Salem, it was frowned upon for a single woman to even *look* at a man. But these boys are youthful and boisterous, not bedraggled and full of pent-up anger like even the young Salem men were. Ursula waves at a few.

"Ursu-*lah*!" one boy booms from across the green. A kid behind him hops on his shoulders, nearly knocking him over.

Ursula turns away haughtily, but I can see her smiling. "Did you have a boyfriend at your old place?"

I nearly swallow my tongue. "What? *No*."

"It's not a crime."

*In my old town, it kind of was,* I think, but I don't say it.

Ursula points out more boys across the green. A few are pretending to dance with one of the Halloween skeletons. "Most are really nice. And you want to have a date to the Halloween dance, right? It's in two weeks—the best event of the school year. Girls ask their dates. It's tradition."

"Uh, pretty sure I'm not going to that."

She cocks her head. "Why not?"

I keep laughing. Agatha and Halloween dances don't mix. Agatha and *boys* don't mix. We're like acid and baking soda: mix it together, and the whole thing explodes.

But just as I'm saying this, a figure steps out from behind one of the huge oak trees. He's tall and lanky, with a rounded jaw, green eyes, and longish golden hair that falls almost to his shoulders. He reminds me of someone I knew long ago. A prince? A warlock? Or no, wait. A dog. A shaggy, happy farm dog like Holdfast, the one I remember back in the 1690s. He found so much joy in romping around, herding the sheep.

The boy looks up and sees me staring. His eyebrows shoot up. A hint of a smile crosses his features. Mortified, I look away. My heart is beating so quickly. My hands feel clammy. My head is woozy. Am I dying? Have I contracted smallpox? I'm feeling so strange. Whatever this is, I don't like it.

I don't like it at all.

# *Five*

Later that evening, Ursula and I stand outside a small cave at the edge of campus. Night has fallen. Creatures rustle in the trees. The wind has picked up, scrabbling fallen leaves and sticks across the forest floor. I hear something howl—maybe a wolf.

"You definitely didn't see anyone following us, right?" she asks me.

"For the millionth time, no," I whisper back.

There were big signs prohibiting students from leaving the academy's grounds and a low iron fence to mark the border. Ursula glances over her shoulder, makes sure no one is watching, and then climbs over the fence easily. I do the same. Technically, we aren't breaking curfew—students are allowed out at night as long as they're at sports practice, another sanctioned activity, or in the school's library. And so, Ursula and I checked out of our dorm, saying we were going to the library to study. When we got to the library, however, we avoided signing our names at the check-in desk when the librarian on duty wasn't looking—that way, when we snuck out minutes later, the librarian would have no record we were missing. We only have an hour, though. After that, the library closes, the dorm doors lock, and the RA will do a head count and realize we're gone. What Conant Academy does *not* allow, obviously, is students wandering free on campus after hours.

But it feels fun to be bad. I've made it through exactly one day of school, and it feels like my brain has been hit repeatedly with a very hard hammer. There's no way I'm going to cram in all the information the teachers want us to learn in time to take any exams. My hope is that I won't be *here* for any exams, but just in case my search for the Darkhold takes longer than I expect, I'm going to have to come up with a memorization spell to help.

Then I hear a strange *beep* from somewhere in the woods. I freeze and look at Ursula. "What is that?"

She cocks her head, listening, too. "I don't hear anything."

We wait a few more moments. I don't hear the beep again. It was probably just an animal. Or one of those Halloween decorations. Certainly not that strange glowing thing I saw out the window yesterday.

"You okay with small spaces?" Ursula asks, gesturing to the mouth of the cave. "The coven meets in there. It's, you know. Witchy."

"I'm fine with small spaces."

And I know this cave, actually. I used to steal away to this very spot when I'd had enough of the coven. Sometimes, Prudence followed me. We'd pass the time by telling stories about Atlantis, the Roman Empire, my time on Mount Wundagore. Prudence loved my tales. Little did she know they were true, personal accounts of things I'd actually lived through.

I feel a pang of dread. Has another day passed in 1691 with no one searching for Prudence? I picture her locked in the Parris stables, maybe, or perhaps their springhouse. She's probably so scared she can barely breathe.

"So listen," Ursula says, and I snap out of my thoughts. "Before we go in, there are some things you should know. The coven might be a little standoffish at first. They don't make friends easily."

I nod. "I'm fine with standoffish." I'd actually *rather* they're standoffish than shower me with more hugs. My main objective, in joining this coven, is to see if Martha is among them.

"Our leader is Ivy," Ursula goes on. "Be sure to say hello to her *first*."

I roll my eyes. "Why does she get to be your leader? Seniority?" Just like Elizabeth Good.

"Sort of, I guess. She's the one who created the coven at the beginning of this year." Ursula's smile twitches. "She's a little intimidating. I think she knows *actual spells*."

I perk up. Could it really be *that simple*?

Then Ursula fans her hands around her mouth and makes a birdcall sound into the mouth of the cave. A moment later, someone inside the cave makes the same birdcall back. *Caw-caw. Caw-caw.*

Ursula nods at me. "That means we can enter."

She ducks into the cave's dark mouth, and I crawl in after her. It's so pitch-black I can't see an inch in front of my face, just like it used to be in 1691. It smells the same, too—earthy, musty, and a little bit like bat guano.

"Sisters, I have a new potential member," Ursula says softly, her voice echoing off the narrow walls. "Show yourselves!"

A tiny light flicks on. There, gathered on the rocks, sit four people. They're all still dressed in their school uniforms, just like I am, but they've jazzed them up significantly. A dark-haired girl with spiky black hair and black makeup wears shredded tights and work boots under her plaid skirt. A tiny, pale, nymphlike girl has a granny-square cardigan slung over her school-issue blouse and wears pink furry slippers on her feet. A lithe Black girl with beautiful cheekbones and a shining nose ring wears a pile of necklaces and a stack of bracelets and has her academy blazer rolled up to her elbows, and a guy with wavy hair to his shoulders and tiny wire glasses wears a giant, rainbow-colored fur coat as a complement to Conant Academy's boring khaki pants.

"You didn't tell us you were bringing someone new," the spiky-haired girl says, her voice sharp. She's got deep-set eyes and a bow-shaped mouth that seems to be in a permanent smirk. My guard goes up.

"Alice is my new roommate," Ursula says. "I think she'd make a great addition. Alice, this is Ivy."

She nudges me as if to say, *This is our leader! Be nice.*

"What's up," I say in a taut voice.

Ivy scrutinizes me unabashedly. The candle's shadows making her features look pointed and ghoulish—and irritatingly alluring. I'm tempted to climb into her mind so I can interpret her thoughts, but I have to be careful. She's giving big Martha vibes. Reading her mind would tip her off about me. A witch always knows when another witch is trying to mind-control her.

The Black girl on the right clears her throat and

shifts forward. "Jamira Atwood. I live in Farnsworth Hall and specialize in tarot and contacting the dead. Aren't you in my Geometry class?"

I blink. "Uh . . . maybe? Is that the dreadfully boring class about the triangles?"

She smirks. "Right. That's how I feel about Geometry, too."

I shake her hand, appreciating her firm but friendly grip. Definitely not Martha energy.

"Francie Jones." The elfin blond doesn't look up from a pile of knitting in her lap. "I'm into love and healing magic."

I doubt she's Martha, either, because her knitting project is so tangled and messy. Every witch I know who bothers with knitting can create perfect stitches every time, thanks to easy stitchery spells.

The guy witch seems downright thrilled. "Evan," he says, moving over so I can sit next to him. "I'm really good at removing evil spirits from rooms. Just give me a smudge stick, and I'll clean out any bad auras. I've seen you across the green, by the way, and I was dying to say hello—I love new people. Also, Alice is the *perfect* witchy name. I mean some people might think *Alice in Wonderland*, but there's also Alice Cooper, you know?"

"Totally," I lie. I have no idea who he's talking about, but I like his happy aura.

"Evan, can you chill with the enthusiasm?" Ivy gives him a sharp look. "We haven't actually approved her yet, so her name is not yet witchy or *un*witchy."

Ursula laughs awkwardly. "But you didn't have to approve us when we wanted to join."

"That's because I know all of you," Ivy says. "I *trust* you. You'll keep our coven a secret. Where'd Alice even come from? Why did you come to the academy two months into the school year?"

"I'll keep the coven a secret," I volunteer. "Being a rat isn't my style."

"She also owns the most amazing witch's cloak," Ursula says. "It's vintage."

"Our craft is about more than *fashion*." Ivy sounds disgusted.

I turn to her. "What's *your* specialty in the coven, by the way? Francie heals, Evan's got his smudge sticks, Jamira's into contacting the dead . . ."

Ivy raises her chin. "I'm the leader. That's my specialty."

"Meaning you don't *have* a specialty."

The other witches gasp, like I've said something taboo. I can't help myself. I love to spar.

"Ivy, Alice didn't mean that," Ursula says hurriedly.

"Maybe she did. How can I tell she's not a spy?" Ivy asks.

I groan. "If you're worried I'm going to tell, I won't. I can't stand authority."

"We'll get in big trouble if the teachers find us out," Ivy says. "And if they *do* find us out, I'm going to assume it was you who said something."

"They have a task force," Francie says without looking up from her knitting. "At the head of it is that new teacher. Dr. Stephen."

I frown. "Dr. Stephen?"

"Dr. Novis," Ursula explains to me. "Some of us call him Dr. Stephen."

"As a joke," Francie says.

"*Never* to his face," Jamira insists. "It really bothers him."

I chuckle. "He's that offended that you call him Dr. Stephen? Sounds kinda sensitive."

"Most teachers don't like us referring to them by their first names," Ursula says. "And Dr. Novis . . . he seems *particularly* old-fashioned."

She leans forward. "Alice was with Dr. Stephen when the latest earthquake happened. She had to hide under the desk with him and the headmistress. He's *so* odd. Always *staring* at us, like he's trying to read our minds."

"And does he even know how to play field hockey?" Francie adds. "Like, has he ever even seen a game?"

Ursula and I look at each other and giggle. Not that I know how to play field hockey, either—today was my first practice—but Dr. Novis, who'd taken over as coach, gave us some random drills he'd found on the internet. I had no idea what I was doing, but half the team stopped and gave him a strange look. Apparently, most of the drills were for soccer.

"Mr. Haverford was a great coach," Ursula sighs. "At least he knew how to use a field hockey stick."

"Wait, what happened to Mr. Haverford, exactly?" I ask, remembering that Headmistress Peabody mentioned that name. "Did he quit?"

Evan's eyes widen. "It was weird. One day he was here, and the next . . . *poof.* I walked into his office after he left, and I got the *eeriest* feeling."

"People don't go *poof.*" Not normal humans, anyway, unless they've been put under spells.

Though . . . wait a minute.

"*When* did Mr. Haverford disappear?" I ask.

"At the beginning of this year," Evan says. "Around the same time Syl . . ." But then he trails off, looking guiltily at Ursula.

"It's okay," Ursula says. "I told her about Sylvie."

"So let me get this straight," I say. "A teacher *and* Sylvie disappeared at the same time?"

"Pretty much," Jamira says. "There were all these

rumors that Mr. Haverford kidnapped Sylvie, but no one believes it."

I'm not sure I believe that, either. Could Martha have gotten rid of them, maybe? I watch Ivy carefully, seeing if she looks particularly guilty or if she's hiding other emotions. She kind of looks annoyed.

"Can we not get sidetracked by Sylvie and Mr. Haverford?" she says. "There are a million rumors, and they're all probably wrong. Same as all the talk about the weird weather stuff. It's not aliens. It's not the government using satellites. It's boring old global warming."

*Hmm*, I think. Interesting that she's trying to get us off the topic of Sylvie and Mr. Haverford. And that sounds exactly like what someone who's trying to cover up that she's bewitching the weather would say.

Ivy turns back to me. "Look, this coven—it needs to be top secret. Also, we do things differently than most other witches. I mean, as you can see, there aren't thirteen of us, and we don't assemble in a nine-foot circle and conjure up dark spirits."

I scoff. "Witches don't actually do that. Same with the pointed hats and broomsticks."

"How would *you* know?"

She glares at me. I glare back. I can't tell if she's really asking . . . or if she's just pretending not to know.

"Anyway," Ivy says, "the point of our coven is to use

our skills *and* our smarts to disrupt the status quo on campus. We're trying to right wrongs. Use our skills to enchant, bewitch, and make things more fair." She crosses her arms. "But even saying that is saying too much. Like I said, if the teachers find out, I'm going to assume it's you—and then I'll have to kill you."

"Not really, Alice!" Ursula laughs nervously. "She's totally kidding!"

"C'mon, Ivy," Evan says. "Just let her join. I like her."

"Same," says Jamira. "You're fiery, Alice."

Francie makes a little "mm" sound that doesn't sound too terribly negative. I'm enjoying this, mostly because it's really making Ivy mad.

Then Ivy smiles mischievously. "Okay. She can join the coven if she passes a simple test."

"A test?" Evan turns to her. "Like truth or dare?"

"Sort of." Ivy shifts closer, and I can smell a strawberry scent on her skin. It makes me a little dizzy. "There's a boy named Jack Poole in Paddington Hall. He isn't a good person. I want you to sneak into his room—it's 124—open his top drawer, and steal a little envelope that's tucked in next to his boxers."

"Hold on," Evan says. "I knew we were going to get Jack in some sort of way, but—"

"We haven't even agreed on anything yet," Jamira interrupts.

"And, Ivy." Ursula looks nervous. "Don't make Alice sneak into the dorms after hours."

"No?" Ivy smirks at me, the candlelight flickering across her face. "Maybe it *is* too hard of a task."

I straighten up. "I'll do it. But why's this guy so bad? I'm not going to do it without a reason."

"He's a jerk," Jamira says.

"A meathead," Francie mutters. "Pounds people's heads in for fun."

"Gives major bully energy," Evan seconds. "*And* he's a cheat."

I cross my arms. "What's in the envelope?"

"Something that will get him in trouble," Ivy says cryptically. "Also, since you asked, *my* skill is psychic powers. I know for a fact that he has something hidden in his drawer that we can expose. I also know he's at soccer practice right now, so the room is empty."

"Your psychic powers told you that?" I say sarcastically, though I feel a little worried. How psychic *is* she, actually? Psychic enough to sense who I really am?

Ivy gives me an exasperated glare. "*No*, Alice. The school schedule told me. And it's a pretty tight window. Practice is over soon. He'll be back to his room thirty minutes from now."

"I'll be back here in fifteen," I say through gritted teeth.

"Alice!" Ursula looks worried. "That's not enough time!"

"Don't make promises you can't keep," Ivy warns me. "If you can't deliver, you're out. And we'll have to kill you."

"Something tells me you'd love that." I stand up, annoyance snapping through me. I hate being told I'm not up for something. "I'll be back."

I turn around and leave the cave, remembering to duck at a deceptively low rock outcropping just before the exit—it's exactly the same as it was hundreds of years ago, when Prudence accidentally bashed her head on it so many times.

There are footsteps behind me. Ursula has run out of the cave, too. "You don't have to do this. I'm sorry she's being hard on you. The group can be so tough."

I shove my hands in the pockets of the sweater she's loaned me. "Ivy likes people arguing with her. I can tell. Also, if she's psychic, then I'm part raccoon." As I say it, I realize it's true. If Ivy actually *were* psychic, she'd already know why I was here and what I was looking for. She would have called me out already, and we'd be locked in a battle, trying to destroy each other.. This doesn't mean she isn't Martha, of course . . . it just means she's a liar.

"As far as the rest of the group goes, they seem fine," I add as I step over the fence and back onto campus. "I want to join. I can totally do this."

Ursula rushes to keep pace. "This isn't fair, though. You might get in trouble. How are you going to sneak in *and* get back in fifteen minutes?"

"I'll manage. Don't worry."

"But someone might see you." She sounds so concerned. "You know what? I'll just come. I'll stand guard."

There's no arguing with her, so I let her follow. It's actually helpful, because she can point me to where Paddington Hall is. We rush ahead down the leafy paths. The air has grown colder even in the past half hour, and the sun is starting to set, turning the sky orange and casting the trees in spindly silhouettes. I notice how neat things look on the green. There aren't downed trees, tipped-over decorations, or even scattered leaves. The earthquake was only yesterday and everything is cleaned up—it's clear a witch tidied things. How nice of Martha. And is Martha . . . Ivy?

"How well do you know Ivy, anyway?" I ask Ursula as we walk.

"Uh, pretty well?"

"You don't sound so sure about that."

"No, I am. I just don't know what you mean. Like, are we best friends? No. But we've always been interested in the same things."

"Like tarot and stuff? Witchcraft? And she's been going to school here for how long?"

"Since the beginning of high school," Ursula answers.

"And she hasn't acted strangely lately? Like . . ." I'm not sure how to ask the question. *Like someone else took over her body?*

Paddington Hall is a two-story stone building with stained-glass windows and a slate roof. Pine trees hem the path to the doors, so I tell Ursula to stand guard out on the sidewalk, where she'll have a better view of anyone coming.

She looks at me worriedly. "How are you going to figure out how to get the doors open? Can you pick locks?"

"Something like that."

I dash down the path. It's long and dark, and soon, I can't even see Ursula waiting on the sidewalk anymore. Sure enough, the front doors are shut tight; I pull at the handles, but they don't budge. There's a little keypad off to the side, but it seems to need some sort of electronic key to be allowed entrance—or, I realize, a special numeric code.

I remember the code I'd memorized from the other night when the RA typed it in. I wonder if this school is lazy enough to use the same codes for all the buildings. I give it a try, but the keypad makes an angry beep, and the buttons flash red. I'm not sure I can risk trying it again—something tells me I can only enter codes a few times before an alarm goes off. And the real code could be anything. A zillion different number combinations.

I glance over my shoulder. Ursula hasn't whistled that anyone's approaching, and I don't see anyone in the lobby, either. Hurriedly, I covertly recite some magic words and wait. There's a metallic *clunk*. The bolt gives way, and the door swings open.

I slip inside and look around. The hallway of the boys' dorm is dim and echoing, and it smells like feet—a scent that has remained exactly the same since Salem 1691. There's music playing inside, light chatter. As I tiptoe past the rooms, some of the doors are ajar, and I can see figures moving inside.

I pass room 115, 117, 119. Room 124 must be close. Suddenly, a door behind me whips open, and a teenage boy with mussed hair wearing sweatpants and a T-shirt steps out. I freeze. In seconds, he'll see me; I don't have time to waste. I whisper some words under my breath, and my body dissolves. The invisibility spell. Relief floods me again that the spell has gone off without a hitch. Maybe I'm getting stronger. See? My powers returning had nothing to do with being true to thineself or whatever.

The boy stops and looks around, maybe sensing a shift in energy. I stay very still, unseen. After a moment, he trundles down the hall in the opposite direction. He opens another door at the far end of the hall, perhaps a communal bathroom. The door slams shut. He's gone.

The silence echoes in my head. I count to three, then cancel the spell—I don't want to practice magic for too long, or Martha might sense my powers and find me to wreak her final revenge. My body shimmers into view again. I glance at the clock hanging in the hallway above the rooms.

Ten minutes left. I bet Ursula's panicking out there.

Room 124 is just ahead. I turn the knob, and it opens easily. The room is empty, meaning Ivy was right about this guy being at soccer practice. The space looks exactly like Ursula's and mine with two beds on either side, two desks, one window—except this room is decorated with pictures of sports stars and popular movies.

Ivy told me to check the dresser on the right, so that's the direction I turn. I yank open the top drawer. Inside is a jumble of a teenage boy's undergarments, things I'd really rather not touch. Still, I plunge my hand into the mess of underwear and feel around for paper. Nothing. Frowning, I stand on my tiptoes and feel to the very back of the drawer. All I touch is cotton. I feel a prickle of fury. *Did Ivy set me up?*

But then, way in a corner, I touch a sharp, square paper corner. *Bingo.* I slide the envelope toward me and tuck it in the sleeve of my sweater.

"Uh, hello?"

I swivel around in horror. A figure stands in the doorway. It's . . . him. Not Jack, but the guy I saw across the quad. The one I couldn't stop looking at.

My mind drains of all rational thoughts. I notice a key hanging from his fist, along with a blocky key chain with his dorm room number on it. I was given one of those. The number on his reads *124*. Meaning . . . this is his room, too.

I scramble to recall my spell that will erase his memory, but I don't feel the normal crackle of energy. It's like my battery has gone dead. *Ugh*—maybe I spoke too soon about my powers being back. I have to handle him without magic.

"Uh . . . hello." I step away from the bureau. I feel the envelope pressed up in the folds of the sweater. "I—I was just leaving."

He cocks his head. "But what were you doing here in the first place?"

I blink. "I, um, know your roommate," I lie. "We're friends. Good friends. We go way back."

A tense moment passes. Then he laughs. "No way. You're not Jack's type."

"What's *that* mean?"

"Believe me, it's a compliment." His expression softens. "You're new, right? Didn't I see you across the quad yesterday?"

My mouth wobbles. *He saw me, too?* But that doesn't mean anything. It's clearly just an observation.

"I'm West," he says, stepping closer. "How'd you even get into this dorm? Last I checked, girls aren't allowed. Which, I mean, isn't *my* rule, but you could get in big trouble."

"Maybe I like getting in trouble," I say.

His eyebrows raise. "Well then, I won't stop you . . . doing whatever you're doing."

His gaze on me makes me feel warm and kind of tingly. Whatever this feeling is, it's making me lose control. I have to get out of here.

I rush past him. "You never saw me. This never happened." And then, before I know what I'm doing, I knock the whole jar of pencils from his desk to the floor. They clank and scatter everywhere, and he stoops to pick them up. The moment he's distracted, I bolt out of there.

"Wait!" he cries, half standing up again. "What's your name?"

I run down the hall, past open doors and sleepy-looking man-children stumbling into the bathroom and a big poster about basketball sign-ups. I nearly knock a boy in slippers over as I barrel out the front door and to the quad, though I'm moving too quickly I don't think he even sees me.

Ursula erupts into a sigh of relief when she sees me

at the end of the path. "I thought something happened! I was so worried!"

"I'm fine. I've got the envelope. We're good."

I start toward the cave, but she grabs my arm. "We won't make it back to the cave in time! Curfew is too soon!"

I touch her hand. "Go to the dorms if you're worried. If for some reason Jenna does bed check early, just tell her I'm in the bathroom."

Ursula bites her lip. "Are you sure?"

I tell her I am. Then I tell her three more times before she feels confident enough to run back to the dorms. I've never sprinted so fast as I cross the green back to the cave—*who bothers running when you can fly?*—and when I reach the coven's meeting point, I know, instinctively, that I've gotten here with no time to spare.

I fling myself back through the mouth of the cave, nearly bumping into the coven on their way out. I guess they weren't waiting around.

I toss the envelope at Ivy's chest. "This what you were looking for?"

"Ew!" Evan cries, scuttling away like a cloud of mold spores have dispersed in the air. "Was that really in Jack's underwear drawer?"

"Alice!" Jamira looks delighted. "You got it?"

I roll my eyes. "It's not like it was hard."

Ivy lifts the envelope to the light she's holding. Her brow is furrowed and her nose is wrinkled. "How'd you get this?"

"With my two legs," I snap, rolling my eyes. "And hands. And eyeballs. Ursula went back to the dorms, by the way. Which is where we should be, too."

"But how did you get into Paddington Hall?" Ivy asks. "It's locked."

"Are you going to keep asking questions, or are you going to thank me?"

Ivy studies me carefully. I smile at her and then, impulsively, blow her a kiss. She flinches.

"Who cares how she did it?" Jamira blurts. "You're being way too hard on her, Ivy! Just let her into the group already!"

"No one saw you?" Ivy asks.

I look away. "Nope." Better not to tell her about West and . . . whatever that was. "So what's in the envelope?"

Ivy opens it up. We all lean in to look. Ivy pulls out a folded-up piece of paper and begins to open it flat. *Chemistry Midterm*, it reads at the top. Below are test questions . . . and all the answers.

"This is for Dr. Stephen's class," Evan says. "But we haven't even had this midterm yet." He looks at Ivy questioningly. "So this is a cheat sheet?"

"What do you think?" Ivy murmurs.

"How did you know this was here?" Francie asks.

Ivy crosses her arms. "I just *did*."

I want to make a snarky remark about Ivy's psychic abilities—I still don't buy it—but we're all too busy staring at the paper.

Then Evan turns to me. "It's common knowledge that he cheats a lot, but he's never been caught."

"He's also at the top of the class, which is really annoying," Francie adds.

"And the teachers *never* do anything about it," Jamira says. "Think the guy walks on water, just because his parents are big donors." She looks at the cheat sheet. "But how's he gonna get an A on the midterm without this?"

"But why stop at him failing a midterm?" I ask. "We should slip the cheat sheet back in his backpack when he isn't looking . . . and then tip off the headmistress to search his things. That way he'll also get in trouble—and there will be no way for him to wriggle out of it."

There's a long pause. "That's not a bad idea," Francie says.

"I have Calc with him tomorrow morning," Jamira says. "I could put it in there."

"I kind of love this," Evan says. "You're a *natural* disrupter, Alice."

I shrug. "I actually thought that was already *part* of the plan. It seems obvious."

Ivy looks like she might explode. She hates the idea, but only because she didn't think of it. Finally, she sighs noisily. "Fine. I'll tip off Peabody once you give me the signal, Jamira."

"And what about Alice?" Jamira goads. "She's in the coven, right?"

Ivy shuts her eyes like she has a very bad headache. "I suppose."

"About freaking *time*," Evan bellows. He throws his arms around my shoulders with so much gusto that I can't wriggle free.

"I totally believed in you," he whispers. "I knew you could do it all along."

But as I break away from him—I can only stand being touched for so long—a wild gust of cold air swirls against us. It's a gale force, strong and sudden, blowing Jamira into a tree, Evan and Francie into one another, and Francie's knitting needles flying into the air.

"What the—?" Ivy cries, covering her head.

We fight to stand upright against the hurricane-level wind. I drop to the grass to brace myself against the impact. This feels just like the tornado that kicked up when I was in Peabody's office. The wind whispers, too—I can hear a voice.

*Agatha*, it screeches. *Agatha Harkness, where are you?*

I don't dare answer. It's Martha. She hasn't found me yet, but she's definitely not wasting any more time.

# *Six*

"I love Historical Society days," Ursula says as she links her arm in mine. "I'm such a nerd, but seriously, you have never seen a town so into its heritage as Salem. *And* it's Halloween. It's like a nonstop party the closer we get to the holiday—you'll see."

It's Friday morning. Ursula and I are volunteering for the Salem Historical Society, which Conant Academy has participated in since the school was founded in the late 1800s. I'm not sure what it entails, exactly, aside from educating visiting tourists on what Salem is all about. Ursula won't stop gushing about it, though.

We've just walked through the school's iron gates,

and now we're on the sidewalk in Salem proper. It's the kind of day where the sunlight sparkles off the leaves and the air smells like apple cider. Most people adore this weather, and while I like autumn a lot, I only like the *gloomy* days. Happy citizens carving pumpkins and drinking their fancy autumn coffee drinks always makes me want to roll my eyes.

"So." Ursula pulls out a tube of lip balm and smears it across her lips. "Can you believe you've been here almost a week?"

"It's been excruciating," I say, which is the truth. Not long ago, if someone had asked me if I would have endured a week of school, I would have cast a soul-manipulation spell on them.

But most of my classes have been . . . fine. I guess. Thanks to memory spells, recall spells, and a helpful spell I remembered that enabled mathematical problems to be automatically solved without me trying to work them out on my own, that is. Thankfully, Martha hasn't detected these powers, and I'm trying to use my magic sparingly. Usually, there's a small window of magic a witch can do before being detected by another witch, so I'm trying to stay under that threshold.

I don't really like all the school's rules, though. Sitting still in class. Wearing the stiff academy uniform, a pleated skirt and itchy collared shirt. I don't like sticking to a schedule, and I'm also tired of everyone coming up to me because I'm the new girl and asking where I'm from and what I'm into and *blah, blah, blah*. I've come up with a standard script: I'm from a few towns over, I was homeschooled, I'm just keeping my head down and trying to do well in my classes. It makes me sound dull, which I can't stand—it's more of my nature to be the most interesting person in the room—but for now, I need to blend in.

I've also learned some other rules about Conant Academy—the rules teachers don't tell us about. For instance, it's taboo to eat the pizza in the dining hall—people will brand you as "weird"—though I absolutely swooned when I ate a slice, as it was the most delicious thing I'd ever eaten. Also, Wednesdays seem to be the days that everyone is allowed to dress in clothes other than their school uniforms, though when I stepped onto the green two days ago, everyone was awash in gold and navy—the school's colors. Everyone except me, that was. I was wearing a bright purple sweater I borrowed from Ursula. Ursula apologized up and down for not telling me sooner.

Field hockey continues to be baffling. It meets for practices so early in the morning even the birds aren't up. The first time Ursula dragged me out of bed to say we were going out to *run*, I considered throwing my shoes at her. Imagine my surprise when a group of girls jogged happily in place in front of our dorm and seemed perfectly willing to set off like spry deer through the meadow. I slogged behind them for a little while, growing more and more exhausted, and finally I felt fed up and cast a simple enchantment on my leg muscles. That helped a lot.

"Wow," Ursula said as I caught up and surpassed all the runners. "You really kicked at the end."

"Indeed," a voice said behind us. And there was Dr. Novis, dressed not in exercise gear but a trench coat, tweed jacket, and a tie. His eyes sparkled mischievously. "That was quite a second wind, Alice."

Dr. Novis sets me on edge. Every interaction I've had with him, he stares at me a beat too long or saying something kind of . . . *knowing*. In chemistry class, he brought up the magic of the science to me nonstop, as though he realizes the word *magic* means something special to me. In the dining hall earlier this week, as I was selecting a hot dog, he looked at me and gave a wry smile. "I believe you'll enjoy that, Alice."

Like he knew I'd never had one before. Like he knew that only a few days ago, I was living in the 1690s.

He also asked me, as we were preparing for our second chemistry lab of the week—something involving baking soda and vinegar—how I was doing in my "search for what I was looking for." I stared at him blankly, forgetting momentarily about our discussion in the headmistress's office. I didn't know what to make of his question. *What does he know? Is he keeping tabs on me?* The coven also said he was on the task force to figure out who's part of the school's secret coven, though—maybe it's that? I don't get a sense that he's Martha, but *something* seems off.

As for my search for Martha and the Darkhold, I haven't gotten as far as I hoped. There's a possibility that Ivy is Martha. I can definitely see her conjuring a windstorm during our coven meeting out of jealousy because I thought up a better scheme . . . but at the same time, I was standing there with her. You'd think I would have seen her perform the spell. Martha can't be *that* covert when doing such powerful magic. And also, I don't get the sense that Ivy wants to *destroy* me. She seems annoyed and definitely doesn't think I deserve to be in the coven, but I'm not sure I detect that kind of violence and rage.

Then again, secret rage has surprised me before. Martha from old Salem times is a perfect example.

I've poked around for the Darkhold, too, but I don't expect to find it that easily—that sneaky little bat is good at hiding. Every closet door I open, every library stack I peer on top of, I have this glimmer of hope that maybe, *maybe* a bat will fly out in hysterics . . . but it hasn't happened. I've also looked at a modern map of where the

Parrises' cellar might be—that's where I found the bat the first time. While the Parrises' street still exists, their home is long gone, which is to be expected. I've tried to look for a crystal ball, too, thinking one will just . . . *appear* somewhere in a classroom or closet, but no such luck.

I look up, realizing that Ursula has said something I've missed. I ask her to repeat it, but she waves her hand. "I'll tell you later." Then she notices a few members of our coven waving. Francie, I'm told, volunteers in the front office instead of participating in Historical Society days—apparently she feels "too shy" to lead the tours. But Evan and Jamira are here, and they wave extra enthusiastically at me.

Ursula raises her eyebrows.

"They *really* like you, huh?" she muses.

"Not Ivy," I point out, noting the sour look on Ivy's face when she notices I'm here.

"Yeah, well, she doesn't like anyone. But the others? Wow." She nudges me. "Don't end up being better friends with them than you are with me!" Before I can protest, she adds, "I'm just kidding, of course."

But I wonder if she's not quite kidding. Ursula is definitely damaged and insecure after Sylvie went missing. Sometimes, at night, she asks to leave a night-light on to sleep. I've caught her looking longingly at Sylvie's picture on the wall. And sometimes she looks so dazed and far away, like maybe she's reliving the whole thing again.

Teachers stride to the sidewalk outside the gates, and I break out of my thoughts. Headmistress Peabody wears a navy wool coat and is holding a clipboard, presumably of everyone's assignments. Dr. Novis accompanies her, dressed once again in a suit that seems too big for his body. When he spies me, he beckons me over. Begrudgingly, I go see what he wants.

"Alice. So glad you could make it. You settling in all right?"

I shrug. "If you want me to say school is fun, you're going to be disappointed."

He chuckles like this is funny. "How about your roommate? You two getting along?"

"I guess. Sure."

"Good. Glad you're getting her out of her shell."

Then the headmistress taps her clipboard. "We should start!"

I hurry back to the coven, glad to be free of Dr. Novis again. Near us, someone in a bright red beret keeps stealing glances at the group. It takes me a moment to realize that it's that new girl, Campbell. Once again, she's snickering with a group of girls. They seem to be pointing at Evan especially, who's once again wearing his fabulous rainbow-colored coat. Just as I note this,

Campbell and her group move toward us, plowing through a freshly raked pile of leaves. With one swift kick, Campbell sends a heap of dusty leaves and dirt flying through the air straight at Evan's coat. He jumps away, but not quickly enough, and the leaves and dirt stick to the gorgeous fabric.

"Hey!" I screech.

Campbell looks back and gives me a fake-innocent look. "Oops," she simpers. "I slipped."

"It's fine, it's fine," Evan mutters, brushing off the dirt.

Ursula grits her teeth. "No, it's not. She did that on purpose. What does she have against us?"

"Do you think she suspects something about the coven?" Evan looks worried.

Ivy shakes her head. "Nah. There's no way. We're so careful. And anyway, people should celebrate us. We're doing good in the world!"

She and Jamira give each other conspiratorial looks. Jamira turns to me and gives me a fist bump. As planned, Jamira slipped the cheat sheet into Jack's backpack. Moments later, Ivy called the headmistress's office with an anonymous tip that Jack had something on him that he could use to cheat. Headmistress Peabody tracked him down that next hour, searched his backpack, and *voilà*—instant suspension. Of course Jack protested that he didn't put the cheat sheet in his backpack, but it didn't matter. So many other voices backed up that he didn't earn his grades fairly that he didn't have a leg to stand on.

As far as everyone in the coven is concerned, the operation was a complete success. Good prevailing over evil. But I know something they don't: *Someone saw me steal the cheat sheet.* Ever since then, I've been waiting to get in trouble. Surely West will tell. Why would he not?

More annoyingly, I keep thinking about my interaction with West *period*. His twinkling eyes, his sneaky smile like he knew exactly what I was doing. The way he *looked* at me, the way he said he'd seen me across the quad . . .

Really, it's taking up entirely too much space inside my head.

Headmistress Peabody claps her hands, and I look up. "Thank you, Historical Society volunteers! Now, as usual, we're in for a very busy morning. The Hawthorne Hotel is filled with guests, and there are more buses from Boston parked by the Witch Museum right now, so we have lots of tours to help out with."

She starts dividing the students into various groups to pitch in at different museums and sites around Salem. The whole thing is so puzzling to me still—I don't get why Salem became so historically significant. Or maybe *all* towns have lots of museums in 2025? Maybe people just love history.

Miss Peabody turns to me. "Alice, since it's your first time here, how about we put you at the Witch Museum? It's Salem's flagship attraction."

Ivy makes a frustrated little sniff. "But, Miss Peabody, *I'm* on the roster to go there today."

Miss Peabody gives her a wan smile. "You can take Alice, Ivy. You'll lead the tour, and Alice will shadow you."

Ivy sets her jaw like she's happy she got her way . . . but annoyed that I'm part of the deal. I don't want to hang out with Ivy, either, but maybe spending some time with her will make her let her guard down and use some magic.

If she's Martha, that is. *Find her before she finds you.*

Ursula is assigned to another museum, but she seems a little hesitant to leave me. "The Witch Museum really is the best place to volunteer. Are you going to be okay with Ivy?"

"I'm not afraid of her, Ursula. It's fine."

"If you just, like, play by her rules, you two might get along."

"But then I'd be playing by her rules. And what's the fun in that?"

"We'd better go, Alice," Ivy says loudly. "You're going to make us late."

I squeeze Ursula's hand and follow after Ivy down the quaint cobblestone street. Ivy walks slightly ahead, like she doesn't want to be seen with me. *Fine*, I think. *I don't want to be seen with you, either.*

It doesn't take us long to reach Salem Square, which doesn't look too different from the Salem Square *I* remember. The buildings along the square are small and old with crooked shutters on tiny windows, not unlike the houses there in the late 1600s. In the center of the square is a statue of a man I find familiar but I don't know why—he has a large, Pilgrim-style hat on and flowing robes, and he has a foreboding look about him. *Roger Conant*, reads the plaque. *The first settler of Salem, 1626.*

A chill runs through me. I recall townspeople speaking of Mr. Conant, though he'd died before I arrived.

I look at the building opposite. It's an enormous, delightfully strange stone church with an enormous pointed window and door as well as four turreted rooftops. There's a gate all around it, and hanging just over the door is a large sign. *Salem Witch Museum.*

I look at Ivy. "Witches are sure popular here, huh?"

She looks at me like birds have just flown out of my mouth. "Uh, *yeah*. Have you been living under a rock?"

This feels like a test, but I don't know the right answer. So I just shrug. "Not really into museums, sorry."

Ivy looks at me long and hard. "Considering how much you claim to *know* about everything, I thought you'd have visited here lots of times."

"Never said I know everything. I believe that honor belongs to *you*."

A church bell rings—it's ten o'clock, and the tour we're to run starts at ten thirty. We hurry through the museum gates and through the front doors into a small, musty room with plaques all over the walls. I catch sight of old drawings—and the lists of names—and some garments and other things in glass cases. Something occurs to me—if this is a witch museum, then maybe I could find a crystal ball *here*.

But before I can look around, a tall woman with chin-length hair and round, wire-framed glasses appears out of a far door and hurries up to us.

"Perfect, Ivy, you're here." Then she looks at me. "Who's this?"

"Alice," Ivy says in a monotone voice. That's all. No other introduction.

"Alice Harvey. I'm new to Conant Academy," I add, sticking out my hand. "Thanks for having me."

The woman shakes my hand. "I'm Jean." She points us through a set of doors. "Go get your clothes on. We have about a full house. Ivy, you're okay with showing Alice the ropes?"

"*Thrilled* to," Ivy says sarcastically.

We head into the small dressing area to change into whatever costume has been assigned. "Let me guess,"

I say. "We have to wear black dresses and pointed hats?"

"Uh, no. We dress like the Puritans." Ivy gestures to some dresses hanging on hooks in the corner. She pulls both down, seems to compare them, and then hands one to me. It's clearly the uglier of the two, the cotton torn and the little hat way too small for my head.

Still, I'm not letting her get to me, so I take the garments as if they're the most lovely items I've ever seen. "Wow!" I gush. "These are *beautiful*!"

Ivy gives me a strange look. "They're totally gross, and they never fit, and I wouldn't be caught dead letting a boy see me in them. Also, be careful putting them on. The museum says they're authentic to the period."

"Uh, don't think so," I blurt.

She turns and looks at me. "Pardon?"

I finger the lace. It feels way too soft. This sort of fabric wouldn't have been available in the late 1600s. Frankly, anything we would have sewn would have disintegrated by now. But I decide to let it drop.

We pull the dresses on over our clothes. When I look at myself, I see a villager staring back, not the witch I once was. I don't get why we're dressing like townspeople. Then again, I don't understand why I'm in a museum *celebrating* witches, period.

"There's a script for the tour, but I'll do the talking," Ivy says. "Just follow me around, hold doors for people. If someone asks a question, refer them to me."

"Why?" I ask.

"Because you don't know the answers, obviously."

"So basically, it's precisely like how you want things to be in the coven," I point out.

She slaps her arms to her sides. "Alice, I *swear*, are you just trying to make my life hard? I still don't trust you. I still think you have some kind of ulterior motive, joining our group."

I grin. *That* sounds exactly like something Martha would say. "I might have an ulterior motive, but it's not getting the coven in trouble."

"So you have an ulterior motive."

"Sure I do. Don't you?"

I look her in the eye. After a moment, she looks away. "You're really annoying."

"Admit it," I whisper. "You hate me, but you also love me."

Ivy's eyes widen. "Are you kidding?"

I enjoy how riled up she's getting. Maybe, if I can continue to push her buttons, she'll slip and reveal her powers. It happens, sometimes, with the more emotional witches—the more they feel things, the more likely their magic just sort of explodes out of them. So far, though, I haven't seen even a spark at Ivy's fingertips. Things haven't levitated. I don't detect a color-changing aura, no animals have acted strangely around her, *nothing*. She's a hard nut to crack.

Jean knocks on the door. "You girls ready?"

Tossing her head, Ivy pushes the door back open. In the few minutes we've been gone, about twenty people have crowded into the lobby. Their faces light up at the sight of us in our Puritan garb. I figure they're waiting for the tour.

Ivy grabs a microphone from the stand, and her voice changes from the taut, annoyed tone she's been using with me to a voice that's honeyed and welcoming. "Greetings, everyone, to the Salem Witch Museum. We're about to start our tour, so show me your tickets as we pass through the doors. Also, no photos or video, and please refrain from eating or drinking." She pulls at a door handle. "Through these doors will be the details of the famous Salem witch trials of 1692. During that time in Salem and its surrounding villages, over a hundred and fifty townspeople were accused of witchcraft and association with the devil, made scapegoats for the town's failing crops, cold winters, disease, and so on. It kicked off a great hysteria where many people believed to be witches were condemned."

I freeze in my tracks. *"Excuse me?"*

The tourists all turn to me. Ivy glances over, too, a mix of annoyance and bemusement on her face.

"Sorry," I mumble. But my head is reeling. *This* is why Salem is famous?

"And as a result of this hysteria," Ivy goes on, her voice

rising, "quite a few of the accused were tortured—and killed. Nineteen in Salem alone were hanged—fourteen women and five men. One man was pressed to death by a rock. Four others died in jail of starvation and illness."

She glances at me like she can tell how much this is affecting me. And it *is* affecting me. There are about fourteen women in my Salem coven not counting myself. As for the men accused, maybe it's some of the townspeople who helped provide materials for our cottages, or tolerated the witches selling their wares in town—who knows? Are my coven members the fourteen Ivy's talking about? I think of Elizabeth and all the members of my coven sitting on the logs, innocently talking about tinctures and herbs. That was 1691. If what Ivy is saying is correct—and this takes place in 1692—well, that's just a few months later.

I think, too, about the paranoia I started to feel in my bones, the strange ways the townspeople had started to look at the members of the coven, especially after the bad weather shifts, the failed crops, the early winter. It would make sense, then, that the Parris family might be holding Prudence hostage even if they didn't see her do magic. They think they've caught a witch.

I knew it. I called it. And Elizabeth didn't believe me.

"Right through here," Ivy says to the group, pushing at the double doors into a dark room.

All the tourists follow. I try to keep my hands from

shaking so I can hold the doors open for them like Ivy asked. A few people glance at me quizzically or even worriedly, likely because of my weird outburst, but I keep my head down, trying to hold it together. My teeth are chattering so hard I think I'm going to grind them to dust.

After all the guests have gone into the next room, Ivy marches over. I can feel her annoyance radiating off her. "What's your problem? Are you sick or something?"

"Um . . ." I search for something snarky to say, but my mind feels clogged with molasses. When I try to take a step, my knees buckle, and I list woozily to the side. I have to catch myself against her arm.

Ivy makes a noise of disgust and moves away from me. "Don't you dare puke all over me! Are you coming or not?"

She passes through the double doors, holding them open so I can follow behind. I creep into the dark space, lean against the wall, and try to catch my breath. A recording plays. A British-accented man's voice welcomes the tourists to the museum. *Do you believe in witches?* he asks in an echoing tone. *Millions of your ancestors did. Worshippers of the powers of evil, the forces behind storms and sickness . . .*

"But that's not true," I whisper. "They weren't evil. Not most of them, anyway."

My head is spinning. I need some light. I back up though the double doors again to the lobby. Then I stare at the wall I noticed when I came in. Words flash before my eyes. *Accused*. And . . . there are names. *Witches.*

The letters swim in front of me. *No*, I tell myself. I can't look. I *can't.*

"Alice?" Ivy sticks her head out the door again. "What's wrong with you?"

But I can't move. My head spins. I feel like I'm going to faint. I can't take this. Panicked, I back up toward the exit.

"Alice?" Ivy asks.

But there's fear in her eyes now. Powerlessness, too. It's a breaking point, I realize—she could so easily use magic to pick me up, erase my fears, even control my mind. But I don't feel controlled at all. And that's when I realize—Ivy is just a frustrated girl standing in a doorway. Not a witch. I can tell.

"I just have to . . ." I mutter.

I flee out the door and into the morning sunshine. I make it to the grass before the oats I ate for breakfast come back up. I vomit until my eyes water and my throat burns. Tears run down my cheeks, but at least it's a good mask—everyone will think I'm just crying because I'm sick with something. Not that I'm scared.

I fall to my knees, coughing and coughing. The grass feels cool against my skin, but it doesn't do much to calm the storm I'm feeling inside. Then I hear footsteps.

Someone kneels beside me. I think it's Ivy, but the hand on my shoulder feels a little bigger and warmer. I look up and see an unexpected face.

"Are you all right?" West says softly. "How can I help?"

# *Seven*

This is not an ideal moment to see West again. Not just because there's vomit on the corners of my mouth, though that's certainly not a plus. Also not just because my Puritan-style dress is now covered with grass stains or because my eyes are wild, my hair is tangled, and my cheeks are stained with tears, though I'm not thrilled about that, either. I have a perfect excuse for looking this way—I've just discovered a hard truth about the possible fate of my coven three hundred years ago. But honestly it's because I don't feel poised and ready to have a conversation with him. With *anyone*, really.

I curl up in a ball, waiting for him to go away. I can tell he doesn't move. In fact, after a moment, he hands me a water bottle. I take it gratefully and drink. There's nothing worse than puke breath. But my cheeks are blazing. Can he *smell* the puke breath?

"That happened to me when I first went in that museum, too," he says after a while.

I scoff without looking up. "Don't try to one-up me."

I keep thinking of all those witches in my coven, innocently making their herbal blends and knitting their sweaters and mostly just trying not to contract smallpox like everyone else. What happened to them? I was too afraid to look. Okay, so I found most of the witches annoying, but I didn't want actual harm to come to them. And what kicked off the trials? Was it the mounting fears about the weather and the crops and everything else, or was there a clearer, sharper inciting incident? Something terrible occurs to me—what if it was the fire inside my cottage? What if someone saw the portal? Or what if Prudence *did* teach Betty how to heal animals, and the Parrises turned on her? That vision I had of Prudence was right, that's for sure. She's in grave danger.

"Okay, I didn't get sick, but that museum is hard-core," West goes on. "I'm from Pennsylvania—I had no idea Salem was so into all of this when I chose to go to

Conant Academy. Then, when I learned more about all of it . . . It's a weird thing to be famous for. It was your first time in there, wasn't it?"

I finally look at him. His hair is mussed, his lips are pink from the cold, and he's wearing a plaid fleece vest. There's a lanyard around his neck that says he's volunteering for the Salem Walking Tour.

"Don't you have a walk you're supposed to be on?" I groan uneasily.

"So . . . you want me to leave?"

"Yes," I say quickly.

"I just wanted to make sure you were okay."

I look away. "You don't have to babysit me, Holdfast."

He cocks his head. "What did you call me?"

"You remind me of a dog I once knew. Holdfast."

His smile widens. "What kind of dog is Holdfast?"

"A farm dog. Herded the sheep. He was just so . . . *patient*. The sheep would nip at him, the farmer made him sleep outside in the bitter cold, but he never seemed to mind."

West leans back and smirks. "So basically you're saying I'm a border collie who's a glutton for punishment?"

"I'm calling you Holdfast," I say stubbornly. "That's your name."

"Okay, whatever," he says. "I can deal."

I roll my eyes. "That's *exactly* what Holdfast would say."

Across the street, Ursula and a boy I don't know lead a group of walkers down toward the harbor. I turn away so she doesn't see me; the last thing I need is for her to worry about why I'm on the lawn instead of in the museum.

I figure that since West isn't going anywhere soon, I might as well talk to him. "So Salem took you by surprise, too?"

"It did and it didn't. This whole state is filled with weird stories and bizarre history of when the colonies were forming, a lot of it not good." He looks at his lap sheepishly. "I actually wrote an essay about Massachusetts's history, and it got me a scholarship to the academy. My parents didn't have the cash to pay the tuition. And actually, at Conant Academy, that's its own witch hunt."

"What's that mean?"

He shrugs. "People sometimes get weird about scholarship students. Say we don't deserve to be here, even though we probably deserve it the *most*." He smiles at me. "You're on scholarship, too, right? I heard Headmistress Peabody say something about your stellar entrance exam."

I snort. "I barely looked at my entrance exam."

West frowns. "What does that mean?"

It occurs to me, after a beat, that he's trying to figure out if I cheated. I shake my head, even though I don't know for sure. “It’s not what you think, but I don’t care about Conant Academy enough to cheat my way in.”

West cocks his head and looks at me sideways. “So you don’t want to be at Conant Academy?”

“No. But I *have* to be here.”

“Why?”

“If I told you I traveled through time to search for an ancient book that’s posing as a vampire bat, would you believe me?”

I nearly gasp. I can’t believe that just popped out of my mouth—it almost feels like someone possessed me to say it. I’ve definitely blown it. West stares at me, his mouth hanging open.

But it’s only for a moment, because then he laughs. “Good one. You should join the Conant Academy Comedy Troupe, Alice.”

My heart slows. I’m relieved he found it a joke. Then I realize what else he said. “How do you know my name?”

He looks caught. “I, um, asked around. I mean, I wanted to know the name of the girl who I randomly found in my room.”

I stiffen. “I wasn’t in your room.”

“You . . . weren’t?”

I hold his gaze. He stares back. I’m not technically manipulating his mind, I tell myself. I’m just gaslighting him. Which is totally different.

Finally, West puts a finger to his lips. “Right. Of

course you weren't. Though . . . if you *had* been, and if you happened to find something in a certain drawer, I won't say anything. Promise."

"Great, but I didn't do that," I repeat, my heart banging hard. "I wasn't there."

"Of course not," West says, waving his hands. "You weren't there."

All around the square, academy students dressed as Puritans give talks to tourists. One of them is Campbell. She takes a moment to turn to look at us and frown. I want to roll my eyes. She's probably disgusted because we're sitting on the grass instead of doing our jobs. She seems like a big rule-follower.

"Look, Jack sometimes asked me to write his papers," West says in a soft voice. He's not looking at me anymore but at the statue in the center of the square. "Actually, not asked, exactly—more like forced."

"How did he do that?"

"Uh, brute force?" He gestures down at his lithe, greyhound-like body. "Guy's in the gym, like, twenty-four/seven. Unlike myself."

I bite my lip.

"So basically, that little trick that got Jack in trouble for cheating?" he goes on. "I'm in total support."

"Yes, but I have no idea what you're talking about."

"I know. But *whoever* got Jack in trouble, I owe them big-time. And if you happen to come upon that person, please ask them what sort of favor they'd like to me do for them in return for their service."

I lean back. "What sort of favor are you willing to do for that person?"

"That *smart* person," West says.

"Smart, *resourceful* person," I add, smiling.

"Smart, resourceful, *intriguingly pretty* person," West says.

I blink, letting what he said sink in. *Weirdo*. Does that actually work with girls?

"Obviously I don't know this person," I remind him. "But if I did, perhaps they'd want a favor like . . . oh, I don't know. Doing their chores for this alleged agriculture class we have to take?"

"You don't think the person likes farm chores?" West places his hand on his chest in mock surprise. "Cleaning up sheep poop and milking goats isn't their cup of tea?" He leans in closer. "This person might enjoy feeding the baby lambs little bottles in the spring. I don't think she's as tough as they let on."

"Uh, that's where you're wrong—I think she's *exactly* as tough as she lets on, if not tougher." But then I smile. "Though, I have to admit. Feeding lambs does sound kind of cute." Not that I'll be here by spring.

"See? It's okay to be a softie." Then West crosses his arms. "Also, that stuff in there?" He points to the Witch Museum. "It's terrible. There's no shame in getting sick over it. As I was saying, I knew about the history of this place, but it was a whole different ball game when I first went into that museum and saw what was in there."

I run my fingers through the cool, soft grass, picturing the names on the plaque. Not that I looked at them. It's like there was a blindfold over my eyes, suddenly, preventing me.

"Some of the people died so young, too—thirteen, fourteen. They must have felt so scared. They probably didn't even understand what was going on. And all those tourists in there—do they really get that? They have their cameras, and they're wearing their Halloween costumes—it's not really *real* to them."

*"Yes,"* I say emphatically, the word slipping from my mouth. Then I cough, trying to rein in my emotions. "The Halloween costumes are ridiculous. This is *all* ridiculous. I had no idea Salem was going to turn into some kind of Circus Maximus."

"Is that a theme park?" he asks.

I shrug. I lived during the time of the Roman Circus Maximus. I've never been to a theme park.

Then West squints. "And what do you mean, you had *no idea*?"

The words freeze in my throat. I've done it again—slipped and talked honestly. I blame it on West being so disarming. Sitting there so friendly and patient.

I've definitely given too much away. West's going to figure me out. I give him an annoyed look. "Is that your thing? To pick apart every little sentence I say? You're the word police?"

West looks hurt. "Sorry. I was just . . . making conversation."

He falls silent, like I've hurt his feelings. I know I've pushed him away, but it was the only thing I could think to do. Also, what am I even doing? I need to be looking for Martha. I need to find that Darkhold. I need *out* of here.

The door to the Witch Museum opens, and Ivy pokes her head out. When she sees me sitting on the grass with West, her expression softens—she looks kind of relieved that I didn't drop dead.

"Is she okay?" she asks West instead of me.

West turns my way. "Are you?"

"I'm fine. But . . . I'm not sure I can go back in."

I brace myself for Ivy's reaction—irritation that I'm slacking off, satisfaction that I can't *handle* something, annoyance because she has to handle everything herself. Finally, Ivy makes a sour face and whirls around. "Whatever," she mutters to herself. "I'll just tell the docent you can't handle life."

There. There's the reaction I was looking for. But she isn't Martha, I can feel it. I'm happy, but also disappointed. It would have been nice to get it on the first try. Now I have to start all over in my search.

The door slams. I lean back on my palms and blow out a breath. West turns to me. "She's actually nice once you get to know her."

I frown. "Huh?"

"Ivy. She's prickly, but she's pretty cool underneath. Just has a funny way of showing it. I had Bio with her last year—we were lab partners. She grows on you."

I scoff. "Thanks for the insight, but who said I actually care?"

He grins lazily—which, admittedly, is way too attractive for his own good. "You're not as hard to read as you think." Then he stands and brushes himself off. "I should go back to my tour."

I look at him impassively, wanting to say something snarky like how it's *about time*, but I find my mouth doesn't really work.

"And also?" West adds as he backs away. "It's a date."

I blink. "*What's* a date?"

"Agricultural class? Doing your chores for a week? I want to make good on my promise." His eyebrows shoot up and down mischievously, sending my heart on another little dive. "See you again soon."

# *Eight*

After my incident in the museum, I tell the headmistress I'm not feeling well and want to head back to the dorms early—which I guess is a thing that's allowed in 2025, though it probably would have been discounted in the 1690s, because *everyone* felt ill mostly all of the time. Maybe a lot of students are rattled by their first experience in the Witch Museum, though, because Peabody makes a sympathetic face and tells me to run along and get some rest.

I let myself inside the dorm room with my key. Ursula isn't back yet from her tour guide duties, and I'm grateful. The last thing I need is for her to see my sensitive side.

My scared side, actually.

I stand in the doorway, sensing strange energy. Our room is as neat as we left it, but something seems off. *Disturbed.* Like someone's been in here. Looking for something, maybe.

I close my eyes, trying to divine the knowledge, but I don't hear my name whispered in the wind. I don't feel the ground shaking. Something seems like it might have happened in here, but whatever it was, it's not here now.

I flop down on my bed and pull up the laptop computer I've been issued. It didn't take long to learn how to use the device, especially the internet. I lift the lid, click the browser icon, and then navigate to the search bar. My fingers waver over the keyboard. I've looked up a variety of topics this week. How to properly clean one's teeth. How many colonies there are in the New World these days. (Boy, has this place endured a lot of changes in the past three hundred years.) What is the meaning of the term *K-pop*. And then my favorite, *Where is the Darkhold?* I mean, the internet seems kind of magical; I figured it was worth a shot. Not that it told me anything.

Now I consider hunting and pecking the words *Salem witch trials*. I really want to know about all the things I was scared to face in the museum. Names. Dates. Atrocities. I *need* to know before I'm caught off guard again.

But my fingers won't type the words. They just . . . can't.

Prudence's terrified face swims in my mind. I try to return to that strange, zapping netherworld she brought me to when I first arrived. *Tell me more,* I beg, trying to conjure her up—or for her to conjure me. *Tell me what will happen to you. Tell me where you are. And who Martha is. Where I can find the Darkhold. Then I'll come back to you and get you out of there. Whatever is about to happen, I'll save you.*

Only . . . what will happen if I go back to my Salem? Will I be risking my own fate, now that I know there are trials against witches—*deaths,* even? I think of the vision I saw when traveling here through the portal—the one where I'm an old woman. That would mean I survive the witch trials. But maybe at too high of a cost—maybe, somehow, it makes me lose my anti-aging abilities.

Suddenly, sparks flash in my brain. I'm falling through darkness again—not in the netherworld with Martha, but flying through the New York City sky. And here's Old Agatha again, waiting at her door. I'm back in that vision.

I look closely at the old version of myself, trying to find any indication of what I've lived through in Salem. Did I lose a lot of the coven? Is that why I'm living in New York City now? What happened to Prudence?

The vantage changes, and I'm now following that

fiery-haired woman as she walks up the path to the little shack. I still have no idea who she is. I thought maybe she was that witch Ursula can't stop talking about, the Scarlet Witch, as she also has red hair—but it's definitely someone else. Someone called Firestar.

Old Agatha doesn't seem surprised that the fiery mutant is here. I watch again as she grumbles, annoyed, *Firestar, why have you darkened my doorway?*

*You need to help us,* Firestar begs. *Things have grown dire. You have to come back to Salem! Only you can save us!*

Voices sound from the halls, yanking me from the vision, but I can't quite join the present yet. I don't understand why I'm being shown this vision. Why am I old? Who is Firestar? I definitely don't remember her from the coven. . . .

Boisterous footsteps thump outside my door, followed by more giggles. Groaning, I rub my eyes and sit up. Then I notice a photograph taped up against the sides of Ursula's nightstand. I hadn't seen it before.

I scoot over to look closer. It's a picture of Ursula and Sylvie. Both are in shorts and T-shirts, squinting in the bright sun. They look so happy, leaning against each other and laughing.

I squint hard, conjuring subtle magic to bring the photo to life. The girls in the picture are suddenly animated; Ursula and Sylvie turn to each other and smile. The image freezes again.

There's something so sad about the photo. In it, Ursula seems so different—lighter, happier. Even her voice is a higher pitch. She's happier. Not yet traumatized, as her friend hasn't gone missing. This happened so recently—only a few months ago. And that teacher disappeared, too. Do the two things connect? Did Martha have something to do with it?

Curious, I pull my computer onto my lap again and type in Sylvie O'Toole's name. After a pause, a list of web links appears. *Student Vanishes from Private School.* The date is late August, seemingly right when the academy started its fall session.

There are photos of search parties through the woods, Headmistress Peabody giving a speech, a frantic family, and a group of students holding a candlelight vigil. I recognize a few students: Jamira's familiar oversize jewelry, Ivy's long braid, and even West sitting at the base of a tree trunk, talking to some boys. Sylvie's family put out a nationwide search, offering money to anyone who saw her or had any information. No one came forward. It was like something had swallowed her up. Her cell phone was last tracked in the woods, and then it went dead . . . but it wasn't found, either.

All through early September people searched, but Sylvie remained missing. A few articles reported that the cops are still searching, but there are no leads. There's a thumbnail image of the reward poster on my laptop screen, though when I click on it to look at it closer, the link doesn't work.

Next, I type in *Mr. Haverford, Conant Academy, Missing*—and I get a ton of results right away. Just like the coven said, Mr. Haverford also vanished at the start of the school year right around when Sylvie did, but his friends and neighbors don't buy that Mr. Haverford would abandon his wife and children. He was a model dad, a loving husband, the quotes say. There are a few speculative op-ed pieces and chats on message boards trying to suggest he kidnapped Sylvie, but it doesn't look like the police took that very seriously.

I pick up the picture of Ursula and Sylvie again. I concentrate hard on the image, trying to scry some kind of answer to what happened. That's the problem, though—to properly scry, I still need that damn crystal ball.

The doorknob rattles. I slam the laptop lid shut just as Ursula walks in and drops her backpack on her bed. "Hey, you want to . . ." she says, whirling around to me. But her expression falters when she sees the photo in my hand. "Oh."

"Sorry," I say, hurrying to tape it back up on her dresser. "I was just . . . I was curious." My cheeks burn. I hate that she caught me snooping. "It's so strange, Ursula," I admit. "People don't just vanish."

Ursula shrugs. "I know."

Then I pull open the drawer to my nightstand. "Is this her handwriting?"

Ursula steps forward and looks at the scrawl. *Darkness is among us.* She blinks hard. Blood drains from her face.

"Do you know what it means?" I ask.

"I—I have no idea," Ursula whispers, looking frightened. "I had no idea this was even there."

"Did Sylvie seem scared before she vanished? What would prompt her to write this?"

Ursula shakes her head. She's practically quivering. A single tear slides down her cheek. She looks up, and for a split second, there's a desperate look on her face. It's a look I want to understand.

"What?" I whisper.

"I . . ." Ursula starts. "I think . . ."

Her eyes flutter closed. She mumbles something about needing to lie down. I remember the headmistress's advice that I should go easy on Ursula, that she was horribly rattled when Sylvie vanished. Maybe I've pushed too hard.

"Never mind," I say quickly. "Forget I asked."

I help her into bed, guilty that I riled her up. Ursula keeps telling me that it's fine—she's just tired—but I can't help but think there's something she's repressing, a terrible clue she's afraid to share. Maybe *she* saw Martha?

Maybe she saw the Darkhold? But maybe Martha doesn't *know* Ursula saw her, and Ursula's doing everything in her power not to reveal the truth?

It feels like I'm circling around something. I just don't know what.

Ursula looks refreshed when she wakes an hour later. She apologizes for her overreaction and says there's even probably a theory for the writing inside the drawer. "Sylvie was always a little dramatic," she says. "All the stories of Salem kind of got to her in a big way. Maybe it was just that." Then she looks at me curiously. "Also, did I hear you almost fainted outside the Witch Museum?"

I was wondering if she'd found out. I mumble that I might have eaten something bad and felt lightheaded. I think Ursula would understand about how one could get woozy from learning about Salem's past, but I don't feel like rehashing it again.

"*And* you were talking to West Delecroix," Ursula points out.

I whip my head up. "Who told you that?"

She smiles mysteriously. "You two would make a cute couple."

I feel my shoulders stiffen. "I don't . . . It's not . . ."

But then I close my eyes, feeling my resolve crumble. I've actually been dying to tell someone about my interaction with West. It's been on my mind since the moment I left him. I can't remember the last time I've thought about someone so much—unless, of course, you count Martha.

"He was just worried because I fell over," I say. "Also—please don't tell Ivy, but he saw me when I stole that envelope from Jack's drawer."

Ursula's eyes widen. She claps a hand over her mouth. "That could be bad. What if he tells on you? He'll get the coven shut down!"

"He promises he won't say anything. Apparently, Jack made him write his papers."

"Really?" She sits down on the bed. "You really think he'll keep quiet?"

"I do. He said Jack getting in trouble is the best thing ever, actually."

This seems to calm her. She smiles. "Maybe he's also keeping quiet because he likes you."

I wave my hand. "Doubtful."

"You sure? I've seen him looking at you."

I snort. Usually, the only time people look at me is when I'm making their lives miserable. But I have to admit I feel sort of . . . *tingly*, too. It's kind of like that giddy rush I get when I'm about to cast a powerful spell, or the thrill I felt back in 1691 Salem when I finally captured the Darkhold bat.

I have no idea, though, why I'd be feeling that for West.

# Nine

It's the Friday-night coven meeting, and I find my cloak, back from the dry cleaner, in my closet and pull it on. It's never smelled so fresh. I keep sniffing it over and over, kind of amazed. When I go back to my Salem, I'm going to detest all the terrible odors that linger endlessly in the air. I really wish I could take some functional cleaning products with me.

*If* I go back to my Salem. I have to . . . right? What will become of Prudence, otherwise? Admittedly, though, the longer I stay in this century, the harder it's going to be. Soft beds, good food, indoor plumbing, and general ease of living really do a number on a person.

Once again, Ursula and I pull the library-studying trick, leaving our names off the sign-in sheet and sneaking out the back door. It's even chillier outside this evening, and Ursula pulls a hat over her ears as we start across the lawn to the cave where the coven meets. Skeletons loom and werewolves tower. I keep seeing them out of the corner of my eye and mistaking them for real live creatures. When we reach the edge of the woods, I scan for spies . . . or that strange specter I noticed looming in the trees the first night I was here.

Except she isn't anywhere. I'm starting to wonder if I really saw her at all.

The other members are already in the cave when we arrive. Ursula makes the birdcall sound, and Ivy lights the candle to guide our way. The group sits tightly together, and there's something flat and rectangular balanced between their sets of knees. Ivy looks vaguely annoyed, but Jamira looks excited.

"Ooh, Ouija!" Ursula squeals. She looks at me. "You like Ouija, right?"

I fake a smile. My "modern stuff" spell has informed me what Ouija is, but sadly, there's no way a silly little board is going to connect people to the dead or predict the future.

"Ouija doesn't work," Ivy says as if reading my mind. "It's for babies. Besides, we should be trying to figure out what our next task is. Taking down Jack worked like a charm. How about Chelsea? Or Dylan?"

Ursula turns to me. "Chelsea Woods is a plain old mean girl. And Dylan Carroll just broke up with his girlfriend, Madison. Rumor has it that he posted pictures of her—pictures she didn't give him permission to take—online."

"Why don't we use the Ouija board to ask if it's really true about Dylan?" Francie says.

Ivy groans. "The Ouija board won't tell us that. I vote we prank Chelsea."

I give Ivy the side-eye. She might not be Martha in disguise, but she still has a terrible attitude. Then something occurs to me. Maybe, instead of sparring with Ivy, I should kill her with kindness. Make her feel special. I knew a witch like her from one of my old covens—she was always downvoting everyone else's ideas, making everyone feel less about themselves because, deep down, that's how *she* felt.

It's a little bit of a risk—I'll have to use magic. But the magic will be subtle, nearly undetectable. It's not like there will be flames shooting from my fingers.

I clear my throat. "You're probably right, Ivy. Ouija is silly. You're really smart about things like that."

"Thank you." Ivy puffs out her chest a little. "Glad *someone* recognizes it."

"But I have heard that Ouija does work, sometimes, if there's a powerful witch around. Which you are, obviously."

Ivy gloats. Jamira gives me a weird look. "Why are you being so nice to her?" I can feel Ursula watching me, too. I give her a look that says *I'm trying to play nice.*

"I feel like your powers combined with Jamira's abilities might actually conjure spirits," I say. "Just a hunch."

Ivy thinks it over. "Fine, but I can't promise anything."

Francie moves over so that Ursula and I can squeeze into the circle. Jamira instructs everyone to lightly place their fingers on the planchette, the little plastic heart-shaped piece in the center. She starts dragging the planchette in circles. Our fingers move with hers.

"Oh spirits," Jamira says dramatically, the candlelight flickering across her face. "Come to this cave. Come to our coven. Speak to us. Tell us what you know about what's happening at Conant Academy."

The planchette swirls. An owl hoots outside. After a while, Ivy lets out a snort. "No amount of my power is going to make this work, I'm afraid."

But then Jamira looks around, her eyes wide. "Actually, I can feel that spirits are here. They're asking who'd we like to speak with from the afterlife."

I perk up, thinking of Prudence. Maybe I could talk

to her again through the board? Or maybe Elizabeth Good, or that fiery-haired mutant in the vision, whoever she is? Or maybe someone who knows Martha . . .

Francie sits straighter. "How about Marilyn Monroe!"

Evan laughs. "Francie, you *always* want Marilyn Monroe, and I always tell you she's way too busy to speak to our coven."

"Can we at least try?"

Ivy shifts. "I don't know if I can get Marilyn Monroe to visit, though."

I smile to myself. *Yes, you can*. I hope.

Everyone places their fingers on the planchette again. "Close your eyes," Jamira says, and we all do.

I take a moment to summon my powers. I haven't done a necromancy spell in a while, but probably doing a teensy little one here won't tip off Martha.

I can feel magic welling inside of me, *working*. Summoning a spirit from the dead is a little bit like dragging a cat out from a hiding spot—there's some fighting and struggling, maybe even some clawing, but eventually, if you have your spell right, you'll be able to get the spirit in your grasp.

After a moment, I feel the essence of a young, beautiful woman. She's an actress—complicated, intelligent, haunted. Marilyn Monroe isn't someone I know anything about, but I can feel that it's her moving through me; it's like we've been friends for a long time. She seems annoyed that I've brought her here—which is normal, as most spirits don't want to be bothered to perform these silly parlor tricks. My magic is strong enough to tether her to our world for a few minutes, though.

*Just do me this favor,* I tell her. *Just spell something out. Answer a few questions. I'll owe you one.*

The planchette starts to glide across the board. Jamira draws in a gasp, looking up at everyone. "I'm not moving it," she says in a voice that sounds slightly panicked. "I swear."

The window in the little tool hovers first over the *I*, then the *M*, then the *H*. "*I-M-H-E-R-E*," Ursula spells out excitedly. "*'I'm here!'* She's here!"

"Oh my God, oh my God," Francie says. "It's really her!"

Evan leans over the board. "Marilyn, is that you?"

The planchette moves quickly to YES. "Guys . . ." Jamira's voice trembles.

"*The* Marilyn Monroe?" Evan asks.

Again, Marilyn, bless her, answers YES.

Ursula gapes. "This is incredible."

"Truly," I say, hoping I'm selling the innocent act.

Ivy smiles self-assuredly, like she knew she could do it all along.

Jamira pulls her fingers off the planchette. "Is no

one else kinda freaked out? I didn't actually think this would work."

Francie ignores her and addresses the board. "Marilyn, do you think James will say yes if I ask him to the Halloween dance?"

"Francie, Marilyn Monroe doesn't know *that*," Evan snaps.

But the planchette moves once more to YES.

"Really?" Francie squeals. *"Yes!"*

Then Ivy shifts forward. "Did Dylan Carroll post those pictures of Madison online?"

This time, the planchette moves to NO.

Ursula looks surprised. "So maybe we *shouldn't* prank Dylan?"

Evan removes his hands and inspects his fingers. "This is weird. How does Marilyn Monroe even know these things?"

"It's scaring me," Jamira says. "Maybe we should stop."

"We don't have to stop," I tell her. "It's safe."

"Yeah, I feel like it's safe, too," Ivy says quickly.

Francie looks up at me. "What do *you* want to ask Marilyn, Alice?"

But before I can say a word, Ursula looks at the board and says, "Marilyn, does someone have a crush on Alice?"

The planchette moves quickly to YES.

"Ooh!" Ursula squeals. "It's West, right?"

The planchette hovers between YES and NO. "Let's ask it something else," I say quickly. I don't want to know about West. West doesn't matter. I think of the thing I really want to know and ask it quietly, in my mind: *Do you know where the Darkhold is?*

Gradually, achingly, the planchette glides over to NO.

Ursula looks puzzled. "So it's . . . *not* West who has a crush on you?"

"Ladies, I love you, but I still don't buy this." Evan taps his fingers on the planchette. "If it's really you, Marilyn Monroe, give us a sign. Something *not* on the Ouija board."

"That's not fair, Evan," Jamira says. "She's speaking through the board and only the board."

Regardless, we all look around, waiting. I still feel Marilyn buzzing inside me, so I know she hasn't left yet, but I don't know what else she's capable of. I'm almost considering using magic of my own to make something happen—just to keep the fun going—when the candle's flame goes out. The cave is bathed in darkness.

"What the—?" Ursula whispers.

*"Oh my God,"* Jamira cries. "It's a sign! It's her!"

"Someone blew it out," Evan protests, but his voice shakes a little.

"There's no breeze, though." Ivy sounds dazzled.

The candle flame flickers to life again. Everyone screams. Jamira jumps to her feet. "Oh *hell* no." Everyone else follows, whisper-shrieking.

I can feel Marilyn wanting to leave, too, so I cut the tether and let her go. *Thank you*, I tell her. *Godspeed, wherever you're going next.*

Outside, the sky is dotted with stars, and branches zigzag over the sky. Our feet crunch on the thin layer of frost on the ground. Jamira leans over her knees, breathing hard like she's run a marathon.

Ivy looks down at herself with pride. "You know, I always *thought* I could conjure up spirits. It wasn't even hard!"

"That was maybe the most amazing thing that's ever happened to me," Evan decides, breathless too. "Is it wrong to say that I consider Marilyn Monroe one of my besties now?"

"Next time, *I* get to pick who we bring back," Ursula says. "Maybe a musician? Or, ooh, Marie Antoinette? Or . . ."

But then she trails off. Her eyes narrow at something in the bushes. I turn around just in time to see branches shivering and shaking and then going still.

A few beats pass. We all glance around at each other, doomed looks on our faces.

"I-is someone there?" Jamira whispers.

"How would someone know we're here?" Ivy hisses. She looks at me. "Did *you* tell, Alice?"

"What? No!" I press my hand to my chest. "I swear!" Though my stomach lurches. It can't be West, can it? He only saw me in the dorms, not in the cave. . . .

The branches rattle again, and we all jump back. It's got to be an animal, I think, but then the bush shimmers slightly, sort of like a thousand fireflies are lighting it up. The light is translucent, the movement fluid. It's kind of . . . ghostly.

Everyone gasps. Francie squeezes my hand hard and makes a little *eep*.

"What the . . . ?" Ursula's voice quivers.

"I don't like this," Jamira whispers.

*"What if it's Marilyn?"* Evan whispers. *"What if she's come back to life?"*

The glow shifts and flows like liquid. It's definitely not a person. It's sort of *shaped* like a person—head, shoulders, torso—but I can't see actual legs. It's sort of . . . floating.

I think of the glowing girl I saw at the edge of the woods, staring up at the school. Is this her again? Only, when I look closer, I don't think so. This flickering, shimmering figure doesn't have her long hair or her flowing dress.

This figure looks like a man.

# Ten

I stand my ground in the woods, watching the shimmering figure before me. *Hey!* I shout telepathically. But the apparition doesn't seem to hear. Before I can move closer, the figure turns and floats away—fast. I'm ready to sprint after it, but then Jamira grabs me by my sweater.

"What are you *doing*?" she cries. "Let's get out of here!"

I glance longingly back at the receding, glowing light—I'm not one to run away from magic. But Jamira tugs at my arm once more. I don't want to reveal my powers by staying here. Reluctantly, I follow her.

The rest of the weekend, the coven lies low. Everyone seems rattled. A few of the coven members truly believe it was a ghost, but to my surprise, though, Ursula insists that it couldn't have been.

"Ghosts don't exist," she whispers to the group when we see each other in the lunchroom. "It was probably just fireflies, or some weird atmospheric disturbance. We've had plenty of those, haven't we?" Part of me wonders if she keeps talking about it as a way to convince herself there's nothing to be afraid of.

I pretend to have no words to explain the strange apparition we saw, either, but I've been thinking a lot about it. It was definitely a ghost—I've seen ghosts plenty of times before. Actually, maybe it was *two* ghosts, because this latest one looked quite a bit different than the girl I saw when I tried to sneak out of the dorms. Only, ghosts from when? Old Salem times? The present? And why are they hanging out at the edge of the school grounds?

Monday morning rolls around, wet and dreary. I have my first Agriculture class, which I'm not looking forward to. I'm to report to the barns at eight a.m. sharp.

The teacher is Mrs. Moon, a healthy-looking woman in a ball cap and a quilted jacket. Because it's the middle of the term, she sends all the students off to complete their daily chores without much instruction, then high-tails it to a little office off the barn and shuts the door. Ursula and I have the class together, and she comes over to me to help.

"Mrs. Moon is like that," she says, then looks at my chore sheet. "But she was easy on you. You just have to add water to the troughs and pens for the animals."

Then she looks up and frowns. Campbell swishes past us on the other side of the barn. As usual, she's with her group of girls. When they see us, they huddle together and whisper. I feel like something's up. I just don't know what.

Ursula seems uneasy, too. "I swear I saw her come out of our room yesterday," she murmurs.

"What? When?" I think of the presence I felt in our room when I came back from the Witch Museum.

"When everyone was still at dinner. She was in the hallway, near our door—and she looked so guilty when she saw me. I don't know what she could be looking for, though." Ursula casts a dark glance Campbell's way again. I do, too. What would she want in our room?

Just then, Mrs. Moon trundles out of her office and stops short at the gate that separates some of the pens. "Where's the key to this?"

Campbell's group blinks innocently. I wonder if

it was her I sensed in our room. Why doesn't she like Ursula? Or is it *me* she doesn't like? Why doesn't she just leave us alone?

Mrs. Moon continues. "This gate needs to be locked at all times. The key is usually sticking out of the lock. Does someone have it?"

"I saw Ursula and Alice messing with it," Campbell pipes up.

"What?" I shoot up straighter. "No we weren't!"

But then another of Campbell's friends, a girl named Ava, points at Ursula's backpack, which is hanging from a hook with everyone else's stuff on the far wall. "Isn't that it?"

Sure enough, a shining key juts halfway out the front pocket. Ursula's jaw drops. "I—I didn't put it there!" She points at Campbell's crew. "You framed us!"

"We did no such thing!" Campbell cries, a hand pressed to her chest.

Mrs. Moon rolls her eyes as she retrieves the key from Ursula's backpack. "Girls, I don't need this right now." She gives Ursula a sharp look. "The key stays in the gate. Got it?"

Ursula nods, looking like she's going to cry.

I clench my teeth. I've had just about enough of Campbell. But as I surge forward to confront her, Ursula grabs my arm. *"Don't."*

"She set you up," I hiss.

Ursula shakes her head. "I know, but I don't want to get in trouble."

I lower my shoulders and turn away, hating that Campbell has won this round. But I honor Ursula's request, going back to my chores. First, I pour water into a bucket and start filling the pans for the animals. As I'm finishing up filling another trough, a gray goat with a broken horn and bristly fur nudges my hip. I glance at her, which is a big mistake, because she totally locks with my gaze and enters my brain.

*I'm hungry*, she tells me.

I want to laugh. *Not my problem*, I telegraph back.

*But you can get me food. It's on the high shelf. I can't reach it.*

*You certainly don't look underfed.* Which I normally wouldn't say—I'm all for body positivity in this day and age, even for animals. On the other hand, I can't have a goat bugging me all morning.

The goat doesn't like this answer. In retaliation, she takes the edge of my sweater in her mouth and clamps down.

"Hey!" I growl. She won't let go. "Come on," I grumble, tugging the sweater until I hear threads ripping. The goat comes away with a square of my sweater in her mouth.

Someone snickers behind me. I whip around, and there's Campbell again, leaning against one of the fences, seemingly doing nothing at all.

I turn back to the goat with the piece of my sweater still in its mouth. *Go bother her. She has food.* Obediently, the goat pivots and trots over to Campbell instead, nudging her gently with her broken horn.

"Uh . . ." Campbell raises her hands in surrender. "Whoa. Not so close." She shoos her unsuccessfully. The goat edges even closer. Campbell backs away, arms raised. Then she glares at me. "Did you make this thing come over here?"

"How could I have done *that*?" I ask innocently, feeling a dart of satisfaction.

The goat lets out a loud, bossy bleat. I wish Ursula were here to see this, but she's gone to do her chores in the horse barn. Then I notice Campbell picking up a rake like it's a weapon.

"Hey!" I call out. "Don't hit her. She isn't doing anything wrong."

"I should be able to defend myself," Campbell says shrilly. Then she looks up at someone in the doorway. "Oh my gosh—I'm so glad you're here. This thing's trying to eat me!"

"Pretty sure goats don't eat people," a familiar voice says.

West swings into the room. He's wearing a grubby sweatshirt, ripped jeans, and unfashionable rubber boots. Somehow, though, he looks great in it. A little swoop goes through my stomach. It's an annoying feeling I'm starting to grow accustomed to, as it happens whenever he comes around.

West reaches out and pats the goat's head. "Hey there," he says in a low, friendly voice. "You bothering people, girl? How about a treat?"

The goat backs away from Campbell and follows him toward a bucket of goat feed stashed on the high shelf.

"West, you're my hero," Campbell swoons. "I literally saw my life flash before my eyes!"

I snort. As if West saved her from a rampaging bear.

West notices me. He smiles and strides over, holding his hand in a wave. I immediately busy myself with filling the next trough like I don't really care whether he's here or not.

"You're quite the hero," I mutter. "Though giving that particular goat food doesn't exactly make you Dr. Dolittle."

"I'm sorry you don't recognize my talents with animals," West teases. Then he points at me. "Also, what's that bucket doing in your hand? Didn't I say *I* would do your chores today?"

I roll my eyes. "I'm very capable of doing my own chores."

"But I said I'd help."

I finally look up at him. "Do you even have this class right now, Holdfast?"

"I see we're still doing the dog-nickname thing?"

"As I said, it suits you so well."

A gate slams shut. I look up, and Campbell is glowering at us. Whenever I'm not doing what I'm supposed to, she's always there.

"Look, I had a free period," West says. "And I remembered this was when you had your farm duties. Seriously, I'll finish up. Besides"—he clears his throat—"someone looks like she wants to have a word with you."

At first I think he means Campbell, but when I turn, the goat that ate my sweater is behind me. She stares with her eerie, rectangular pupils.

*I'm still hungry*, she says.

"Oh my God," I mutter to her. "How much have you eaten today already?"

West leans toward the goat. "I'll handle her. Janice and I have an understanding." He gives her some more feed from his palm. She gobbles it up like she hasn't eaten in a week.

I point at him accusingly. "Don't give in to her! It's obvious she's a chowhound! Also, *Janice*?"

He smiles. "That's her name. She told me."

I blink. "You can talk to animals?" I almost say *too* but catch myself.

He looks over at me, the sneakiest look on his face. "Can't you?"

My heart swoops. But it's fine. He's just kidding.

West says he'll help me fill the last trough at the

chicken coop. As we walk there, Janice trots behind. So does Campbell, I notice, though she lurks at a distance, pretending to do something with the garbage cans just outside the goat pen. I also spot Ursula in the horse barn. She sees me, too—with West—and her eyes light up with glee. I pray she doesn't come over here and make a big deal out of this.

"What else is on your task list?" West asks.

I look at the list again. "I need to gather up some eggs, and that's it."

He holds the coop door open for me, and I pass through, swooning a little at the milky scent of his skin. My coven had some chickens, and I have to say our hen house didn't look much different. The chickens scatter and cluck. When I turn, Janice is on our heels again. I wouldn't be surprised if she tried to eat a raw egg right out of my hand.

We gather the eggs in the little baskets provided, and we deposit them in cartons. The front of the cartons have familiar symbols—pentagrams, cauldrons, and the egg of fertility. *Enchanted Eggs from Salem*, the label reads.

"Enchanted?" I repeat. "Really?"

"They're plain old eggs," West says. "Saying they're enchanted drives up the price at the farmers' market in town. They make a great souvenir."

"Souvenir?" I narrow my eyes and consult my modern-day-everything spell.

"You know, a memento of your travels." West searches my face. "You look like you've never heard the word."

I quickly cover my tracks. "Just not really a souvenir person." It's not like you can carry keepsakes through portals.

West closes the carton. "*Never?* No goofy hats from an amusement park, or a little snow globe, or a foam finger from a baseball game?"

"I am pretty much souvenir-free."

We take the cartons to designated bins. "Well," I say, hands in my pockets. "Thanks, I guess? Though to be honest, you didn't help much—except show me that you're a pushover with Janice the goat."

West turns and pets Janice, who is still lingering. Then he says, "But now that we both have a free period, how shall we spend it?"

I feel heat rise to my cheeks. He's suggesting we do something . . . *together*? I spot Ursula still with the horses—she's keeping an eye on us. She'd totally tell me to go if I asked her.

It sounds kind of . . . nice, actually. It's so easy to talk to West. I feel like my funniest self around him—he gets my jokes. For so many centuries, with so many covens, my jokes fell flat. And his skin smells so good. . . .

I cast the thoughts out of my mind with a start. Hanging out with West isn't why I'm here. I have a mission. A compromise pops into my mind then. A use for West.

I look up. "Will you show me where the shops in town are?"

He smiles. "Like the witch shops? Do you want to get . . . *a souvenir*?"

"Maybe so." What I really need is a crystal ball. It seems like a perfect excuse to go searching for one. "Lead the way?"

West smiles and starts down the hillside. When I glance over my shoulder, Ursula is still peering out the horse barn, beaming. There's a crash by the garbage cans, too—Campbell is still there, emptying something into the barrel in a noisy, almost angry way.

Halfway down the hill I glance to my right and see something else—a flash of something red hovering at the edge of the trees. I slow. Someone is walking around at the edge of the woods, not far from where I saw that first shimmering spirit. It's a real person this time, though, not a ghost, but he holds something glowing in his hand. Sweeping it back and forth, back and forth, as though looking for something.

Dr. Novis.

In the front office, West and I secure passes to leave the school grounds, and soon enough, we're on the sidewalk of regular old Salem. Cars speed past. A couple out for a stroll glides by us, their held hands swinging. I see the Witch Museum in the distance, but I avert my gaze, trying not to think about what's inside.

As we walk, West tells me that at the moment, he doesn't have a roommate—because of Jack being caught cheating, he has been suspended for two weeks.

"It's kind of lonely. Not that Jack was good company, but I grew up with a bunch of brothers and sisters. I'm used to noise. A quiet room—that's unfamiliar." He glances at me. "You got any siblings?"

Agatha Harkness, *siblings*? What a quaint little question. Though it occurs to me I have no idea if I do or not. It also occurs to me it would be very strange to answer that way.

"No," I decide.

"Ah. So maybe you'd be used to an empty room, then. But you and Ursula seem to get along."

"Sure. I like her a lot." I pause to wait at a crosswalk. "But it's terrible about what happened with her old roommate. Everyone tells me that it's good I came along to help her out of her slump, but I can't help but wonder if she, like, *witnessed* something she doesn't want to talk about."

West frowns. "You think?"

"She just shuts down sometimes when I ask her about it. But the only reason I *do* ask her is because it seems like she wants to say something . . . but she almost physically can't."

"Like she's traumatized?"

"I don't know."

The light changes for us to walk, and we cross and head down a side street, passing old-timey streetlamps and a blue post box.

"I don't know Ursula that well," West admits. "Though I will say, when it all happened, she was really upset. It wasn't that long ago. She's probably still grieving for both of them suddenly vanishing."

"Both of them?" I squint. "You mean . . . Mr. Haverford? She knew him, too?"

"He was Ursula's adviser—mine, too, though I didn't see him much. Ursula leaned on him a lot, I'm pretty sure. I always saw her in there for homework help, and he was also the field hockey coach. Nice guy, really. So strange."

I navigate around a large sandwich board for a coffee place. "I didn't realize she was close to him, too. Poor Ursula."

"Certain teachers make all the difference. You were homeschooled before coming here?"

I shrug. It's the story I told Ursula, the story I'm supposed to stick to. Lies can come in handy sometimes, but I'm having a hard time keeping track of all the things I've said. Also, homeschooled Agatha sounds really boring.

"Was that weird? Did you feel isolated? Who taught you, anyway—your parents?"

"Yes? No? I don't know." I'm starting to feel itchy. "I don't really like talking about myself, sorry."

"Why?"

"There's not much to tell." I don't feel like making up lies is more like it.

He laughs. "I don't believe that."

I skirt around a sewer grate. The sun ducks behind a cloud, and we're bathed in shadows. Then West adds, "I was just wondering because you seem different. In a good way. So many people here come from, like, the same places with the same family setup. You seem, I don't know—worldly."

"I've moved around a lot, I guess."

"Okay, where?"

I give him a slightly withering look, and he returns it with an apologetic smile. "Have you heard the phrase *pulling teeth*? Throw me a bone here, Alice. I want to get to know you."

I roll my jaw, annoyed. Then a mischievous thought occurs to me. What if I tell him the truth? It worked before, in front of the Witch Museum.

"Okay. I've lived near the Himalayas. And Eastern Europe. And at the bottom of the ocean."

He stops and stares at me. Just when I think he actually believes me, he lets out a sigh. "So that's how it's gonna be, huh? You're going to joke the whole time?"

"Who said I'm joking?"

But then I wink.

We stop at another intersection, letting two bikers whiz past. "And you're also here on a time-traveling mission? Where'd you come from, anyway?"

I smile mysteriously. "Long, long ago."

"And you traveled here . . . how? In that fancy car from *Back to the Future*?"

Ursula and I watched that movie in the common room the other day. I shake my head at all its ridiculous, nonsensical details. "A portal is a much more elegant way to travel through time than a silly car."

"Ah, right, a portal. You know, I've always wondered—what does it feel like to travel through a portal?"

"Sometimes, you feel nothing. Other times, it makes you feel a little dizzy. And then other times, you see things. Visions."

"What kind of visions?"

"Well, this time, I saw myself as an old woman. Which, I have to say, was alarming, because I never thought I'd grow old."

West raises an eyebrow. "Everyone grows old."

"I won't. Or that's what I thought, anyway."

West rolls his eyes. "You really should take a creative writing class."

We turn down another street, this one bustling with shops and shoppers. In many of the windows are common witchy emblems and tarot designs. *Wiccan and Witchcraft Altar Supplies*, the signs read.

I make a beeline for them, suddenly excited. In the first store, crystals hang from gossamer threads and twinkle in the light. There are jars of eyeballs and freeze-dried frog legs and honorific statues of Cernunnos, Baphomet, and Freya.

West chuckles at them. "What are these even used for?"

"They're placed at an altar as a sign of worship." I point to Cernunnos, with his humanlike body and giant deer head. "This guy is the god of animals. He has superhuman strength, stamina, immortality—basically all of the good stuff—and helps with fertility and bounty. The Puritans should have worshiped him more, actually—maybe they would have had better harvests. But of course they didn't, because he was a false god." I touch the statue's head. "I met him once."

West laughs. "You *met* this giant horned dude?"

"Well, I *think* I met him. He'd inhabited someone else's body, because obviously he can't roam the earth as he is, but I'm pretty sure it was him."

"How about this guy?" West points at Baphomet. "Have you met him, too?"

"I don't think so, not yet. He's a demon." I notice the weary smile West is giving me. "What?"

"Are you ever going to tell me anything serious about yourself?"

"But isn't it more fun this way?"

"Is it because you don't like getting close to people?"

I snort. "That's a weird thing to say. And completely wrong."

"Is it?" West pretends to be really interested in a box full of old bones. "I had a good friend once who was a pathological liar. I talked to a therapist about him. The therapist said that my friend's lies weren't cruel—they were often a way for him to control his surroundings. Because he didn't reveal anything real, no one would ever criticize who he really is, and he'd never get hurt."

My heart starts to ramp up. "Are you accusing me of being a pathological liar?"

"I'm accusing you of protecting yourself."

"What's wrong with protecting myself?" Then I pivot. "Let's try another store."

The next store smells so strongly of incense sticks and candles that it instantly makes me nauseated. I poke around a little, though it isn't the kind of place that would have a crystal ball. I'm starting to wonder if any of these stores will, which is beyond frustrating because this is a *town of witches*. Behind the counter is a woman with purple hair wearing a pointed hat with stars and moons all over it. A woman wearing a T-shirt that reads *My Other Car Is a Broom* holds one of the candles in her hands and asks the shopkeeper if it actually casts a spell.

"Oh absolutely," the shopkeeper says, speaking in a Scottish accent that sounds a little bit fake. "This is our Love Spell candle. Burn it, focus your energy on the person you want to fall in love with you, and soon enough, they'll be yours."

I snicker. I can't help it. Candle spells aren't actually a thing.

The shopkeeper looks up and frowns. "Don't believe me? I made this candle myself, lassie, using my ancient practices."

I glance at West. "She's not a real witch," I murmur. "Don't be fooled."

The shopkeeper might not be a witch, but she must have *very* good hearing, because she beckons us forward. "Come hither, children!" She shows me the candle the tourist was asking about. "I guarantee this will make him fall for you."

"It's fine," I say quickly, my cheeks blazing. "We were just leaving."

"You don't think love spells work, lassie?"

"Not at all," I blurt, not able to help myself.

She doesn't look fazed. She points at West. "I'll make him fall in love like that." Her fingers snap. "How about this? I'll enchant you for free. Right here. Right now."

"Ooh, I want to see!" says the other customer, clasping her hands together.

This is my worst nightmare. I'm not about to be some charlatan's guinea pig, and I definitely don't want her to put a fake spell . . . on West . . . to fall in love with *me*.

I turn to West with a look that I hope conveys that I absolutely don't support this idea. But to my surprise, he whispers, "The shopkeepers sometimes do this to entertain the tourists. I bet if we stay and get her to sign off, it will count as our Historical Society credit for the week."

I stare at him. "You want to *do* it?"

He shrugs. "You said yourself it won't actually work. What are you afraid of?"

Something's caught in my throat, but I try to swallow it down. Maybe I should adopt West's cavalier attitude. Clearly he doesn't care about doing the spell because there are no emotions at stake for him. I'm just a random girl. And he's just a random guy.

I can feel everyone waiting. If I say no now, I figure, it will seem like too big of a thing, too great of an emotion. So I coolly shrug, too. "Fine. Let's do it. As long as it's quick."

The shopkeeper whoops with delight. Then she makes us sit on little pillows in front of her own altar behind the counter. The altar is covered in crystals and tapestries. There's a sharp, sandpapery sound as she lights the match, and the candle flame leaps into the air.

Then she shoves two horned helmets from behind the counter at us. "Put these on."

"Why?" I cry, staring at the thing in my hands. The horns are old and dirty. The inside smells like manure.

"We want the gods close. Those are the actual horns of the Horned God of Wicca." The fake witch sounds like she absolutely believes in what she's saying.

West's expression is mock serious as he puts on the helmet, so after a moment, I put mine on, too. It's so heavy that it feels like it's pressing down on my brain. When I look across the circle, West's helmet is perched on top of his head, maybe a size or two too small. He meets my gaze across the candle, and his lips start to twitch. I feel a laugh bubbling inside me, too. A snort escapes from his nose. Tears well in my eyes. I have to pinch the inside of my palm to stop.

"I'm going to give you a sweetening spell," the shopkeeper says. "I want you to stare at your man's forehead when you speak."

"Do I have to?" I ask, surreptitiously wiping my eyes from the laughing fit.

*"Yes,"* she says sternly. "That's how it works."

I begrudgingly gaze at the spot between West's hairline and his eyebrows. *This is ridiculous*, I tell myself, but suddenly, my heart is pounding.

"Now"—her skirts rustle as she moves closer—"concentrate on his forehead like you're entering his mind."

I grit my teeth. The problem is that I *can* enter his mind. So it's almost like I'm putting the brakes on so I *don't*.

"Now think to yourself, *My name in your head, my image in your mind*," the shopkeeper says. "Repeat it to me, out loud."

I glance at her in horror. "There's no way I'm saying that."

"You must maintain eye contact with his mind!" she snaps, spitting a little as she does. She points back to West's forehead. "Say it! *My name in your head, my image in your mind*."

"My name in your head, my image in your mind," I say in monotone, feeling my magic stirring within me but trying desperately to tamp it down.

"Now say, *You and I are intertwined*."

This is so cheesy it makes me writhe with humiliation. But I say it all the same: "You and I are intertwined."

"*Reach out to me, this I plea*," she says.

I repeat it.

*"As I ask, so mote it be."*

I squeeze my eyes shut. "This is the worst spell ever."

"Say it, lassie! Otherwise the spell won't work!"

My lips tremble. "As I ask . . ."

But then I pause. Across from me, West now has his eyes closed, and his face is neutral. I can't tell what he's thinking. Surely he's just sitting for this to get the credit. Or what if he feels bad for me, and he's humoring me because he thinks *I* have a crush? A heat comes over me, an embarrassment I've never felt the likes of before. I can't do this fake enchantment. Not because I don't want it to happen—but more because I *do*.

"Sorry." I leap to my feet. My movements are so abrupt that the horned helmet falls off my head with a clunk. "I, um, have to go."

West opens his eyes, too. "Alice?" he cries. "Alice, wait!"

But I shake my head and hurry out. This was a mistake. And so I continue down the sidewalk and all the way to school, not looking back even once.

# Eleven

A*gatha . . .*

*Agatha!*

My eyes flutter open. Blurry shapes slide past. Someone laughs in the distance. *Martha?*

*I've got you where I want you.* The voice is an icy whisper.

"No you don't," I murmur. "I know for a fact you have no idea who I am. And I've been careful. Really careful. There's no way you've found me."

*Not careful enough. I can't believe you haven't found me yet. I'm right here. Right in front of you.*

I look around, as if she means it literally. "Listen, if you have me where you want me, why don't we battle already? Why don't we end this?"

*What's the fun in that?*

There's a loud *boom*, and my eyes snap open. I'm in my bed in the dorm. Outside, it looks like the source of the boom is that one of the large Halloween skeletons has fallen over, face-first. A few people are gathered around him, trying to stand him back up, but the thing is so tall that they're having a hard time.

I stare down at my hands on top of the covers. The dream was unsettling. It feels like Martha was dangling over my bed, taunting me. *What's the fun in that?* The words rush in and out. Sure, Martha might be having fun right now . . . but if that crow was correct, her goal is destruction.

Eventually, she'll get tired of the games . . . and end me.

Later that morning, I stare at my breakfast in the dining hall, not hungry for the first time since I arrived in Salem. The other coven members have early classes, so it's just Ursula and me. I still feel jittery from the dream. Uneasy about the interaction I had with West. Uneasy with *everything*, really.

"So," Ursula says as she stabs a piece of turkey bacon. "Who are you going to ask to the Halloween dance? It's in a few days."

I look at her and realize she's not kidding. "Uh, no one."

She sets down her fork. "Why not?"

There are way too many reasons to list. I want to tell Ursula it's because I probably won't be here, but the rate things are going, maybe I will. My strange dream swims in my mind. What did Martha mean that she couldn't believe I'd figured her out yet? That she was *right here*? Right *where*?

"Well?" Ursula asks.

I sigh. "Why do *I* have to ask someone? Can't it be the other way around?"

"That's just the tradition. Girl asks. How about West?"

I nearly choke on my scrambled eggs. That bizarre scene in the witch shop keeps flashing in my head. I ran all the way back to the dorms before West could catch me, though I sensed him trailing me the whole way. I didn't know how to explain myself—it was just that the fake ritual suddenly made me so uncomfortable. I also didn't like how much I hoped for it to work. I don't like hoping for things. It's so eager. Vulnerable. I'd rather plan, scheme, plot, and divine my destiny on my own time. I should have stayed and endured that silly spell, acted like it didn't bother me.

"He seems into you," Ursula says. "All that chatting

he was doing with you at Agriculture? And then you left together!"

"He's not into me."

"You could at least test the waters. You're running out of time."

"Are *you* taking someone?"

She shrugs and takes a bite of bacon. "I'm just going with the coven, I think."

"Why can't I do that, too?"

"Is that what you want?"

She looks at me challengingly. What *do* I want? Is it silly that I'm not exploring a possibility with West? I think of his weird little psychoanalysis of me—that I'm hiding behind my lies, protecting my feelings from getting hurt. He's not wrong. It's just that I've never *not* protected my feelings. Actually, I'd rather not have any feelings at all.

Experimentally, I explore the idea of West and me going to the dance together. We'd probably have fun. But would we have to dance? That means we'd have to hold hands. My body flushes hot. I push the idea away again.

Ursula points her fork at me. "Okay, how about this? I'll help you come up with a plan to ask him. And if it doesn't work out, then we'll all go together as a group."

I sigh. "If you're going to be annoying about it, what other option do I have?"

But deep down, I'll admit it. I'm kind of excited.

As luck would have it, Ursula and I have a free period this morning, which means, she says, that we can strategize. She tells me to go back to the dorms and wait—she has a few things she has to gather up.

I try to study, but I feel antsy. Is this a huge mistake? I don't ask boys to dances. I think about that dream again, too—Martha saying she's found me. It makes no sense. I've been careful. I haven't used big magic. I haven't been *able* to. It's got to be my mind playing tricks on me.

About an hour later, Ursula returns to our room from the school store, carrying a black poster board under her arm. "You're going to *love* this."

She spins the board around. On the border of the poster are artistically drawn white vines and candles. There's also a penciled skeleton head at the top. And in the middle, in big, spiky writing, it reads, *You have been SUMMONED to go to the Halloween dance with me! From, Alice.*

"What on earth is *that*?" I screech.

Ursula's smile doesn't falter. "It's the dance proposal. Everyone makes a poster asking people to the dance using funny puns and whatever. I thought it would be cute because of Halloween."

"That's the stupidest tradition I've ever heard of!" Is this truly how people have evolved in 2025? I gesture at the skeleton head. The use of *summoned*. "It's basically advertising that I'm a witch."

"You *are* a witch." Ursula searches my face and seems

startled by my reaction. Then her shoulders droop. "You don't like it. That's fine. It's just that I made Sylvie *her* proposal sign last year, and I wanted to do a good job with yours. . . ."

Now there are tears in her eyes. *Perfect.* I run my hands down the length of my face, desperate to make it stop. "Oh God, *whatever.* It's great, you're amazing, we're best friends, *la la la* bonding moment, bonding hug. Are we good now?"

Ursula blinks at me like I've just spilled hot water all over her. "You don't have to make it *worse.*"

"Ursula. I don't do cheesy friend stuff, I'm sorry." I glance at the poster again. "It's fine. It's not like West is going to say yes anyway."

"Yes, he will! You need to think positive!" And then she drags me up by the hand and plunks me down at her desk. "Because after classes, we're going to give you a makeover."

Imagine giving a cat a makeover. Trying to paint a cat's claws and put mascara on a cat's eyelashes. If you tried to swipe lipstick across a cat's mouth, you'd definitely get bitten and probably have to go to the hospital because everyone knows that cats' mouths are way dirtier than humans'. That, in essence, is what Ursula, Jamira, Evan, and Francie go through in dolling me up for my big proposal to West. Even Ivy comes, though she smirks at me the whole time.

"Do you even know how to wear lipstick?" Ivy teases. "You're eating it all off."

"And you're acting like we're trying to poison you," Francie says when I swat away a blush brush.

"It's like you've never seen makeup before," Jamira jokes after I flinch when she gets too close with an eyeliner stick.

"I've seen makeup," I snap, which isn't entirely the truth. "I just don't like it on my face."

Doing my hair isn't much easier—witches tend to be quite sensitive, so whenever Evan rakes a long brush through my locks I resist the urge to start screaming. "Am I hurting you?" He looks horrified, and then, to my surprise, I see tears in his eyes.

"It's not *that* bad," I say, rolling my eyes. "I usually don't admit things like this, but I might be acting a tad dramatic."

"Sorry, sorry." Evan fans his face. "I'm just a little jumpy." He leans in closer and whispers, "I asked my crush, Simon, to the Halloween dance. But he said *maybe*."

"Maybe?" I wrinkle my nose. "What's that mean?"

"I don't *know*!" He drops the brush to the dresser. "It's beyond frustrating. It took me so long to work up the courage to ask him, period. Even a year ago, I would have died before asking Simon to the dance. It's so . . . *awkward*."

"Don't I know it," I say dourly, because I feel exactly all the things that just came out of his mouth.

"But that's different—it's tradition for girls to ask. Besides, West is totally going to say yes. Anyone would, with you."

"Liar." I meet his gaze in the mirror, shocked by how easily he accepts me. How he thinks the whole *school* accepts me.

"Are you kidding?" He picks up the brush again. "You're a breath of fresh air."

Huh. Usually I'm referred to as a breath of stale air, or even noxious air that suffocates and poisons. You'd think I'd put a spell on all of these people to like me, except I know I haven't. They *actually* feel this way.

As Evan gently brushes my hair, a very strange feeling comes over me. I kind of *like* that people like me. And even weirder, it kind of makes me want to be nice too.

"Strong people do the asking," I tell him. "Weak ones sit back and wait to be asked. And if he doesn't say yes to you, then it's his loss."

A little smile plays on Evan's lips. "You think?"

"Yep. You need to go in there and be confident. Ask for what you want. He'll say yes. I feel it." And I do. A tiny clairvoyant glimmer of Simon feeling a little overwhelmed by Evan's forwardness but then happily agreeing to go.

He pets my shoulder. "You're the best, Alice."

He finishes combing out my hair and then uses a curling iron to give me some waves. After all my pampering is finished, my reflection in the mirror looks a bit like a psychotic clown that's been electrocuted, but everyone keeps saying I look *so much better.* It makes me wonder how terrible I looked before.

But, okay, it's been slightly fun. A tiny bit.

Due to her "psychic powers," Ivy knows that West has soccer practice this afternoon. Since I'm wearing uncomfortable high-heeled shoes, Francie helps to steady me down the stairs. I'm now clad in a soft purple sweater of hers that she says "works great with my coloring." All of us walk across the green in the morning sunlight, the proposal sign tucked under Ursula's arm. When we crest a hill and I catch sight of the boys playing on the soccer field, there's a nervous buzz in my stomach.

"This is going to go quite badly, I can feel it."

"No it won't." Francie's arms swing merrily at her sides. "This is how people ask people to the dance. I did it last night with James—*and* he said yes."

"But you knew he would say yes," Ivy points out. "Marilyn Monroe said so. All because of me."

I stifle a smile. I'm a little sad I won't be here the next time Ivy and the group consult the Ouija board, even though it won't work quite as well.

Soccer practice is just wrapping up as we approach the bleachers. The boys head to big jugs of water on the sidelines and start pulling on sweatshirts. The field is teeming with players, coaches, and a lot of random people milling around, watching.

I turn to Ursula. "Maybe I could find a more private time?"

Ursula shakes her head. "Come on, Alice! You've got this!" She raises her arms in a V.

"I thought you disliked cheerleaders," I say darkly.

"I'm all for cheerleaders if it's about cheering for you!"

I practically rip the poster from her cheerful little fingers. Then I stomp across the field. I'm almost right up against the group of boys when West looks up and sees me. A curious smile spreads across his face.

"Alice. H-hey."

"Hello, Holdfast," I say shakily.

He looks around. "Were you . . . *watching*? Are you . . . *into* soccer?"

"What?" I snicker. "Oh. God. No. I hate organized sports."

West's gaze travels over my face. "You look . . . different today. Did you get a haircut or something?"

"I was abducted. Made to put on makeup and these terrible shoes." I lift my foot, showing off the heel.

"Ab—"

"By my friends. They tied me to a chair and put all this goop on my face and lips and all of that. It's giving me hives."

He laughs. "Oh. Well, that's better than being abducted by aliens." Then he looks curious. "You . . . haven't been abducted by aliens before, have you? You know, after time-traveling through portals and everything else."

"Not that I'm aware of. But I suppose there are parts of my life that I don't remember, so who knows?"

There's an awkward pause. Then West shifts. "So . . . what's up? You feeling better after that whole spell thing at the shop?"

"Sorry about that," I admit. "That, um, helmet was giving me a migraine, and that Scottish woman kept spitting when she talked . . . I had to get out of there."

"Of course," West says, though his expression is skeptical. "So it had nothing to do with the spell, then?"

"Absolutely not."

I glance across the field. My friends are watching. Jamira makes a rolling motion with her hands—*speed it up*.

"Anyway." I sigh and awkwardly hold up the sign. "Here. Sorry. This is hideously embarrassing."

West cocks his head confusedly at the poster. That's when I realize I'm holding it upside down. I groan and turn it right side up, but that seems to puzzle West even more. He looks from the words to me to the poster again. That's when I realize the words have shifted on me. Now they say *Beware All Ye Who Enter Here!*

Oops. I think I was so appalled by the idea that I had to do this that I inadvertently magically changed the wording.

"Hang on," I say quickly, turning the sign around to face me again. I need to enchant it back to its original message, but for the life of me, I can't bring myself to make it say that stuff about summoning again. That would make it seem like I care entirely too much.

So I change it to the most blasé message I can think of: *Maybe we can go to that dance together because sitting at home is boring?* Ursula will be disappointed but, well, she doesn't have to know.

West studies the sign once more . . . but then he shifts uncomfortably. "Wait, you want to go to the Halloween dance together?"

"It appears that the sign says that, yes." My voice comes out garbled. It sounds like I'm choking on my tongue. Why is he making this so difficult?

"I . . . I didn't think you were *into* dances, though."

"I'm not," I say quickly. "At all. Dances are awful. My roommate put me up to this. Although, um, it wouldn't be too terrible, I guess—you know, if we went together."

I peek at him, but he's shaking his head slightly. My heart stops in my chest. I'm not sure if he's disappointed . . . or disgusted . . . or something else, but all of a sudden I want out of here immediately.

"Alice," he says. "I'm sorry, but I already told someone else I'd go with them to the dance."

"Oh." The poster flutters from my hands and crashes to the ground. I wish I could disappear. I need to open a portal in the earth. "Uh, okay . . ."

"It's just—after we went to that store yesterday, and you ran out, and then someone asked me last night. Actually, I think you know her."

All of a sudden, I know what name he's going to tell me before he says it out loud. I don't even have to use mind reading to do so, it's just so obvious.

"It's Campbell," he says quietly. "She's . . . new."

"I know who she is," I blurt. "Goat girl."

It makes so much sense. The way Campbell was spying on us at the farm. The way she said *West, you're my hero*. Of course she has a crush on him. I can't believe I didn't see it then.

"I'm really sorry." West leans down to pick up the

poster. He offers it to me, but there's no way I'm touching it again, so I sort of bat it out of his hand and it flutters to the ground. Then I turn to leave.

"See you later!" I cry. I'm so mortified that I can't even see straight. "Well. Pretend this never happened, then. It was all just a bet, anyway!"

I kick off my heels and practically sprint across the field, having to pass at least a hundred soccer players as I go. It feels like everyone is staring at me. Oh, how I wish I could use my powers. I'd turn them all into turnips. I'd suck out their voice boxes. How dare they make fun! How dare they think I'm suffering!

Instead, I glare at several players who really don't look like they were doing anything wrong. "What are you looking at?" I growl, my anger so palpably forceful that one of them wheels backward and almost trips over his heels.

It makes me feel slightly better.

# *Twelve*

Ursula and the others are gaping at me as I march past the bleachers.

"Alice?" Ursula says in a small voice, hurrying after me. "Wh-what happened?"

"He's taking someone else. But it's fine. Really. No problem at all."

I walk up the hill past the tennis courts. Then I beeline for the dining hall. I can stuff my face with macaroni and cheese to drown out my humiliation. I use my sleeve to rub off my makeup. It leaves tan and black smears on the fabric, so I can only imagine the messy smudges it left behind on my face.

Ursula keeps pace with me, and I can sense the others lagging behind. "But who is he going with instead of you?"

"Campbell."

She stops in her tracks. "You're kidding."

"I don't care. Honest." I try to tell myself this is true.

"I—I had no idea that was going to happen," Ursula stammers.

I stomp through a raked pile of leaves, disrupting them just for the heck of it. "I'm not saying you did. But you also didn't have to push me into asking him."

Ursula's chin trembles. I know I've hurt her feelings, but I'm just so humiliated. Lashing out feels terrible but also good.

Jamira runs up and puts an arm around my shoulder. "Come to the dance with us. We'll go as a big group."

"Totally." Evan takes my hand. "Coven power. We've got this."

Even Ivy falls in step. "The worst thing you can do is show Campbell you care. You'll have a better time without a date anyway."

I grumble in a noncommittal sort of way. I'm in such a black mood that I don't feel like going to the dance at all.

Ursula eyes someone standing near a few of the

skeletons on the green. Campbell is giggling with her friends. Before I can stop her, Ursula marches straight up to her.

"Ursula, *no*!" I whisper, rushing over to her.

But Ursula stands her ground. Campbell jumps when she gets close.

"Do you even like him?" Ursula demands.

Campbell wrinkles her nose and steps away from Ursula like she's covered in germs. "Who are you talking about, weirdo?"

"You know." Ursula has her hands on her hips. "Do you actually like West, or did you only ask him because Alice likes him?"

"I don't like him!" I screech.

Campbell's gaze shifts from Ursula to me to her again. Then she smirks. "As *if* West would like Alice!"

I blink. "What's *that* supposed to mean?"

"I think you know," Campbell says.

"I don't know," I challenge. "Care to explain it to me?"

Campbell just looks at me with that infuriating half-smile. My mind reels. Is she saying I'm not as pretty as she is? As charming, as smart? For a second, I wonder if she's *right*—it's not like I know how to do crushes and relationships. I'm so furious I can feel magic tingling in my chest. I want to turn her to stone or ice. I want to give her a pig's tail.

Then I tug at Ursula's arm and whirl around. "Let's get out of here."

Ursula follows, as does the rest of the coven. Behind us, we can hear Campbell whispering.

When we're far enough away from Campbell, Ursula says, "Emergency coven meeting. Tonight."

The group exchanges a cautious glance. "Wait, why?" Jamira asks.

"She's out to get us, guys. This is the last straw. We need to plan—in private."

"Yeah, and you confronting her just made her *more* out to get us," I grumble.

Ivy clears her throat. "Also, we don't meet on Tuesdays, Ursula—you know that. Mrs. Gersh is on library night duty, and she's a real stickler for evening rounds."

"But we need to make this right," Ursula pleads.

I let out a breath. "Do we, though? Do I think Campbell is obnoxious and judgey? Yes. Do I wish Campbell would accidentally get shot to the moon? Absolutely. But I don't really care."

"Why not? It's not fair!" Ursula's eyes flash, and her cheeks are flushed. I'm surprised at how worked up she's getting. "Campbell is a manipulative bully, and she's been watching us. I swear she snuck into our room. And what about all the other things she did? Put that key into my backpack to get me in trouble? Kick leaves all over your coat, Evan? And it's clear West likes *you*, Alice. What's she going to do to us next? We have to teach her a lesson!"

Jamira glances at Ivy. Evan shifts his weight. "But she seems sort of onto us. At least, with the others, we were anonymous vigilantes. With Campbell, she's probably expecting us to retaliate."

"Which is why we need to figure out a plan to take her by surprise," Ursula insists. "And we can't do it in the dorms. She might be listening."

"I don't feel great about sneaking out, though," Francie says. "It isn't the right night."

"Maybe we could be sneaky enough to evade Mrs. Gersh," Ursula protests.

"Can't this wait another few days, until our normal meeting?" I ask.

But Ursula shakes her head. "What if she does something worse between now and then?"

Everyone shifts their weight. I suppose Ursula has a point. Campbell has been coming after us sort of hard. And the stuff about her sneaking into our room . . . we never did figure out what that was about.

"It's possible, I guess, she has something even worse planned," I murmur.

Jamira sighs. "We could give sneaking out a try."

Ivy shrugs. "I'm in. I think Campbell's a little snot."

"But please don't do this on my behalf," I beg them.

But they all wave their hands. "We're doing it for you, but we're also doing it for all of us," says Evan.

"We stick by our girls," Francie says.

Ursula puts her arm around me. "We'll make this right."

And I have to say, their support feels pretty good.

Which is alarming.

I really have to stop feeling things.

The evening is full of bad omens about the night we're about to have. In the library, Ursula and I made sure to sneak past the sign-in desk without adding our names as usual, but even so, Mrs. Gersh is on constant patrol, her blocky loafers clonking down the marble hallways every few minutes to make sure students are in their seats, studying. After what seems like hours, when she finally excuses herself to the ladies' room, we slip out of the building.

But it's hazy outside, with no moon—which isn't great for navigation. The paths are extra dark, almost too dangerous to traverse without a flashlight. Ursula almost stumbles over a rock. I lose my footing walking down a steep grade. A guard strolls unexpectedly past the main building and we have to duck behind a tree.

I start to second-guess why we're even doing this.

"We should turn back," I whisper to Ursula after our third time of having to hide. "It's probably better that we leave Campbell alone."

"And let her pick on us? No, Alice. And it's not just because of West. There's something up with her. Why does it seem like she knows, somehow, that we're a coven? Does she have a sixth sense?"

Her words rattle through my ears. *Does* Campbell have a sixth sense? I can't believe it hasn't occurred to me before.

I look at Ursula. "Wait. When did you say Campbell came to school again?"

She hunches her shoulders as she walks. "At the beginning of September. A few weeks after school started, I think."

"Around the time Sylvie vanished? And the teacher, Mr. Haverford?"

Ursula flinches. "I guess. But what does that have to do with anything?"

*Maybe a lot*, I think. "Do you know where she's from?" I ask. Ursula shakes her head. "She's never mentioned another school, a town, a family?"

"I don't really know her. And it's not like I'm siding with her, but I wouldn't hold that against her." Ursula chooses her words carefully. "Because you don't mention your past, either."

*Exactly*, I think. I have no family or past I can speak of because my truth is so bizarre—I mean, I tried to tell West, and he laughed me off.

*What if* Campbell *is Martha?*

It could make sense. Maybe Martha wouldn't hide in a coven—it's an even better cover to pretend she hates witches. And there have been more hints, too—sneaking around in our room, for example; maybe she has a sense about who I am and wants to prove it. Even the timing of when the atmospheric disturbances began lines up with when she arrived at Conant Academy.

I mean, she and I are the only two new students this year. Of *course* she's Martha.

But what of that dream I had? *I've got you where I want you.* What's that mean?

We reach the cave. Ivy lights the candle for us, but when we creep through the cave's mouth, the mood seems off. Evan and Jamira are in the middle of an argument. When I ask what's going on, Jamira turns to me with a loud sigh.

"Evan forgot half our talismans and good luck charms. I reminded him a million times!"

"I'm sorry," Evan protests. "I left in such a rush. The schedule was messed up today. My RA wouldn't leave the common room, so I couldn't sneak past him."

"If we don't have our talismans, we're not protected!"

"You'll be okay," I say. "We'll be safe."

"But what about what happened with the Ouija board?" Jamira whispers. "Spirits are all around us!"

"And there's that . . . *thing* in the woods." Francie sounds frightened.

"Maybe that thing wasn't real," Ivy points out. "It was probably just a solar light, or someone's dropped phone."

"Uh, it was definitely a ghost," Francie argues. "It looked right at us! It . . . it didn't have legs!"

"Did you think it looked like a guy?" Evan whispers. "This is going to sound weird, but I swear I saw a necktie."

"Yes!" Jamira's eyes widen. "I saw that, too!"

"So we have a dressed-up ghost?" Ivy scoffs.

"Can we talk about Campbell, guys?" Ursula interrupts. "Why do you think she went after the one guy Alice liked? And how can we take her down?"

But suddenly, a twig snaps outside the cave. Everyone goes still.

A few seconds pass. Nothing. *"What was that?"* Francie mouths.

Evan puts his finger to his lips. More silence passes. I can feel the group holding in a breath.

"Maybe it was nothing?" Francie says after a while.

"Just an animal," Evan says.

But I suddenly have a terrible feeling that someone

is nearby. Watching. Here in this cave, we're as good as trapped. The only chance we have is knowing they're coming before they get here. And that calls for magic.

I scoot backward from the group a tiny bit, praying they won't notice anything about me that's off. Then I close my eyes and, in the darkness, cast my soul outside my body, floating outside the cave to the woods beyond. Astral projection isn't a spell I use often—it makes me feel queasy afterward, and while I'm in the middle of the spell, if one of them talks to me, I won't be able to answer back. Between that and the fact that it's the strongest spell I've performed so far at school, let's just hope I get my answer quickly.

At first, I see nothing in the woods besides trees and bushes, sleeping birds and squirrels. I drift around this way and that, desperate to find some kind of information. And then I see the glimmer of a lantern. The light shines against three tall, adult bodies. They're walking quickly, heads down, shoulders hunched. They're on a mission.

I snap back to myself inside the cave, right where I left everyone. *"They're coming for us!"*

Ivy looks at me. "What do you mean?"

"How do you know?" Ursula cries.

"It's Peabody. And Novis . . . and a security guard. They're in the woods—they're *coming.*"

Evan looks confused. "Can you hear them or something?"

"Sort of," I fudge. "*Yes.*"

Jamira starts gathering her things. "I can't get in trouble! My parents will kill me!"

"They'll shut down our coven," Evan whispers.

"We'll probably be suspended," Ivy adds. "It'll go on our records."

And Ursula just stares at me, eyes wide, too shocked to speak.

"We have to get out of here!" I beg them. "Now!"

"How?" Ivy whisper-shouts. "If you're so sure they're coming, they'll see us if we go through the front."

"Actually, there is another way." I'm still a distance away from the group, so I close my eyes and press my hand against the rock at the very back of the cave. Slowly, I can feel it start to give and crumble to dust. Performing yet another strong spell is a huge risk, but I don't know what else to do.

I pretend to be pushing leaves aside and then shine the candle toward the back of the cave. "I'm pretty sure this is a tunnel that empties to another spot on the other side of the campus."

Francie looks alarmed. "Since *when*?"

Evan's face goes slack. "How *big* of a tunnel?"

Ivy gives me a strange look. "How did you even know it was there?"

"I, um, was feeling around the leaves last time we were here, and I felt a draft. And then when I was on the other side of campus, I saw a cave through the rock—I looked on a GPS topographical map—it all seems to link up." I'm babbling for sure, trying to come up with something that sounds logical. "Listen, we have to try. It's the only option."

"You're *sure*?" Jamira sounds horrified. "But what if it's a dead end? Then we'll *really* be trapped!"

"It won't be." I can still feel the infinitesimally subtle vibrations of the rest of the rock crumbling away. "We'll be safe. I swear. We'll crawl out the other way, run back to our dorms, and sign in there. We didn't sign in at the library, so our names aren't on the list. They'll assume Mrs. Gersh was off with her head count."

The group just gapes at me, but they have to get on board. If my estimation is correct, the headmistress, Dr. Novis, and the security guard are only a few minutes from discovering us, so we have to act fast. I can only hope that my magic has created a tunnel wide enough for all of us to pass through—and that the rock above us doesn't collapse on our heads. Fingers crossed I'm not leading the coven to certain death.

I move toward the tunnel, pushing aside more leaves. "Come on," I urge. "We all have to do this together. They're coming."

Everyone breathes nervously as we squeeze into the space. I go first, then Ivy, then Evan, then Francie,

Jamira, and Ursula. The tunnel is dusty and crumbly from all of the rock I had to magically disintegrate, and it's hard not to cough.

Then dim voices ring out from the mouth of the cave.

"Hello?" It's Dr. Novis. "Who's in there?"

*"Don't answer him,"* I mouth over my shoulder.

"Hello?" calls another louder voice. An *angry* voice. I'm guessing it's the security guard. "Come out right now! You're in violation of Conant Academy rules! We'll call the police!"

I can feel the coven going totally still. I pray no one makes a sound.

"No one is in here, Dr. Novis," Peabody says after a while.

"But there *must* be," he argues. "The tip I got was credible."

I bite down hard on the inside of my cheek. Tip . . . from *whom*?

"Let's go," I whisper to the group, and we keep crawling again.

The tunnel ceiling gets lower as we go. My back bumps against the hard, unforgiving rock ceiling, and I have to keep my head low. Behind me, I can hear Jamira softly whimpering.

Evan keeps saying we should go back. "Maybe they'll

leave," he says in a quivering voice. "And we could just go out of the cave the normal way."

"Or maybe we should give ourselves up," Francie says.

"We have to keep going," I urge them. "We'll come out the other side. I'm sure of it."

Except the tunnel shrinks even more. It's so thin a gap that we have to crawl on our bellies. Behind me, Francie starts to hyperventilate.

"Come on, Alice, we have to go back," Ivy whispers. "There's no way we can get through this. We can barely fit."

"Please," Jamira blubbers.

I hesitate. Even I'm not sure this is a good plan. We could get wedged. The ceiling could collapse on us. There's no way I can use magic to widen this tunnel, though. The others would definitely notice.

I stop crawling abruptly, and Ivy bumps into my feet. "Why did you stop?" she whisper-shrieks. "What's wrong?"

I draw in a ragged breath. "Maybe we should . . ."

But then I notice something ahead. *Light.* A tiny pinprick, possibly from one of the overhead lamps scattered around the campus paths. It's the opening. My eyes adjust, and I can see just enough to tell that the tunnel isn't too thin—we can make it after all.

"We're almost there," I assure everyone. "I see the exit!"

I crawl urgently, not caring that the rock is scraping my knees raw and chewing up my vertebrae. With every inch forward, I see more light. The group behind me sees it, too, because everyone starts crawling faster. Twenty feet to go. Ten. *Five.* I can touch the exit. Wide open space.

I scramble through the mouth of the tunnel and roll onto grass. I've never been so happy for wide-open space in my life.

But almost the exact moment I do, the sky opens up with a thunderclap. Rain pours down in buckets, the deluge so sudden and strong that I'm instantly drenched.

I scream, cover my head, and stagger for shelter under a nearby tree. The rest of the group spills out of the cave and dart away from the rain, too. Only once we're all gathered under the tree do I look around to see where we are: a remote corner of campus by the sports fields. There's no one here waiting to get us in trouble—no teachers, no guards. We did it.

Except the raindrops turn to hail. We shield our faces to avoid getting stung. I've never seen a storm this violent; tree branches break off right and left, whipping through the air.

"It's another weird weather event, don't you think?"

Evan screams over the wind. "Like the tornadoes? The hurricanes?"

I nod, my body suddenly so freezing and wet. It makes me uneasy. This is Martha's—*Campbell's*—doing. Maybe she's angry again. Mad that we didn't get caught. Is *she* the one who told on us?

I'm sure curfew is soon. There's no way we can stay under the tree for long. We need to check in with the RA, or all this suffering has been for nothing. After a little reprieve, all of us sprint across the playing fields toward the dorms. Our feet slosh in the mud. We nearly slip in the wet grass. Dry paths are now flash floods, and we have to avoid a few routes unless we want to get swept away in rushing currents. At the rate the rain is going, the school will be underwater in an hour.

*Is that what Martha wants?* I wonder. *To drown all of us?*

Finally, we make it to the dorms. Before we peel off to our separate quarters, Evan grabs my arm and pulls me close into a wet hug.

"You saved us, Alice!" he screams over the sound of the deluge. "Thank you."

Jamira hugs me, too. So does Francie. Even Ivy gives me an appreciative—though spooked—nod. "I guess we can't use the cave anymore," she yells.

"We'll find somewhere new," Evan assures her.

And then everyone sprints to his or her dorms. We're

all so wet we don't even bother to cover our heads anymore. As Ursula and I get to the door of our lobby and sign in, the large clock inside says it's a few minutes to curfew. We've slid in just under the wire.

Never before have I been so happy to be inside the dry, warm lobby. We stand for a moment on the mat just inside the door, our bodies dripping. Jenna the RA peeks out her door and raises her eyebrows.

"It's *scary* out there," she says. "Glad you guys made it back okay."

Jenna gives us a few towels so we can dry ourselves. Still, it feels the best to finally peel off our clothes in the dorm room, dry my body again, and put on clean, dry pajamas. As I'm toweling off my hair some more—I'm not sure it will ever get dry—I feel Ursula standing next to me. She looks positively waterlogged. She's been quiet, too—not the reactive quiet because of the rainstorm, but more like contemplative. There's a troubled look on her face.

"This was all my fault," she says quietly. "I almost got us in huge trouble."

"You couldn't have known it was going to happen," I assure her. "Nobody did."

She turns away slightly, the towel lifted to her face. "*You* did," she says in a small voice. "How did you know they were coming?"

I don't make eye contact, pretending to be intensely concentrating on my towel drying. "It was just a hunch. I have good hearing."

"And how did you know that tunnel was there? That cave is so dark normally. And I swear I've gone all the way to the back. There was nothing."

I stand and walk to our little bathroom in search of a brush. "I told you. There was a wall of leaves and dirt, not rock. And I looked at a map online."

Ursula doesn't respond. Her silence feels pregnant and pointed. Finally, I look at her. Her eyes are sad and wounded, like she doesn't believe me.

"Alice." Her voice catches. "You know you can tell me anything, right?"

Outside, the rain is still barreling down. When I look at myself in the bathroom mirror, I realize that the stinging sensation on my cheek is a big scrape, likely from climbing through the tunnel. I poke at the little bloody spots.

Maybe anyone would realize I'm lying. Maybe the whole coven does. But while I feel only a twinge of guilt covering things up with them, with Ursula, it's different. I can't deny how close we've become. I see her like a sister, sort of—it's a relationship far deeper than the one I felt with Prudence or . . . *anyone*. But how can I tell her who I really am? There's absolutely no way. Even what I tell West—he thinks I'm joking. It's too bizarre for these people to be real. Ursula would be terrified of me if she knew the truth. She'd want nothing to do with me. She'd break off our friendship.

And, I realize, that's something I don't want.

"Thank you. I know I can," I say gently. But then I let my own silence fill the air between us. I can tell her anything, but I won't.

For the sake of the friendship.

# *Thirteen*

By the following morning, the campus is still waterlogged, and classes are canceled. Building basements have flooded. Leaks have sprung everywhere. The staff and maintenance crews assess the damage. Half of the Halloween decorations on the green floated away, too. Some of them made it all the way to the Witch Museum downtown.

People are whispering things, too. Lots of students heard that right before the storm hit, Mrs. Gersh the librarian's head count was off, and some people were missing. Then students saw Peabody, Novis, and the security guard, Mr. Haines, head across campus toward the caves, though no one knows why. No one is sure what happened next, either, because it started to rain so hard. *What if someone else disappeared?* go the whispers. *It's like Sylvie and Mr. Haverford all over again.*

There is talk of a serial killer. An ax murderer. A wolf in the woods. Naturally, the coven pretends we have no idea about any of it. Jamira shows us how to use makeup to cover the bruises we got from hurtling through the cave. Ursula's face is puffy this morning, which makes me think she was crying last night, and she spends fifteen minutes with cucumbers on her eyes to bring down the swelling. I wish I could use a spell on her that would de-puff her instantly. I know so many good ones.

By lunchtime, the rumors have ballooned into wild exaggerations—people are convinced a serial killer is *here*, on campus, looking for his next victim like a psycho in a horror movie. In math class, a girl screams at something in the window, certain the serial killer is watching. This sets off a cascade of more screams and panicked efforts to hide under desks. Someone even faints. As it turns out, it's only a buck. The animal stares at us from across the clearing, then calmly walks back in the woods from whence it came.

It's no surprise, then, that when classes let out, an announcement comes on the PA system that all students need to report to the chapel for an important meeting. I fall in step with Ursula, who's pale and acting twitchy.

"It's going to be okay," I whisper to her. "We aren't going to get in trouble. No one saw us in that cave. No one knows *we* were the ones who left the library."

She looks at me helplessly. "Are you sure?"

"Yeah. Lucky we got that rain, actually. It made it even harder for anyone to spot us going back to the dorms."

"Right." Ursula's expression is uneasy. "But who do you think told on us?"

We both look at each other. It's clear we both think it's Campbell, annoyed with Ursula for confronting her, maybe—or just fed up with us in general. Only, how did she know we were at the caves? Unless, of course, she *is* Martha. Then she'd have lots of senses normal people don't.

The door to the chapel is propped open. The inside is small and cozy, with stained glass windows across every wall. It's much prettier than the Puritan church that stood near here way back when—the Puritans more or less thought that creating something beautiful meant you had too much time on your hands.

Headmistress Peabody stands at the pulpit, looking distraught. Many of the other teachers sit behind her—Mrs. Connelly, who teaches English, Mr. David, who teaches Geometry, Mrs. Rose, who teaches History. I spy Dr. Novis sneaking in from the back, a piece of paper in his hand. He weaves his way through the teachers and then stands next to Headmistress Peabody. They lean their heads together to whisper. At one point, Peabody looks up—and straight at me.

I look away, trying not to feel paranoid.

Finally, once all the students have filed in, Peabody raises her hands to indicate that we quiet down, and the murmurs die away. She sighs in the microphone. "Thank you for coming, everyone. I promise this won't take very long. I want to discuss some rumors that have been swirling and set things straight. I'd like to say that there's no cause to panic . . . but perhaps there is."

Everyone starts to whisper. Jamira and Francie glance at each other in terror.

"Maybe you've heard that we'd had a tip that some students went missing last night," Peabody says. "I know we're all on edge because of Sylvie O'Toole, understandably. As it turns out, we were mistaken—no students are missing. Everyone is accounted for. The head count was off, that's all."

Shoulders lower. People sigh in relief. I don't even realize how tense I am until I look at my palm and realize I've pressed my nails into my skin so hard that there are sharp half-moon indents in my flesh.

"That said, there's still cause for concern," Headmistress Peabody says. "I've received a viable tip that there is a group of students meeting somewhere off campus after hours—we thought they were meeting last night, and we thought we had the correct location, but possibly not. Groups like this are not only forbidden, but they can be dangerous. And that's not all. It's my understanding that these students are engaging in illicit activities. Activities that could be affecting the entire school."

I shift in my seat. *The entire school?* That seems a little exaggerated. We literally got one person in trouble, and he deserved it.

"Perhaps you've noticed the academy has looked a bit different lately. And felt a bit different, too. For a while, we've tried to look the other way, make excuses, but I'm afraid that we no longer can. I'm talking about these strange weather occurrences."

People shift in their seats. A crack forms in my brain. I turn and stare at Ivy, both of us slowly understanding.

"I'm sure all of you noticed the violent rainstorm that came out of nowhere yesterday evening. It caused a flash flood and a lot of damage—and not only that, it swept away one of our students, Jared Scott. He's in the hospital now, recovering from a broken leg."

More murmurs. Ivy grabs my hand. My heart starts to pound.

"For a while, I thought that these weather disturbances were just, well, acts of nature. But it has come to my attention that it might be something more than that. Students might be controlling this themselves. Harnessing dark powers, gathering strength as a group."

*"What?"* Evan whispers.

Ursula covers her mouth.

"The rainstorm last night coincided with a search Dr. Novis and I conducted for this group in question," the headmistress continues. "I have reason to believe that this storm was *created*, by this group, as a diversion."

Jamira stares at us.

Francie has gone pale. "They're going to blame us for this?" she whispers. "It doesn't even make sense!"

"It's just . . . a coincidence," I murmur.

Or maybe not. Maybe someone's trying to frame us.

A hand pops up in the audience. "So are you saying there are *witches* on campus? Real witches practicing magic?"

Peabody glances at Novis, who says, "Look, I don't want anyone to panic, but I'm a bit of an expert on matters such as these. It's possible there are witches, yes. But we're working very hard to expose them and shut them down before they can cause any more destruction or danger."

"We'll be on the lookout for anyone involving themselves in this type of activity," Peabody warns. "And if you know something, say something. This isn't a simple school prank. Tornadoes, hailstorms, flash floods—all of it can be very dangerous."

"Whoever you are, you'll be punished," Novis adds. "Expelled and arrested. So if there's anyone in this crowd who knows something—*anything*—and if you don't come forward, you'll be implicated as well. You must share with us what you know. This is a matter of life or death."

People start to chatter again. Some people start crying. My coven members fidget in their seats. "Maybe it's okay," Evan says, looking at me. "Besides the person who told on us—who doesn't know anything—there's no one else who knows it's us."

"It's Campbell," Ursula says. "She must have followed us to the cave one night and that's how she knew where to send Dr. Novis and the headmistress. That thing we thought was a ghost—maybe it was her."

"But I'm not sure that makes sense," Francie argues. "Wouldn't Campbell have told on us by name? Peabody doesn't know who was meeting at the cave. Like whoever made this tip knows *someone* is . . . but not that it's us."

"Right," Jamira says. "We would have gotten in trouble after the fact. They would have come to our dorms last night or this morning if they knew it was us in there."

"So who else told?" Evan asks. "Who else knows something?"

I can feel Ursula's gaze on me. I know someone else who knows something: West. He knows I was in Jack's room and had a hand in getting him in trouble. And let's not forget all the ridiculous stories I've been telling him—about portals and time travel and having met strange Wiccan gods. But the same argument about Campbell applies to him, too—why wouldn't he call us out by name?

Unless he's trying to spare me. Unless he's trying to warn me to stop before things get out of hand.

That's the question, I guess: Did whoever told do it as a punishment . . . or a warning? I think, too, of the threats Peabody made—and the wild accusations that we caused the hurricanes and earthquakes. *Ecoterrorism. Prison sentence. Call the authorities.* This isn't just a simple slap on the hand anymore.

If we're blamed, this could change everything.

# *Fourteen*

On campus, everyone glances suspiciously at everyone else, probably wondering who the secret witches are, why they're stirring up the elements, and how they can get caught. In any other circumstance, I'd celebrate all the suspicion—it's sort of like I have a whole bunch of helpers along for the ride on my Who Is Martha? quest. The problem, however, is that everyone suddenly pretty much believes the bad guys are Ivy, Ursula, Francie, Jamira, Evan, and me.

It's an abrupt change. Everyone who was nice to us before—which was mostly everyone at school, save for Campbell's group—now looks at us with suspicion. We hear talks of how we look like witches: me in my ancient cloak, Ivy with her goth-black hair and fingernails, Evan and his pale skin and penchant for fur, Jamira in her layered scarves and heavy metal jewelry, Francie with her awkward granny outfits and feverish knitting. Ursula isn't picked on for her looks or style, but Sylvie was her roommate—she's guilty by proximity.

The rumors spread like wildfire, and I suspect Campbell's behind it. When I pause on the green after lunch and pick a dandelion—I've always enjoyed scattering the seeds—a few students whisper to themselves and I swear I hear the words *to use in her magic cauldron*. When Jamira and I are walking, a girl neither of us know starts to convulse violently, claiming we've "hexed" her, before collapsing into giggles. The looks I've been getting from teachers and students alike aren't that different from the suspicious side-eyes I used to get from the Salem townspeople in my time. What's that expression? *Those who forget the past are doomed to repeat it.*

Ursula takes the rumors hard. "People are saying *I* did something to Sylvie now," she says tearfully when she comes back to the room this evening. "As if I'd ever!"

"Of course it wasn't you."

But the rumors do help me to form connections. The same person who's affecting the weather *might* have done something to Sylvie. So Campbell, then? It would make sense that she would be trying to put the blame on someone else.

I stare at the ceiling, trying to figure out a way to get to the bottom of it without using magic. "Maybe we could figure out who made that anonymous tip?" I voice aloud. "How do students usually anonymously report things?"

Ursula shrugs. "I wouldn't know. Maybe they left a note. It could be anything."

"Could we ask?"

"Wouldn't that expose us?" Ursula sounds doomed. "Peabody would wonder why we care."

"True," I mutter.

But I don't feel settled. I close my eyes. I'm able to peel myself away from my body quickly and float over to Peabody's office. The room is dark; she's gone for the night. I look around her desk, desperate for an answer. The problem with astral projection, though, is that you can't actually disrupt anything in the space you visit. I can't open drawers, I can't use the mouse to wake up her computer. Her desktop is neat and organized. There certainly aren't any crumpled-up notes telling on us.

"Alice?"

I snap back into my body. On the other side of the room, Ursula has turned over and is facing the wall. I ball up my fist, annoyed that I didn't find anything.

After a moment, Ursula lets out a little whimper. I sit up. "Are you okay?"

She doesn't answer.

I place my feet on the ground, unsure if I should comfort her. "Are you thinking about Sylvie?" I venture.

Ursula's shoulders shake. "I just hate that they're blaming me."

"They're being idiots. Don't worry about it." And then I pause, trying to figure out how to say this. "You know, sometimes, it seems like there's something you don't want to say. Like maybe something you saw . . . with Sylvie. Like about who did something to her. But maybe . . . you're afraid?"

Ursula goes still. There's a long silence. My heart thumps in my ears.

"It's okay," I go on. "The same goes for you—you can tell me anything."

The sheets rustle. In the dim light, I get a glimpse of Ursula's face, and she has that look again—her mouth is opening and closing like she's trying to talk but can't. It almost seems like she's forming words, but there's no sound.

But then the energy shifts back to normal, and Ursula lets out a sigh. "I wish that were the case," she says sadly. "I wish I knew something. I'd definitely tell you. But things were great between me and Sylvie. I have absolutely no idea why she's gone." Then she yawns and gives me a morose look. "I'm tired, Alice. I think that's why I'm so emotional. See you in the morning?"

"Sure," I murmur uneasily, and we fall silent, leaving me to puzzle for hours in the dark, dark room.

By the next morning, some of the tension toward the coven seems to have abated. When I walk down the dorm halls for the front door, I don't get the same side-eyes as I did yesterday. Maybe it's because the Halloween dance is nearing. Maybe it's because people have very tiny short-term memories. Even Ursula bounds up to me cheerfully at field hockey practice, a completely different girl from the day before.

"You know, just because we had to disband the *you know what* doesn't mean we can't still enjoy ourselves. We should go to the dance, don't you think?"

"The Halloween dance," I repeat. In the flurry of activity, I kind of forgot it still existed.

"Yeah, as a big group! They can't stop us. We still have rights as students. Francie's going with James, but the rest of us don't have dates—Evan still doesn't know about Simon. We can go all out dressing up and forget all about West and Campbell."

I eye her sideways. "Like . . . in costumes?"

"Totally."

"Where do we get those?"

Someone clears his throat. We swivel around, and Dr. Novis is lurking nearby. I instantly bristle, thinking of him standing outside our cave not so long ago. Did he know it was *us* inside? What did this anonymous tipper actually say?

"I couldn't help but overhear, ladies," he says. "There's a great costume shop in town—Gino's Halloween Emporium. It has any costume you can imagine."

He gives me a pointed look. I lower my eyes.

But Ursula smiles at me. "That could be fun."

Novis says he can arrange a pass for us to leave campus. I wonder why he's being so nice.

As much as I hate taking any of his advice, I wouldn't mind dressing up and going with the coven. Our friendship doesn't have to be all about lurking in a cave. And also, we have nothing to feel guilty about. We *should* be allowed to go to that dance as much as anyone else.

And so, an hour later, thanks to two passes admitting us off school grounds, Ursula and I stand in the doorway of Gino's Halloween Emporium. It's on one of Salem's many side streets, not far from a place called the Witch Dungeon Museum, which makes me shudder to think about. The costume shop's building is in a narrow row house, but when we step into the shop, racks of costumes stretch endlessly into the distance, and outfits hang all the way up to the ceiling.

"*Look* at all of this," Ursula gushes, touching the fabric of the costumes hanging on the walls, on racks, and stacked on tables. There are dresses and hats, cloaks and gowns, intricate jackets and masks. I see versions of some old friends—Valtorr, the Loch Ness Monster—in rubber form. And there is, of course, the typical "traditional" witch garb—pointed hats, black dresses that look like they're made from scarves, and so many infernal broomsticks. Ursula tries on a green rubber nose with warts on the end.

"Boo," she whispers.

*"Shhh,"* I whisper, looking over my shoulder. It would be just our luck that someone from the academy would be walking by. Besides, I really don't know where the whole "warty nose" idea came from. Some of the hottest women I've ever met have been members of my various covens.

We spend a half hour trying on plumed pirate hats, terrifying rubber masks, and "bustle" skirts that fit over our waists and make our butts look huge. Ursula giggles when I pull a mask over my head that makes me look like a pig smoking a cigar, and I can't help but chuckle when she gets a large pumpkin stuck on her head and starts to panic when she can't get it off. We have a fake battle with plastic swords, axes, cleavers, and even a giant pair of scissors, and when the shop's proprietor, a frizzy-haired man in tiny spectacles, starts to glare at us from behind his desk, it makes us laugh even harder.

"Girls," he says, "if you aren't buying anything, then you need to leave."

We heap costumes into our arms and go into the dressing room. "Here," Ursula says, handing me a felt costume that's a giant slice of pizza. I pull it over my head and snort at how dumb it looks. Then she pulls a costume out of a bag labeled *Wanda Maximoff.* That fancy-schmancy witch, I remember. As she pulls on a bodysuit and tights, I roll my eyes. What kind of witchy wardrobe even *is* that?

"But seriously," Ursula says, hands on hips as she surveys all the costume options, "we need something dramatic and strong. Not witches, obviously . . ." Then her eyes light up. *"Yes."*

She marches over to a costume and pulls it from the rack. *"This,"* she says, handing it to me. I stare at the item in my arms. It's a dramatic purple dress with a full skirt and a crown. A dark queen. Ursula has selected a red robe with fur accents and a glittering tiara for herself.

"We'll match," she says, "but we'll also stand out."

"Rulers of different universes," I murmur.

"But, like, never at war with one another," Ursula says quickly.

We hurry back into the dressing room to try them on, and of course they look incredible. Ursula is transformed into royalty in her long robe and crown and me, well, I swear I've worn an outfit kind of like this in earlier days. (I've always thought purple suits me.) Ursula twists this way and that, making silly faces in the mirror. "You too," she says to me.

I shake my head. "That's okay."

"Come on! One pose! Please?"

I roll my eyes but then do a little hip pop for the mirror. Ursula whoops. Outside the dressing room, I can hear the shopkeeper let out a very loud sigh.

Our costumes decided, we shed the robes and pack them back up for purchase. As I'm changing, something on the wall just outside the dressing room curtain catches my eye in the mirror's reflection. The dressing room is littered with costumes that haven't been put back, discarded hats, empty cardboard boxes. There's also a bulletin board advertising local hayrides, haunted houses, and random businesses. In the upper left corner is a flyer. *Lost*, it reads. I recognize the girl in the picture.

"Oh," I say softly, squinting to read the rest of the words. They must have made a poster when Sylvie

O'Toole went missing. It states her name and when she was last seen—on the Conant Academy grounds. It mentions she's from Boston, what color her eyes are, how tall she is. *Reward*, it reads, plus a phone number, presumably her parents'.

Ursula follows my gaze, seeing it, too. Her expression droops, but then she shakes her head. "It's fine."

Just as I'm about to pull the curtain closed again, I notice something on the flyer. "Wait, I thought you said Sylvie was from Connecticut."

"Huh?"

"Her sign. It says her family's from Boston. Did they get it wrong?"

"Oh. Uh, no. They're from Boston. I knew that."

"But you said—"

"I must have misspoken," Ursula says hurriedly. She plucks her backpack from the little chair in the dressing room. "I'll get our costumes, 'kay?"

She weaves around a bucket of scythes and other accessories toward the register.

After the total is tallied, Ursula hands over her credit card and then turns to me. "Dressing up is going to be really fun. If we can't be witches, queens are totally the next best thing."

I look down at the purple robe she's bought for me. In it, I'll look like some sort of grande dame ruler of the universe. It's exactly what I want to be in real life, too . . . but the goal seems so faint and far away.

Or maybe not. Because then I notice something on a shelf near the register, half hidden under a few amulets, some fake skulls, a rubber rat, and other Halloween trinkets. I have to hold in a little squeal of delight. Finally, a win. Finally, something has fallen into my lap.

It's a crystal ball.

# *Fifteen*

The morning of the Halloween dance is my favorite kind of weather: gray, windy, dour, dismal. It's a day full of shadows. A day where your bones just can't get warm.

Ursula peers out our dorm room window and sighs miserably. "It's going to be such yucky weather for the dance—what a bad omen."

"Nah." I plop my pillow at the head of my bed and pull up the quilt to meet it. "Bad weather is always good luck. You've never heard that before?"

She turns and gives me a hopeful smile. "You think? At least I'll be warm in my queen's robe."

My gaze drifts to the robe that's hanging on her closet door. Next to it is the purple gown and tiara that I'm going to wear. They aren't the only things I brought home from that costume shop, though. After we paid and left, I hurried back inside the shop, telling her I'd forgotten my school ID on the dressing room floor. I waited until the shopkeeper was distracted with another customer, then snuck over to the shelf where the crystal ball was sitting. All it took was some quick sleight of hand for me to remove it from its spot on the shelf and hide it under my shirt. As for the nosy shopkeeper not catching me . . . well, I might have cast a small spell on him and his store cameras to forget it happened.

It's not stealing if I'm going to put something to good use, right?

Anyway, I've hidden the ball at the back of my closet, under one of my school uniforms—I don't want anyone finding it on me and accusing me of witchcraft, even Ursula. But I can't stop thinking about it. I'm terrified that Martha will come into the room when I'm not here and steal it. I've poked my head into the closet at least six times this morning just to make sure it's still there.

As for when I'm going to use the ball, a plan has come together in my mind. Any witch knows that the most accurate time to scry for answers is during a full moon—which, as luck would have it, is tonight. Also, the best *place* to use a crystal ball is where the energy is strongest, where I think I can divine the clearest path. That's a little trickier for me to figure out. The energy at this school has been caustic, problematic, and confusing. There's nowhere I've felt a particular sense of peace or fluidity. However, I've always loved open spaces where I can see the moon, and the soccer field is perfect for that. Also, it's not like the soccer players are going to be practicing tonight—they'll all be at the Halloween dance. I'll be alone.

My plan is to sneak away from the coven at the dance, ask the ball my question about the Darkhold and Martha, and hopefully get my answer. Then I'll have the key to where the Darkhold is hiding. Maybe I'll be able to even find it tonight. And then, well, the possibilities are endless.

Only why don't I feel more excited?

When I arrived in 2025, I had a clear vision. Find the Darkhold. Attain the power. Oh sure, there were a few side quests—make sure Prudence is okay, get rid of Martha—but for the most part, retrieving the Darkhold was my only endgame. Now, though, my intentions feel muddled. Do I go back to my Salem immediately? Can I really leave Ursula and the others? I have to admit I'll kind of, well, *miss* them. It makes me queasy even to think that way . . . but at the same time, wherever I go next, I'm already dreading the loneliness.

Well. Maybe I won't worry about that for now.

There's a sharp knock on the door, and then it flies open before we can answer it. Jamira walks in first, arms raised. The others follow behind.

"It's my favorite part of any party!" Jamira cries. "Getting-ready time!"

Everyone holds garment bags, makeup caddies, hair tools, and costume accessories. Evan's got a large pair of horns under his arm and says he's dressing up as Loki, the famous shape-shifting god in Norse mythology. I almost say I've met him . . . but then bite my tongue.

Jamira tries to use one hand to lug a large cardboard box with the torso of a half wolf, half man attached to the back of it. Ivy's already got on her costume, a form-fitting feathered outfit with full wings and an alluring mask. She looks like a goddess—albeit an annoying one.

Francie slides in last. She's already in her outfit, too, a fitted pin-striped suit complete with a fedora and a gun holster. "I'm Bonnie from Bonnie and Clyde," she explains when I peer at her blankly. "You know? The gangsters? What, you don't like it?"

"No, you look good," I say, though I have no idea who Bonnie and Clyde are. "Very . . . striped."

"I'm afraid I'm going to get sick all over it." Francie looks down nervously. "I shouldn't have asked James to this dance. It's going to go terribly."

"It'll be fine," Evan coos, sliding over to pat her shoulder. "You're always so nervous, girl." Then his face lights up. "Maybe we should smudge-stick you?" He starts digging in a canvas tote. "I definitely brought one . . . unless we think maybe I shouldn't use them? Are they too witchy?"

"Definitely too witchy. And anyway, no weird-smelling stick is going to clear my negativity."

Francie rubs her temples. Her fingernails are chewed down. Her skin looks unusually gray. I want to tell her that if she's dreading going with this boy so much she *shouldn't*, life's too short—and that's coming from someone who's lived hundreds of years.

But then she notices me watching and whispers, "I just really want this to go well. I like him a lot. What if he's heard all the gossip about us being the ones controlling the weather? Maybe it's amazing he still even wants to go?" She clasps her hands together. "Alice, what do you think?"

I almost want to laugh. She thinks *I* should give advice? But she's looking at me so imploringly, like my opinion really matters.

I sit down next to her on the bed while everyone starts to unpack their costumes. If only there was a spell for giving good advice. "First of all, the gossip about us isn't true. You know that. And if he believes it . . . well, he isn't the person for you anyway. So if he's still your date, he's already passed that test. Remember, he's passing *your* tests, not the other way around."

Francie twists her mouth. "Easier said than done." But then she thinks a moment. "I do sort of like that idea of it being about *my* standards, not his. That way, if something does go wrong, it'll be him failing, not me."

"No one's going to fail. But yes—you deserve to have standards. Also? He's probably just as nervous as you are."

"I don't think anyone could be more nervous than me," Francie says, but then she hits me playfully and smiles. "Though he *has* emailed me five different times, asking how I'm going to dress."

"See? If that's not nerves, I don't know what is."

Francie leans her body into my shoulder. "Thanks, Alice."

"You're welcome," I muster. I bite down hard on my lip. Too much sweetness. Too much friendship stuff. And even worse, it's making me feel all . . . *fuzzy* inside.

Ursula and Ivy have settled at Ursula's vanity, and Jamira is styling their hair with a curling iron. I figure I'll have her do mine next—I've never figured out how to do my own hair successfully—but then I spy Evan in the corner, affixing his Viking horned hat to his head. Like Francie, he looks worried.

"Hey," I whisper, sidling over. "Whatever happened with Simon? Are you guys going together?"

Evan sighs and then explodes with words like he was just waiting for someone to ask him. "I don't know. Yesterday, we talked for fifteen minutes after class—at least it seems like *he* doesn't suspect that I'm the person who's literally creating tornadoes out of thin air. But there's no word on whether we're going together. I *think* he likes me? Or maybe he hates me?" He looks down at his costume. "I wish I could truly be like Loki and shape-shift into someone else."

"Just go ask him to the dance. If he's talking with you for that long, it sounds like he likes you a lot."

Evan's eyes bug out. "But if I show up at his dorm door and he *doesn't* want to go with me, and never intended to, I'll be so embarrassed. But if I don't—"

"You'll have missed an opportunity. The embarrassment won't last forever. No one will even remember."

He nods slowly, thinking it over. "Maybe you're right."

I'm about to say that I'm *definitely* right, but then something makes a *clonk*. The wolf-man part of Jamira's costume has pulled away from the duct tape holding him to the box. Annoyed, she sets the whole thing down on the ground and reaffixes the tape along the cardboard, but she swears under her breath when he keeps listing to one side.

"I was literally up *all night* trying to get this right," she groans.

Evan and I help her to get wolf man upright again. Jamira pulls the box over her head and affixes cloth straps on her shoulders to show us how the costume works. Her body fits through a whole in the box, and the wolf man looms behind her as if about to attack.

"See, no matter how fast I run, he's always chasing me," she says with a laugh.

"That's genius," Evan says.

"You made that yourself?" I ask incredulously. I can barely operate scissors without using magic.

"I've been trying to get Best Costume ever since I was a freshman," Jamira says, then rolls her eyes. "Though I don't know why I bother. Gigi Collins always beats me."

"Yeah, but that's because Gigi's parents pay this famous theater costume designer in New York to make her costume," Francie jumps in. "It's not fair. She doesn't lift a finger, just literally picks up a UPS package that morning and, *voilà*, wins the prize."

I put my hands on my hips. "Gigi Collins. Why do I know that name?"

"She's one of Campbell's friends," Ivy says.

"Probably spreading rumors about us, too," Ursula jumps in.

Jamira waves a hand. "Which is exactly why I don't want to make waves. I don't need Gigi and Campbell doubling down on their little witch hunt."

"It isn't fair, though," Evan protests. "Every year, you have an amazing costume that you work really hard on."

"It is what it is," Jamira says dejectedly.

"Or maybe it's not." I crunch a cookie in my mouth. "This sounds like something the coven should take care of."

Ursula looks anxious. "The *coven* does not exist anymore."

"Yes, but a group of vigilantes still could," I point out. "Not all revenge-seekers are witches."

Jamira sinks into her hip. Ivy holds a curling iron halfway to her head. I can tell they're considering it.

"What are you thinking?" Evan asks tentatively.

I look at Jamira. "Do you know if this amazing costume has been delivered yet?"

"It hasn't," Francie interjects. "I heard her bragging about the delivery coming this morning, but I haven't seen the truck on campus. It usually shows up about a half hour from now." She smiles excitedly. "Finally, a perk of working in the front office instead of the Historical Society—knowing when all the deliveries happen."

Jamira holds up a hand. "We aren't doing anything to her costume, guys. I don't want to be blamed for that."

I smile. "We wouldn't be, technically. But what would happen if Gigi's costume showed up a day late?"

Ivy slowly smiles. "That would be so tragic!"

Jamira doesn't seem convinced. "I want this to be fair. No tricks."

"It's not fair, though," I point out. "If Gigi actually made her costume like everyone else for the dance, *then* it would be fair."

"We could make sure she gets it for Halloween," Ivy says. "She can still wear it for trick-or-treating or whatever."

I smile at her. Look at us, conspiring together.

Francie mulls this over. "I kind of love this. We're no longer a coven . . . but we can still fight for what's right."

"We don't really *need* a cave to conspire," Evan muses.

Francie's eyes sparkle. "And as it happens, the delivery driver and I are like this." She entwines two fingers together. "What if I just, I don't know, asked for a tour of his truck? And then maybe kicked a certain package to the back where he can't find it?" She checks her watch. "But I'd better go if he's on his way to campus."

"Are you sure?" Jamira looks nervous.

Francie blows her a kiss. "Anything for you, my love."

"Wait!" Ivy cries just as Francie is leaving. "How about a potion before you go?"

Francie pivots on her heel. "Of course! I can't believe I forgot!"

"Potion?" I ask.

Evan smiles at me. "Francie makes us potions for every social event."

"It's *my* special talent." Francie leans down to a cardboard box at her feet and unearths six glass bottles with stoppers on the top. Each bottle is filled with liquid that's a pink so bright it definitely doesn't occur in nature, and each is labeled with our names.

"When did you have time to make these?" I ask.

"Oh, I'm full of secrets." Francie giggles. "It's just some herbs and spices mixed into an energy drink. It's not *actual* magic."

My mind spins. The thing is, I kind of *want* them to be magic. What if tonight's my last night with these people? What if the crystal ball tells me everything I need to know, and I find the Darkhold? At the very least, I have to return to my Salem to save Prudence. But what if I don't make it back? What if my newfound power sends me somewhere else?

This might be the last time I see this coven. I kind of want to give them little parting gifts.

I excuse myself to the bathroom and shut the door. Safely inside, I close my eyes and concentrate on the potions Francie made in my mind's eye. On Francie's bottle, I cast a spell of relaxation—things will go great as long as she takes a breath. For Evan, I give him a more overt love spell—nothing like the silly one the Scottish fake witch tried to cast on West and me at the shop, but an actual one that will enchant Simon into taking one look at him and realizing what he's missing. For Jamira, I can't help it—I charm her costume with a tiny spell that will hypnotize the costume judges into choosing her costume over all others. For Ivy, it's trickier, but I can't help but sense that she's insecure deep down. I decide to enchant her potion with a spell of self-acceptance. A spell that makes her believe that she's good enough, no matter what. Maybe it will also make Ivy slightly less annoying.

And Ursula. I picture her hands cupping the little bottle as she waits to take a sip. I wish I could bring Sylvie back to her, especially if I'm going to leave. A witch can sometimes raise someone from the dead . . . but it's extremely difficult. One also has to find where the deceased person is, in ghost form. It's a whole rigmarole.

But maybe answers will give her some peace. That's what I can give her, later, when I sneak away. So I leave her potion untouched. She'll get an even greater gift later.

I step out of the bathroom just in time to see the coven members raising their little cups in a toast. We all swallow the potions, and I hide a smile, a warm sensation washing over me. It almost feels like magic, like maybe I drank one of my conjured potions by mistake.

But after I double-check that, no, everyone *else* got my magic potions, I realize what the feeling really is: the well-being of doing something nice for someone else. I sort of want to slap myself back to normal. What's come *over* me?

But in the moment, I don't really care. I drink my potion, too, uncharmed as it is. The liquid pools in my mouth. The sweetness hits my tongue. It's basic soda, really, the same stuff I've guzzled from the dining hall plenty of times now. Man, am I going to miss soda when I have to travel back three hundred years.

The main hall has been transformed into a graveyard. Mist swirls dramatically through the air, making it difficult to see. Headstones jut up this way and that, a lot of them spouting funny epitaphs like *Here Lies Good Old Fred, a Great Big Rock Fell on His Head.* Fake spiderwebs hang from every nook, and some of the ghoulish decorations—including Samhain—have been moved inside. Eerie electronic music with a thumping beat pumps deafeningly through speakers. Save for Francie, who is coming with James, the rest of us enter the party together in a group five people wide. I have to admit we look fantastic—Ivy in her gothic feathers, Evan in his horns and cape,

Ursula and I twin queens, and Jamira literally with the wolf man breathing down her neck.

We pass zombie cheerleaders, psychotic clowns, mummies, and Frankenstein's monsters. Headmistress Peabody, dressed as a spider, talks to Jenna the RA, who has transformed herself into a glowing skeleton. In the corner is a built-out shack that students are nervously entering—above it are the words *Haunted House*. Screams ring out from inside.

I chuckle to myself. Silly humans and the things that frighten them.

It also seems like any animosity and suspicion people have felt about us over the last few days has been suspended for the evening, because students left and right approach us to say that our costumes are fabulous. Especially Jamira's—even Dr. Novis marvels over how she constructed the costume.

"It's truly genius." He inspects the way the box fits over her shoulders. "It should win Best Costume for certain."

But then a whiny voice sounds behind me. "Yeah, but only because she cheated."

I spin around. I should have known Campbell would dress up like a fairy princess. She's even got on a fake wig that seems to be made of cotton candy and holds a bejeweled staff that could pass for a walking stick. My gaze swings to the person standing next to her, and I almost burst out laughing. West is dressed up like a border collie. He's got dog ears, he's wearing a fluffy one-piece suit, and he's even got a tail. It isn't sexy, but I can't help but feel kind of . . . pleased? I want to tell myself that he didn't choose that costume for my sake or because of my nickname for him, but why on earth would he dress like a dog otherwise?

West notices me, and his cheeks turn pink. "Oh," he says softly. "Greetings, Your Majesty."

"Greetings, Holdfast," I say in a queenly voice.

Campbell glares at me. "What's *Holdfast*?" When I don't answer, she reaches for West's hand and holds it tightly—like, no pun intended, West is on a leash. "Don't look at them directly," she snaps. "They're probably going to put a curse on you."

"That's not nice," Jamira mutters.

But it's like Dr. Novis doesn't notice her little barb. "What's this about cheating?" He looks back and forth between us.

"We didn't cheat," Ivy says hurriedly. "Jamira made her costume fair and square."

Campbell snorts. "Sure, but Gigi told me how much Jamira wants to win the costume contest. Jamira definitely did something to *Gigi's* costume because she's jealous that Gigi wins every year."

Francie looks at Dr. Novis. "That's not true. Honest."

Campbell's eyes flash. "You people are such liars."

"Campbell," West warns. "Leave them alone."

"Yes, Campbell." It makes me feel better that Dr. Novis is paying attention to Campbell's nastiness. "It's not nice to make accusations if you don't know the full story."

"What else do I need to know?" Campbell asks. "It's obvious they're the ones messing with the weather. They're . . . *weird*."

"Now, now," Dr. Novis says. He's about to say something else, but then Peabody calls him away to help move a speaker.

I decide to ignore Campbell completely. I focus on West instead, pointing at his fuzzy ears. "I see you're embracing your inner beast."

He smiles bashfully, subtly pulling his hand out of Campbell's grip. "Yeah, well. It's *really* comfortable. Like wearing pajamas."

"I fully support sleepwear as costume."

Campbell inserts herself between us. "You *should* have chosen the king costume, West. Then we would have matched."

"But you're a princess," I point out. "So . . . he would have been your dad?"

Evan giggles.

"Actually, if West wore the king costume, he'd match *Alice*, not you." Ivy snickers.

Campbell turns a unique color of pink. She wheels around to West. "*They* probably did something to the king costume to make sure you'd have to dress up as the dog instead—just to humiliate you."

"I'm not humiliated at all," West says. "I chose this costume."

"Oh, come on." Her eyes narrow. "That costume is silly! Did they manipulate your mind into believing it was cute?"

"Campbell, no." West looks uncomfortable.

Campbell's voice rises to a higher and higher pitch. "They put spells on things! They're the cause of all the problems around school! They even made that girl go missing at the start of the year!"

"Whoa, whoa, whoa!" Evan cries. Ursula looks a mix between enraged and sick.

"Let's get out of here," I tell the group, disgusted.

We storm away. I can feel Campbell glaring at us. I can also sense West's sheepish energy, like he doesn't know what to believe. It hurts—Campbell is so toxic, and maybe dangerous—but I don't turn back. Soon enough, I'll have my answer about her. The crystal ball will tell me if she's Martha. And then I'll make my move.

As we head to the haunted house, Francie sidles up

to me. "I was telling the truth, by the way. I didn't do anything to Gigi's costume. I wasn't able to catch the delivery guy before the package arrived."

I skirt around a fizzing cauldron of what looks like root beer. "What's Campbell talking about, then? She made it sound like something happened to Gigi's costume."

Francie's gaze turns to the door. As if on cue, a familiar girl I've noticed a few times in Campbell's orbit appears in the doorway. She's wearing a strange, incredibly short green dress, high green boots, and a green cape and is holding a stick of some sort of globular green object in one hand.

"*That's* Gigi's costume?" Evan splutters. "I can see why Campbell thought we messed with it."

"Is she some sort of green superhero?" Ivy whispers. "What's that elongated weird thing on the stick?"

"It looks like a pickle." Ursula starts to laugh. "Is . . . *she* dressed like a pickle, too?"

We all stare in bafflement. The costume makes no sense. The dress is so short that Gigi can barely walk. It doesn't look remotely pickle-like, either. Gigi has a smug look on her face like she's pretending she looks amazing, but I can see the humiliation in her eyes, too.

"I saw Gigi arguing with the driver earlier today," Francie whispers. "She opened the package while he was still there, and she told him he'd given her the wrong item. He showed her again and again how the box had her name on it and where it was from, but she just didn't believe it."

I giggle. "Her handmade costume is a dud."

"I mean, it's not *that* bad," Jamira says diplomatically. "She still could win."

But then we all burst out laughing. We're laughing so hard that Campbell looks up from her slow dance with West. Her eyes narrow, and then she whispers something in his ear.

But I tell myself to focus on more positive things—like Francie, who I've just spotted on the dance floor, too, her arms around James. Thanks to my potion—maybe—her skin is glowing, and there's a contented smile on her face. Even better, her date looks thrilled to be dancing with *her*, like he's the one who won the prize.

She notices me, waves, and then points at herself with a gesture that seems to say, *Look at me! Look how chill I am!* I give her a thumbs-up and then mouth, *"Your rules, remember?"* She nods.

And after another song, Evan, who I didn't even realize was missing, rushes back over to me. *"Alice,"* he says dramatically, out of breath. "You wouldn't believe what just happened. Simon? He just came up to me, *furious.*"

"Why?"

"Because apparently, he'd been waiting in his dorms for me! He was under the impression we were going together all along! Of course I told him that he'd said *maybe*, and that that was confusing—and then he apologized profusely, because he hadn't meant to play games . . . so anyway. We're totally here together now. And I don't know if it's the soap I used today, but he's *fawning* over me. I had to tell you."

"Told you." I guess that love spell I charmed worked a little *too* well. On the other hand, maybe it isn't only the spell's magic. Who *wouldn't* be into Evan?

I drink some punch. I collect a pile of cookies from the dessert table and eat them all. I check my watch for when the full moon is rising, but it's not quite time. After a while, Ivy pulls Jamira, Ursula, and me onto the dance floor for a few songs, though I stand staunchly by my philosophy that Agatha Harkness doesn't dance. The best I can do is bopping back and forth from foot to foot. Ivy, on the other hand, swings her arms and shuts her eyes and spins like a ballerina. She seems . . . happy, I realize. I only hope that my spell lasts forever.

Ursula thinks Ivy's happy for another reason. "This was such a good idea to come together, especially after we had to escape from the cave like that," she says. "Not that Ivy will admit it, but there's nothing like having really good friends."

I rejoin the girls on the dance floor, but no sooner do I reach them than Headmistress Peabody cuts the music short and taps the microphone. "All right, everyone. The moment you've been waiting for. The judges have voted for tonight's best costume, and the results are in."

A hush falls over the crowd. Jamira jiggles nervously. "Gigi still could win, though," she murmurs. "For all I know, she bribes the judges, too."

"Jamira." I give her a level stare. "She's a *pickle*."

Jamira starts laughing all over again.

The headmistress's microphone screeches with feedback. "At Conant Academy, we only choose one costume as a winner, and this year, there was a clear standout. And that was . . . Jamira Atwood!"

Evan screams. Ivy wolf-whistles. Ursula claps so hard it looks like her hands hurt. Everyone surrounding us looks pleased, too, seemingly supportive as Jamira winds her way to the stage to accept her prize. On the way, random people catch her arm.

"The costume is so good," someone says.

"You're so crafty and cool," says another voice.

"You know, I never thought she was a witch, but even if she is, who cares?"

"She cheated!" cries yet another voice, and I bristle. Of course it's Campbell. She points at Gigi. "Gigi should win! They sabotaged her costume!"

But to my surprise, her accusations get swallowed up and then canceled out. People keep talking over her. People don't *care*. Campbell stiffens with fury; I watch as her mouth moves, as she spews words, but it's too loud to hear what they are. It's the most satisfying thing to watch ever.

Onstage, Jamira shakes Peabody's hand, then bounds down and runs straight to us. "Yes!" we all cry, surrounding her to look at the plaque. When it's my turn, I hug her tightly, feeling a heightened sense of contentment. My spells worked. My coven is happy. Everyone has what they want—even Ursula, who looks thrilled that we're all together.

It's a perfect moment, really, if you're into sappy stuff. I wish I could perform a time-freezing spell to hold on to it a little longer. But when I look at the clock hanging on the far wall, the time reads just a little bit after nine. The moon is high in the sky. I don't have a lot of time left. If I'm going to scry, I need to do it soon.

It's time for me to get my wish, too.

# *Sixteen*

As I head away from the noisy festivities, the school grounds are extra quiet. I keep thinking I see things out of the corner of my eye, but when I turn to face whatever's lurking there, all movement stops.

Still, I'm very on edge. What if Martha saw me slip away?

The playing fields are desolate without players and spectators. With the floodlights off, the field looks like a flat, endless graveyard. The goalposts loom overhead like twisted monsters, and the empty bleachers are bathed in jagged shadows. There's an off-putting sound of metal clanging against metal—it's a flag on a flagpole, logically, but I can't stop imagining that it's a ghost dragging chains.

Which means, in other words, the energy is perfect.

I step to the middle of the field and pull the crystal ball from under my robe. It's cool and smooth in my palms. I set it on the grass and settle cross-legged in front of it, positioning it so that I can see the moon's reflection in the surface.

*Crack.*

I whirl around. The sound came from the bleachers. Has someone followed me? Campbell, trying to catch me out, prove I'm a witch? Then again, I can't see her leaving her precious dance . . . or West.

Seconds pass. A minute. No one reveals herself. I let out a breath and turn back to my task. I wave my hands over the top of the ball, stirring up the energy. It takes a moment, but soon enough, the ball awakens. Clouds start to drift from its surface. I gaze deep into its reflection, trying to make sense of the patterns within. I pray my weakened powers are strong enough for this.

*Help me,* I say to the spirits. *I need some guidance.*

For a few minutes, nothing happens. I grit my teeth and concentrate harder. *Please. Please help.* Finally, thin smoke gathers inside the ball. It twists and whirls, turning so translucent that I can see straight through it to the grass below. I breathe out. I can tell the magic is weak, and there's no way I'll be able to hang on for very long of a prophecy, but maybe I'll be able to get some answers.

I shut my eyes and cast my questions through my hands. *Where is the Darkhold?* I ask first. *Where is it hidden?*

I feel the ball forming a response. Finally, an image appears: jutting stones, a dark, dismal cellar, chains on the wall. It's a familiar sight . . . but not for the right reasons.

"No," I tell the ball, frustrated. "That's where the Darkhold *was*, three hundred years ago—the Parrises' cellar. I mean where is it *now*?"

I concentrate again, but the image inside the ball doesn't change. In fact, it gets lighter and brighter, zooming in on the bat wriggling in that same cellar, waiting to be found.

Is this thing broken? Is it because of my weakened power?

Shadows pass over the moon. Clouds are moving in; soon enough, there won't be moonlight to scry. I run my hands over the ball, deciding to come back to the Darkhold question later. I move on to my next quandary: *Who is Martha?*

Smoke swirls beneath the crystal surface once more. It curls and loops, and this time, it starts to form words.

They flit by so quickly I have to rush to read them before I miss them completely.

*Someone you know. Someone you feel strongly about.*

"What does that mean?" I ask. "Show me their face!"

The words vanish in a puff. Finally, a new image appears: *my* image. It's the picture Ursula took of me at the mirror on the first day of school.

I grit my teeth. "*I'm* not Martha. That doesn't make any sense. Are you even listening to my questions?"

But again, the image doesn't change. I groan. Honestly, I have no idea how lower witches with limited skills get through life.

Again, I decide to move on. I remember my last question, the gift I intend to give to Ursula. *Where is Sylvie? What happened to her?*

I think hard. I also convey to the ball that this question isn't for me but for a friend—maybe it'll give me an honest answer this time. The smoke grows dark. An image of trees appears. It's the woods on the edge of campus. And then I'm shown the cave where the coven meets.

"Sylvie's in the cave?" I ask, then bite my lip. "That doesn't make sense."

The image in the ball pans across a particular bush outside the cave, bright with hydrangea flowers in summer. It zooms closer and closer until I can make out individual branches and leaves. There's a red ribbon around its stubby trunk. I sit up, stricken. Hydrangea bushes grow wild in the woods, but how many of them have red ribbons tied around them?

I picture all of us running out of the cave when Marilyn Monroe blew out the candle. A similar bush with a ribbon around it, though its flowers had all dried up. It was the same bush that shook vigorously . . . and then glowed.

I lean toward the ball. "Are you trying to tell me she's a bush . . . or that she was the thing *behind* the bush?" I concentrate on the glowing figure in my mind. "Are you telling me Sylvie's the ghost?"

The ball keeps showing me that same bush. I close my eyes, letting my own intuition wash over me. The theory doesn't surprise me. I think I've suspected that the ghost in the woods was Sylvie for a while now.

I think of something else. "What about that other glowing thing, the one with the tie—is that the academy teacher who went missing? Mr. Haverford?"

But the ball doesn't have to answer—I already know. It's heartbreaking. Two ghosts, doomed to haunt those woods. Something terrible must have happened to them. Only . . . *what*? I really want to know for Ursula's sake.

I cup the sides of the ball and concentrate with all my power. *What happened to them?* I ask. *Who did it? Why?*

The ball lights up, and images flit by in quick succession. A flash. A rigid hand. A frozen scream. Sylvie's face as she backs away . . . and then Mr. Haverford standing in front of her like a shield. I gasp with how sharp and certain the ball's answer is. It's clear I'm seeing the moment they were both hurt. And then the vantage shifts . . . I'm about to see a face of the person who did it. . . .

"Alice?"

I wheel around. A figure stands at the edge of the field. I have to blink a few times when I realize who it is. Quickly, I hide the ball under my robe.

"You scared me!" I sputter. "Don't you know it's rude to sneak up on people?"

"Don't you know it's rude to leave school dances?"

I can barely see West in the darkness, but I can tell when he takes a few steps forward. "Why are you doing out here in the dark anyway?"

"I, um, needed somewhere to decompress." With shaking hands, I stuff the ball even deeper into the robe's pocket, praying he hasn't seen me practicing witchcraft. I want to know how long he's been standing there. I wonder how loud I was shouting my questions. "Also, there's no rule anywhere that you have to stay at a school dance if you don't want to."

"Okay. Fine. I made that up."

He stops at the edge of the field, watching me. It makes me uncomfortable. I can feel the crystal ball pressing up against my abdomen.

"Did you follow me here, or what?" I snap.

West clears his throat. "No? Yes?"

"Well, which is it?"

"It's . . . neither. Both?"

"Are you spying?" I think of Campbell and her beady, narrowed eyes, the way she whispered in his ear. "Did someone tell you to come?"

West frowns. I see the exact moment on his face when he realizes what I'm asking. "*No*, Alice. Absolutely not. No one even knows I left. So actually, I guess I'm being rude, too."

His voice is soft and low. The moon reflects off his ridiculous dog ears.

"But you have a date," I blurt out. "You should probably get back to her, don't you think?" I can't keep the bitterness out of my voice.

West looks down. "About . . . *her*." He coughs. "She said some pretty harsh things about your friends."

"It's fine. I ignore her, as a general rule."

"Also . . . I didn't know you wanted to ask me, Alice. I had no idea."

I wave my hand. "It doesn't matter. Really. I don't care."

"You . . . don't?"

"Nope," I say airily. "Dances aren't really my thing anyway."

"But you asked me to go with you," he points out. "You had that poster. And . . . I saw your face, when I said no. You looked . . ."

"I was just embarrassed. Not about *you*—about the bizarre ritual! That silly poster!"

But maybe it's not the right answer, because I feel his energy shift. "It's not a crime to feel stuff, Alice," he says in a sad voice. "It's not a crime to be disappointed."

"I wasn't disappointed," I say emphatically. "I *wasn't*!"

But then I sigh. It's probably so obvious I'm lying. It's probably a smell wafting off me, like bad perfume.

"Okay," I mumble. "I was possibly *slightly* disappointed, because I think it would have been fun to go with you. It was also embarrassing because all these people were watching me fail in public. But I'm over it. Truly."

"What would you think if I told you that I really, *really* wanted you to ask me?" West says quietly. "That I was kind of hoping you would have asked me when we went into town to those magic shops?"

I look at him in the dim light. It takes me a few moments to muster up a response.

"Why didn't you say something about it?"

"Would you have asked me if I had?"

"I don't know," I say in a small voice. "I'm not sure

I was even thinking about the dance then. But maybe? Only, I thought you were with me at the shops just to humor me. Or to get out of studying."

He laughs incredulously. "I let a woman with a funnel on her head do a love spell on me! I thought I was sending a pretty clear message!"

"I'm not a mind reader!" But then I realize how ironic that is. Because actually, I kind of *am*. When I want to be.

I settle down on the grass, careful not to break the crystal ball that's still hidden under my cloak. I'm not sure how to feel. Giddy that West wanted me to ask him. Annoyed because I missed the chance. Irritated, too, because I believed Campbell when she said West wouldn't go for someone like me. Since when am I insecure?

West steps onto the field and sits down next to me. For a while, we stare up at the sky. Our silence is comfortable. I don't feel like I need to fill the air with words when I'm around him.

"Where are all the stars?" I ask. Three hundred years ago, the sky was brilliant at night, always.

West sighs. "You have to go out to the country to see them. Too much light pollution here."

"Light pollution?" I make a face. It's like a giant jewel box has been taken away. "Do better, 2025."

"Agreed," West says. Then he turns to me. "Tell me something real about yourself, Alice."

I side-eye him. He has a faint smile on his face, but he also looks determined, like it's something that would mean a lot. I'm about to say that I've *already* told him things that are real. Or maybe I should tell him that I can't tell him anything real because it's dangerous. It's funny: I've been absolutely myself and absolutely *not* myself with West, something I've never done before.

I know what he wants: to know something about how I *feel*. What I hope for. What my dark secrets are. What I want in life, probably. I close my eyes, wondering if I even know what those answers are. The knee-jerk answer: to find the Darkhold. Yet over the last few weeks at Conant Academy—with the coven, talking to West—I've realized that other things could make a person happy, too. The pull toward those other things is undeniable, especially sitting here in the moonlight.

"I'm not sure I want to leave here," I whisper. Only when the words fall from my mouth do I realize they're kind of true. "I wish . . . I wish I could stay."

West looks at me. "Then stay." He doesn't understand what I'm saying, clearly, but in some ways, it feels like he totally does.

"I don't want to leave . . . you," I say next, so softly I can barely hear myself—or *believe* myself.

But West hears. I feel him soften. "Then don't," he says simply.

It's like there's a moth let loose inside my stomach. Excitement for sure, but also another kind of loosening—like a knot is finally coming undone. My powers? The electricity in my fingers seems to surge.

But I can't think about my powers right now. Slowly, West reaches out and touches my hand, first curling one finger around mine, then another. My heart starts to bang. Every ounce of my self-preservation wants to pull away and laugh like this is a joke, but I don't let myself. I want to see where this goes.

He tips my chin toward him, and we're looking at each other. The moon makes his skin look silvery and magical. There's a faint smile on his face. He reaches out and touches the edge of my cheek, and I can't help it—I swoon and close my eyes.

I feel him shift closer, so I shift closer, too. My heart is banging faster and faster, ready to explode from my chest. I can smell his milky-sweet scent as he brings his face close to mine, and then suddenly our lips are touching. My whole soul lets go. Everything turns bright in my body, and my mind stills, and all my swirling thoughts stop.

Then he pulls back and presses his forehead to mine. He's breathing as hard as I am, and when I move my chest against his, I can feel his heart banging against his ribs. It's strange to be in such close proximity to another being's heart—usually, when I'm in this position, I'm ripping the heart out, or messing with it somehow, or ignoring it completely. But feeling his heartbeat against me—it's a different kind of magic. A warming kind.

"What are you thinking about right now?" he whispers.

"Ripping out hearts," I whisper. "But how I don't want to do that to you."

"Well, that's a relief." He pulls away and takes my hands. "There's something I need to tell you, though."

"What?" I whisper.

He squeezes my hands hard. "I saw your—"

*Flooom!* Suddenly, an icy wind thunders from out of nowhere, catapulting us both into the air. I feel myself flying, weightless, and then thudding back to earth. I land on my side near the goalpost, but the turf, once cool and soft moments ago, is now freezing and unforgiving.

I sit up groggily. There are giant snowflakes swirling in the air. The ground is covered in several inches of snow—it's all happened in *seconds*. It's like a portal in the sky opened and dumped it in.

Then I look over—West is on his back on the track. Slowly, he sits up, too, battered but okay.

"What's going on?" he shouts to me over the screaming wind.

I bite my lip, pretty sure I know. "I think it's another weather thing. It's happening again." I rush to West's side to help him up. "We need to get inside. I have a feeling it's going to get even colder."

The snow comes down harder and thicker. We have to fight through it just to get off the soccer field. Snowdrifts have appeared within a minute, and we slog through them, our feet and legs soaked through, running as hard as we can until we see the main building. The snow has turned to icy balls; each little pellet that hits us stings like tiny needles.

"Why is this happening?" West screams. "Is someone really doing this to the school?"

I don't know how to answer, but I wonder, too. Maybe Martha created this particular storm because I've escaped. Maybe she *is* Campbell, and she's mad because I'm with West, too. For all I know, maybe she's even seen us kiss.

*Kiss.* My stomach flips over, despite it all.

Then West stops short in front of me, and I nearly crash into him. "What?" I scream, snow flying into my mouth and eyes. "What's going on?"

There are icicles hanging off West's eyebrows and dog ears. He points a shaky, frozen finger ahead, and that's when I see it. The main building doesn't even look like itself anymore.

It's encased in a lattice of ice.

## *Seventeen*

West and I are able to pry our way through the snow and ice to the main hall's entrance, but it's no better inside. Jagged icicles hang from the ceiling. The entire table of food is shrouded under snow crystals. The ground has flash-frozen, and students struggle for their footing as they cross to safer ground. The chandelier in the center groans under the weight of several inches of ice on each individual candle.

And the students? Everyone is screaming. Panicking. People run for exits, but the other doors are frozen shut. At least thirty people barrel past West and me to get out the door we've opened, but when they see the catastrophic weather conditions, they turn right around and come back in.

"Out of the way!" Dr. Novis bellows to some party guests standing under the chandelier, and not a moment too soon—the giant fixture makes a terrible groan, and then the chain snaps, and it crashes to the ground.

Shards of ice and glass fly everywhere, sharp as knives. It's not the only thing that's collapsing—most of the Halloween figurines fall over from the added weight of the ice. Ice-laden paper pumpkins hanging from the ceiling snap from their wires, transformed into miniature bombs.

Students scatter and yelp. Someone's feet go out from under her, and she skids into a group of at least ten kids, creating a pileup on the ice. A lot of people are bloodied; someone cries out that they've broken an ankle in a fall.

I glance around for my coven and spot most of them over by a giant animatronic skeleton. Jamira has shrugged off her costume, and she looks pale and scared. Francie cowers behind her date. Ivy tests out walking on the ice but immediately skids. Ursula finds me across the room, her eyes wide and terrified. The only one I don't see is Evan. Maybe he's with Simon. Hopefully somewhere safe.

West and I are still next to each other, and we

exchange a panicked look. "This is bad," he says. "We need to find a phone. Call the police. Or an ambulance. *Something.*"

Then Headmistress Peabody slides across the middle of the ice with a megaphone. "This has gone too far! Whoever is behind this, show yourselves!"

Then a group of girls point at Ivy, Ursula, and Francie. "It's probably them! They're witches! They did this!"

"Yeah!" cries another voice. "They're evil! They made the ice!"

Chants rise. Costumed students surround my coven and start shouting more accusations. My coven backs up, cornered. The teachers try to place themselves between the two groups, but the yelling continues. It's not fair. My coven has absolutely nothing to do with the dance's giant freeze.

But I'm pretty sure who does.

I spy Campbell on the other side of the hall, shivering next to some of her friends, including Gigi. She peers at me, too, her eyes narrowed, clearly spying West by my side. She's furious. And maybe, if she's suffering, she wants everyone else to share in her misery, too. The crystal ball is wrong. Campbell is Martha. She's got to be.

A scream rises up. *"He's trapped!"*

There's a stir of murmurs . . . and then bloodcurdling sounds of panic. I swing around and suck in a gasp. In another corner, by a large display of pumpkins, stands an enormous, human-size block of ice. The voice is right—someone is trapped in it. My heart jumps to my throat when I realize who it is.

Evan.

*"No,"* I whisper.

I run-slide across the dance floor toward him. Simon, his date, stands next to the giant block, pointing to it with trembling hands. "He was fine a few minutes ago! How did this *happen*?"

Evan is suspended in the ice, his eyes bulging in horror. I don't think he's dead, just enchanted, but it's still a horrific sight. I have no idea how long he'll be able to survive this.

My heart pounds. I can feel magic snapping in my fingers, but saving Evan means revealing myself. I try to make eye contact with Evan's frozen pupils behind the ice, praying he's still with us. *Don't worry. We'll get you out soon.*

"Someone get the heat lamps!" a teacher screams. "We need to defrost him!"

Panic erupts. Everyone starts to scream. "Call the police!" someone says.

"Aren't there plenty of other witches in this town?"

someone else shouts. "It's Salem! Can't they come out here and battle her or something?"

"Everyone!" yells Headmistress Peabody suddenly. "Out of the building in an orderly fashion!"

People stampede for the exits. I skid back across the ice and grab Campbell as she weasels her way out the door.

I grab her arm, and she shrieks and rears back. "Let me go, you witch!"

"You need to stop this!" I growl, pointing at Evan. "Undo what you've done."

It takes her a moment to understand. Her eyes flash with confusion and outrage. "You think *I* did this? You think *I'm* the witch?"

I move my face close. I'm at my breaking point. It's time to bring out the big guns. "It's me, Agatha—though you've already figured that out, haven't you? It's why you froze Evan, isn't it? To get back at me because West followed me out to the fields? You want revenge. You want it on my whole coven, but really, you know it's me you're looking for."

Campbell shakes her head ever so slightly. "C-coven?" She licks her lips. "You're . . . actually witches?"

"Stop the act," I hiss. "You're Martha—admit it. You've been casting the spells on the weather. You're looking for the Darkhold. You *lost* the bat, coming through that portal, and now you're trying every trick in your book to make it come out of its hiding spot. Hurricane winds. Driving rain. And now ice—bats hate ice, don't they? But it doesn't seem to matter that you're hurting people left and right on the way."

Campbell backs up. "Wh-what are you talking about?"

"It's all you, Campbell! I *know* it! It's so obvious!" I wheel around to point at Evan. "Free him! Undo the spell before it's too late!"

Tears stream down Campbell's face, and she suddenly looks small and timid. It takes effort for her to even talk. "Y-you're scaring me." Then she backs up. "*You're* the witches. You said so yourself. Get away from me!"

A crowd has formed around us. Angry murmurs rise up when they hear what I'm saying. It's students I barely know, but behind all of them, I notice a few familiar faces. Ursula, Ivy, Jamira, and Francie gawk at me in shock. Behind them, West stands slack-jawed. They've heard everything.

"Alice," Jamira says. "Why would you expose us?"

Ivy narrows her eyes. "I knew you'd betray us. I *knew* it."

And Ursula just stares at me, lips parted, eyes wide, seemingly too terrified to speak. Or maybe too disappointed.

"No." I shake my head vehemently. "No, I didn't

mean—I was trying to save Evan. I thought she . . ." I point helplessly at Campbell. "It's obvious it's her. She hates us. We all know it. She controlled the weather to . . . to hurt us! To hurt me!"

"And she traveled through a portal?" Ivy says, deadpan. "Looking for a . . . a bat? What's *wrong* with you?"

"Maybe she's the one controlling the weather," Francie says in a haunted voice.

"She *definitely* is!" Campbell says, hysterical. She looks at West. "*Now* do you understand why I've been so afraid of her?"

Ivy shakes her head. "No one is a witch. Alice is just . . . sick. Deranged. I told you we shouldn't have included her. She ruined everything."

"I—I'm sorry," I sputter. "I didn't . . . I was trying to *help*. I didn't make this happen! West and I weren't even here when the storm hit! Tell them, West!"

I look at West, but his eyes are empty and emotionless. Finally, he looks away. My heart snaps in two.

Then Campbell reaches out to someone behind me. "Help us. Please. She's gone off the deep end."

Dr. Novis cuts through the crowd and takes her arm. "Alice, step back. I need to have a word with you."

"Me?" I'm flustered. "B-but she's the one who—"

He cuts me off. "Go," he says to Campbell. "Get out of here." She doesn't have to be told twice—she slide-sprints as fast as she can for the door.

I slap my arms to my sides. "You're just letting her *leave*?"

He gives me a measured look. "Yes. I am. Your accusations make absolutely no sense."

"But . . ." My brain snags. My tongue feels too heavy in my mouth. This isn't right. *I'm* not the bad guy. Could I have gotten this wrong? Maybe Campbell isn't Martha?

"You need to listen to me, Alice," Dr. Novis says sternly.

But then there's a *bang*. Several men in jumpsuits and work boots burst in through the front doors. They push large heat lamps on wheels across the ice.

"Where is the person who's frozen?" one calls.

"This way," Dr. Novis says, gesturing toward Evan.

We move out of the way. The men maneuver carefully toward Evan. Quickly, they find a working outlet, plug in the heater, and aim it straight at Evan's block. But even with the heat cranked up to high, I can tell it won't make any difference. No water droplets appear on the floor. The ice isn't melting.

*It's a spell*, I want to tell them. *It's not going to work.*

Splintering wood sounds from above. When I look up, the skylights are starting to give way. Snow starts to rain in from tiny cracks in the glass.

The maintenance guys see it, too. One of them sucks his teeth. "The whole ceiling's on the verge of coming down. We gotta get out of here."

"But what about Evan?" Ivy shrieks.

The maintenance guy's gaze doesn't leave the endangered windows. "You gotta go. We can leave the heater running, but—"

"You're just going to abandon him?!" Jamira screams.

There's another ominous *crack*. Dr. Novis wastes no time herding the group. "It isn't safe here. We all have to get out—you, too, Alice."

He tries to grab my arm, but I twist away, planting my feet. "You're leaving Evan, too?"

Dr. Novis looks conflicted. "Chances are, there's nothing we can do," he says in a defeated voice. "And it's my responsibility to keep everyone else safe."

"Well." I cross my arms. "I'm not going anywhere."

He narrows his eyes. "Miss Harvey, if you don't come right now, it will be grounds for expulsion—*if* you even survive."

"Come on, Alice," West says shakily.

"Don't be stupid," Ivy adds.

I turn back to Evan, motionless inside the ice block. The only hope of him surviving this is if I use my magic—and I'm running out of time.

There's a terrible shuddering noise coming from the roof. Snow and ice rain down in enormous clumps. Everyone screams and starts to run—including the maintenance guys. Dr. Novis glances over his shoulder at me, noting that I haven't moved, but he doesn't say anything else to convince me.

"Alice!" Jamira calls from the doorway, but I just shake my head. They don't understand. I realize this might get me in huge trouble, but I can't leave Evan like this.

The door slams, shutting me inside with the deteriorating ceiling. It's eerily quiet save for the hum of the useless heat lamps. More snow and ice pour through the skylights. More cracks and groans ring out from the ceiling. I may have a minute, tops, until the whole roof caves in and buries me.

I place my hands against the bare ice, trying to feel Evan's body. I close my eyes and conjure up a warming spell. At first, I feel nothing inside me, only emptiness. "Come on, come on," I whisper, panic rising. I thought I felt my magic surge with West on the field. I need to harness that power now.

Out of the corner of my eye, something large and dark falls through the air almost in slow motion, banging loudly against the ice floor. Chunks of slate tile from the roof slide and scatter, a piece narrowly missing my leg.

Still, I squeeze my eyes shut and concentrate harder. I *need* this to work. I need to save him. I think, suddenly, of the lore I heard about how a witch can regain her powers after traveling through a portal: all that nonsense about *being true to thyself* or whatever. Maybe it's real. Maybe it's true. It's not like I have anything to lose.

"I'll tell the truth," I say out loud. "I'll tell the truth about everything."

More tiles crash to the floor. My eyes pop open and I glance at the ceiling—there's now a gaping hole, and tiles are crumbling fast. Outside, I hear the wail of an ambulance. We're going to need it.

There's a lump in my throat as I turn back to Evan in his icy shell. This isn't his fault. It isn't *fair.* I press against the ice hard, my palms numb, my fingers going stiff. I have thirty seconds, maybe. Twenty . . .

"I'll tell the truth!" I scream again. "I'll tell everyone I'm the witch! I'll even take the blame for everything, even if it means risking exposing myself to Martha! Just . . . I need to save my friend!"

And then I feel it. Heat zings through my fingers, finally penetrating the ice. I straighten up, positioning my hands firmly against the block and watching with relief as water begins to stream to the floor. But more tiles are crashing to the ground behind me. I'm running out of time.

The ice block is half what it once was. My fingers feel like they're going to fall off, but I keep going despite snow swirling around me, stinging my eyes. Inside the block, Evan's finger twitches. Then his arm. I blast the rest of the block, and suddenly the whole thing dissolves into a gush of water, sweeping me off my feet. I leap up and find Evan flat on his back, choking on water.

"What the . . . ?" Evan gasps and coughs.

"You're okay," I tell him, rolling him to his side and letting him cough it out. But I can't let him stay like that for long—there's a jagged chasm in the ceiling, and I watch in slow motion as the whole thing starts to disintegrate. A deafening roar rings out of the entire roof finally breaking.

"Come on!" I yank him up. There's only one way to escape in time. I pick Evan up in my arms and lift off the ground. I spy a huge window toward the back that has shattered and zoom out at the speed of light. And just in time, too—there's a *whoosh* behind me as the rest of the roof finally falls.

We watch from outside as the building folds in on itself.

"What the . . . ?" Evan then cries. "Why are we . . . ?"

I look down. I'm still holding him. We're still suspended in the air. Hurriedly, I sink down and set him on the cold ground, but Evan scrambles backward like a crab.

"Wh-why were you . . . ?" he screams. "What *are* you?"

"I'm a witch. Like, for real." Guess I have to keep up

with my end of the bargain and tell the truth. "And I just saved you. But you have to get out of here. There's an ambulance on the sidewalk. Let them treat you."

Evan blinks hard. There are still icicles on his eyelashes. His skin is still tinged blue. "Wh-what about you? Where are you going?"

"I can't go back to school," I say quietly. "Never again."

I point him toward the ambulance—I can see the red and blue lights shining in the sky—and Evan seems too shocked and scared to argue. He runs as best he can with frigid legs to the dorms. As for me, I wasn't kidding when I said I couldn't go where he's going. I've said too much. People know too much. And Martha—whoever she is—now, surely, knows who I am. I guess there's one silver lining.

At least I can freely use my magic. Guess that lore was right after all.

## *Eighteen*

Martha's icy enchantment extends halfway across the school grounds. While I'm tempted to use my magic to de-ice the lawn, that would draw a big bull's-eye on my location, which I don't want. So I slog all the way across the border, where there's literally a line of demarcation between snow and grass. As I cross it, I've never been so happy to crunch on dry fallen leaves and shiver in the chilly but not subzero autumn air.

But I still know I'm not safe. Only when I plunge into the woods do I start to breathe easier. It's also when I realize the magnitude of what I've done.

The gossip has probably spread wide and fast. By now, everyone likely knows who and what I am. They'll hunt for me. They need a scapegoat for the floods, the earthquake, the main building falling to pieces, even Evan being trapped in that ice. They'll want to ruin me. Burn me at the stake.

And Martha—she's got to be salivating over this, whether she's heard the rumors or detected my magic outright. She must know who I am—I'm back to square one. She'll be able to catch me unaware. I'm a sitting duck.

How did I get it so wrong thinking Campbell was Martha? I don't feel she is anymore—she was so *terrified* just now at even the idea of magic. I don't think a witch could fake that—plus, I've never seen Martha show fear, ever. The vision of West and the entire coven hearing my accusations flashes back to me, too—the uneasiness on their faces, how they slowly backed away from me, how they've probably written me off forever. And forget about West, too. Even Dr. Novis left me for dead in the ballroom, probably in hopes that the roof would crush me dead.

I have no one left here. No support. No allies. I need to get out of this world . . . but I still don't have the Darkhold.

I check inside my robe, but my pockets are empty.

At some point in the scramble back to the frozen dance and the effort it took for me to thaw Ethan, the crystal ball must have rolled away. Not that it matters—the ball didn't work. It told me the bat's *old* location, not the new one.

I sit down on a rock and put my head in my hands, feeling more hopeless than I've ever felt in my life. Why did I even come to this godforsaken place? Why did I make an effort to interact with people? Everything that has happened is *so* out of character for me. Making friends, kissing a boy, enjoying life on a school campus—what was I *thinking*? I should have just stayed in my lane. I should have just looked for the Darkhold and that's it.

From now on, I'm going it alone. No more covens. No more friends. Definitely no more *boyfriends*. No more helping people, or giving people the benefit of the doubt, or being part of a community. Agatha Harkness and community don't mix.

Behind me is the faintest, softest whisper, a sense of movement. It makes the hair on my arms rise. When I spin around, something flashes through the trees, then disappears. It makes me think of the torches I saw in the woods moments before I followed Martha through the portal all those centuries ago. Maybe torches are coming for me now, too. A new witch hunt. It's only fitting.

I close my eyes and recite the invisibility spell. My

body goes transparent, and I watch for whatever it is coming down the path. No torches appear, though. Instead, something softly flickers. *Two* somethings. Ethereal figures drift down the path, sometimes blinking bright, sometimes dimming darker, only vague versions of bodies without legs or feet.

I remember the other thing the crystal ball told me about these spirits. I snap my fingers and make myself visible again.

"Hey," I whisper to them.

The spirits halt. Turn. They see me. I can feel them watching.

"It's okay. I'm friendly. Who are you?"

Silly idea, though. Spirits can't talk. They hover there. Quivering.

So I guess. "You're Sylvie and Mr. Haverford, right?"

The wind rustles. There's only silence, but in my experience, when you're wrong about a question, a spirit will let you know in his or her own unique way. There seems to be a pregnant, anxious pause in the air, like even the trees are nodding yes.

"Did someone do this to you? At the beginning of the school year? Maybe . . . maybe because you knew too much? Or saw something you shouldn't have?" The scrawled message inside Sylvie's nightstand drawer haunts me. *Darkness is among us.* She could have written it as a warning. Maybe she knew something terrible was going to happen to her.

The apparitions flash and then dim. They seem to turn to each other like they're conferring. "And this person," I go on, "she had bad energy. She was dangerous."

Now the spirits glow brighter. I'm on the right track.

"She's a bad witch disguising herself as someone on campus. I'm sorry this happened to you. She's trapped you like this. Made you voiceless. Stuck in these woods."

The spirits move closer—it's clear they can hear me now. The wind is so still, the forest so quiet, that I can hear my heartbeat and the sound of my breath. It's strange to see something ethereal moving through the air and not disturbing anything solid as they pass. They don't rustle a leaf. They don't crack a branch. They interrupt nothing.

I stay very still, waiting to see what they'll do. Even though they're closer now, I still can't really make out their features—only that they have heads and necks, legs and arms, a general semblance of humans but not human at all. I think they've come closer because they're starting to trust me. In fact, they're starting to *depend* on me. I can feel what they want from me as easily as if they'd said it out loud. Despite all of my thoughts just moments ago of not sticking my nose in things any longer, my heart goes out to them. Martha did this—they've all but confirmed it. Undo the spell, and they might live again. It's actually an easier spell to cast than resurrecting someone who's truly dead . . . but only just.

"I'll help you," I whisper. "I can bring you back, if you give me some time." The smartest thing to do is get rid of Martha first.

I turn to their shimmering auras. "But in exchange, I need to know who did this to you. How about I say some names of students, teachers—and you give me a sign if that was the person who did this?" I'll go through the whole student directory if I have to. It's not like ghosts have sleep schedules.

But then there's a snapping sound behind me for real, an actual living being disturbing the earth. I whirl around to check. Shadows pass. My eyes play tricks. I don't think I hear anyone.

I turn around again, but the two flickering ghosts are gone.

"Hey!" I whisper. "Come back!"

Silence. I peer behind trees, around bushes, off into the distance, but they've vanished.

Another crack sounds behind me, and then another. Suddenly, I can make out soft footsteps on the path. Before I can run, someone's hood emerges through the forest. My heart leaps into my throat. I'm just about to turn myself invisible again, but the figure looks up and flicks on a flashlight, beaming it *straight at me*.

I freeze, my bones turning to liquid. Should I shoot the person with a beam? Freeze time? But then I see who it is.

"Alice," Ursula then says in a gentle, shaky voice. "Please don't run. It's okay."

"Don't come any closer," I warn her. "You don't know what I'm capable of."

Ursula halts, stricken. "Are you going to hurt me?"

I look down at my hands. Then I feel my shoulders deflate. "The whole school must be after me. You don't want to be anywhere near me unless you want to be hunted, too."

"But you *saved* Evan, Alice."

I stare at her. "How do you know that?"

"Because I saw the ambulance loading him inside. And I know you. You have a big heart. He was stuck in ice that heat can't melt—you were the one who got him out of there."

I run my tongue over my teeth, trying to wrap my mind around this new perspective. My head feels like it's detached from my body.

"Look, I'm upset that you didn't tell me the truth about who you really are, but I'm trying to understand," Ursula says. "You didn't want to be blamed for the weather stuff. And you're in hiding here—you're from somewhere else. Is that even close to being right? Could you tell me what's going on?" Ursula takes a tentative step forward, and I can see the pain on her face. "I thought we were friends. I don't want to lose you."

I swallow hard. I can't help it—her words affect me. I don't want to lose her, either. But I don't want to put her in danger.

"There's someone I'm trying to hide from," I say quietly. "I couldn't really tell anyone anything about it. Well, except for West." I sigh. "I told him a little, but I phrased it like it was a joke. He never believed it was the truth."

"And . . . this person you're trying to hide from—it's the person who's messing with the weather, right?"

I nod. "And it's someone right under our noses. They've been trying to undermine us with all that weather stuff and other things, too. I think they've been looking through our room. I'm also pretty sure they told on us to Peabody and Dr. Novis—all in hopes of catching us. Making things hard for me. I thought it was Campbell. It made so much sense." I shake my head. "Also . . . I think they're the one who hurt Sylvie, too. And Mr. Haverford."

Ursula's eyes widen. *"What?"*

"I can't figure out why quite yet, but yeah." I glance through the woods, considering telling her about the ghosts, but then I decide against it—for now. "Maybe they've taken over someone else's body, or maybe it's someone who's new to the school—that's why I thought it was Campbell."

"Campbell seemed really scared, though."

"I know. That's exactly what I thought."

Ursula stares down at her shoes for a moment, like she's debating saying something. "Why are you hiding from this person, anyway?"

"Because they're dangerous. And they're looking for me."

"Why?"

"I followed them here to get back something of mine that they took. Apparently, they've lost it, too, so we're both looking for it."

"What is it?"

I shake my head. "It's not for regular people to know about."

Ursula shifts closer. "I won't tell anyone, I promise."

"I don't want to scare you." I think of how rattled she gets even talking about Sylvie's disappearance. This is a million times stranger.

Ursula steels herself. "I can deal with it. Please tell me, Alice."

I watch her for a moment, then sigh. "My real name is Agatha."

She waits. I press my lips together. Can I really tell her the rest? I stare up at the lack of stars. The darkness makes me feel lonely, insignificant. My secrets feel heavy inside me, like they're literal stones weighing me down. Maybe I owe Ursula an explanation. She's been nothing but a good friend, especially now.

And so I get into the story. I tell her about Salem, about the bewitched bat, about Martha and the portal and waking up in Ursula's dorm room. That I used the name Alice Harvey, my safe name. About how Prudence came to me in a vision, telling me Martha was close but didn't know who I was, and that I needed to find her before she found me. "I knew she was here because of the weather," I explain. "She was able to affect the weather in old Salem, too."

Ursula's eyes are wide when I get to this part. "So you're actually a witch from . . . *back then*?"

I nod.

"That explains your old cloak," she says thoughtfully. "So did you endure the witch trials?"

"I went through the portal before they began. I didn't know they were going to happen, though I had a feeling. But I couldn't even go through the museum or look at the list on the wall. I didn't want to see the names of my coven on there. My hope is that I find the Darkhold and use it to go back there."

"To save your coven?"

"To at least save Prudence." But then I let out a groan. "Though I guess I could save the others, too."

"Why do you sound so annoyed about that?"

"Because . . . I'm not the hero. All my existence, I've been on my own. I've only looked out for myself. Even when I was in Salem three hundred years ago, I couldn't stand my coven. I got away from them every chance I had."

"But something changed," Ursula says faintly. "Being here changed you."

I don't answer, but I know it's true. I'm still trying to figure out what it is, specifically, about this coven that changed my mind. I've been in plenty of covens before, and usually they've driven me batty. But I think about how the whole group cheered when Jamira won the costume contest, and how everyone gave Francie that pep talk about James, how devastated they all were when Evan was stuck in the ice. Even how they all cared about *me*, giving me that makeover when I asked West to the dance, waiting in the wings to pick me back up when he said no. In my past covens, we banded together for power, sharing secrets and tips, but we weren't actually friends.

It's a foreign concept, friends. I've never gotten the hype. But now, maybe I do.

Ursula's hair is still wet from the blizzard disaster, frozen at the ends. My mind catches on something she said, something I want to ask about, but I feel so addled I can't remember what it is. The night has been so strange and stressful with so many highs and lows; everything feels so jumbled in my head.

"So this bat you're looking for," Ursula says after a while. "You have no idea where it is?"

"Nope." I explain how I used the crystal ball to scry out a clue . . . but that the clue doesn't make sense. "It showed where I found it the first time."

Ursula strokes her chin. "And where was that?"

"It doesn't matter. It wasn't there."

"Are crystal balls reliable?"

"In my experience, yes. I mean, sometimes they can be cryptic and downright obtuse, but usually they give an answer that makes sense. Then again, when I asked who Martha was, it showed me a picture of myself—so maybe this one is a lemon."

"What was the picture, exactly?"

I call it up in my mind's eye. "I'm standing at the bathroom mirror in our dorm room, staring at my school schedule. But I'm not Martha. That doesn't make any sense."

Ursula thinks about it for a while. "That picture I took of you? On the iPad?" I nod, and she stands straighter. "Wait. Alice. I remember that photo. Maybe the point wasn't to show you at all."

"But there's no one else in the picture."

"Yes, but you said you were looking at your schedule,

right?" I nod. "There are names on your schedule. Teachers' names."

The wind whisks down my back, and I shiver. She's right. In the image the ball showed, my schedule was turned outward toward the mirror. The photo reflected a name or two, especially ones at the beginning of my schedule. My first-period teacher, for example.

Someone new, like me. Someone strange. Someone I've never felt I could quite trust.

*Dr. Novis.*

# Nineteen

Ursula and I stand at the edge of the woods, surveying the school grounds. In the distance, lights flash in the sky: emergency vehicles, probably, tending to more students injured in the ice storm and assessing the damage in the main building. A lot of people are outside still. Voices shout. Dogs bark. Flashlights zigzag across the grass.

They're looking for me. Of course they are. They're not going to let a witch run free, especially one who brought on such injury and destruction. Chances are, the emergency crews went into the main building to see if I had been killed in the collapse. When they didn't find me, well, they called in the authorities.

I look at Ursula. "I really don't want you mixed up in this. If they find us together, you'll be blamed, too."

"I'm already too far into this to turn back now." Ursula shifts thoughtfully. "But wait. Can't you just make yourself invisible? I already know your secret. You might as well use your powers."

I suppose she's right. Besides, it would help with sneaking up on Dr. Novis. The only hope we have now is that he thinks I haven't figured him out yet so I can catch him unaware.

I'm still baffled about Dr. Novis, though. He's strange, that's for sure, but I never got the sense he was Martha. But maybe I've lost a bit of my mojo. Besides, the timeline of when he arrived at Conant Academy matches up. And maybe he wasn't measuring the earthquake activity in the woods but checking that the ghosts he doomed there hadn't left.

And really, he did an abysmal job pretending to be a field hockey coach. That should have been the biggest red flag.

"I knew there was something odd about him," Ursula whispers after we discuss the likelihood of the crystal ball's prediction. "Dr. Novis never seemed afraid of the weather stuff, not like the other teachers were. That would make sense if he was the one controlling it."

"He wasn't afraid of me, either, at the dance," I add. "He just seemed . . . matter-of-fact." I feel another pang, recalling everyone's terrified faces when I revealed who I was. "But this is dangerous for you, Ursula. He knows we're friends. What if he sees you—or anyone sees you—and tries to interrogate the truth out of you?"

Ursula crosses her arms. "That's a chance I'm willing to take."

I feel uneasy, but it's clear she won't back down. So I close my eyes and cast the invisibility spell on my body. It happens quickly. One moment, I'm solid matter, the next, I'm just vapor.

Ursula's eyes are the size of saucers. *"Wow,"* she breathes to the negative space next to her. "That's amazing."

Icicles hang dangerously from trees. Enormous snowdrifts block entrances to some of the buildings. I feel only slightly safer crossing back to campus—the moment Dr. Novis sees Ursula, it's possible he'll know I'm near. When we get close to the emergency vehicles, we duck behind a big tree and spy on the crowds of people dealing with the ice emergency and forming the search parties. There's a large group of first responders, police officers, and school staff, but I don't see Dr. Novis's tall, craggy form among them. To our right, a large group of people in reflective gear head off into the woods. Quite a few of them hold German shepherds and scent hounds on leashes. Dr. Novis isn't part of my search party, either.

I clear my throat. "Did he leave?"

"Weird," Ursula whispers.

It doesn't feel right. Dr. Novis has been at the center of the hunt to seek out the person controlling the weather; why would he just vanish? A trick is coming, I can feel it. I need to outthink the guy—outthink *Martha*.

"Maybe he's gone somewhere private so he can cast another spell?" Ursula asks. "Affect the weather again. Do something to draw you out and make it impossible for you to hide."

"Do you know where Dr. Novis lives?" I whisper.

Ursula nods. "This little house off campus. I'll take you."

We pivot toward the campus fence. The front gates, normally locked, are blocked by more emergency vehicles, but there's no way Ursula could slip out without someone seeing her. "It's okay. There's this little hole in the fence that some students have talked about, though," she whispers.

She hurries to a little ravine at the back of the school. Sure enough, through some bushes, some of the iron fence has eroded away. It's just wide enough for Ursula to squeeze through. Invisible, boneless, and weightless, I have no problem at all.

There's one good thing about being outside the academy gates: The ice spell doesn't extend out here. As in the woods, we're on solid ground again, and the air is significantly warmer. I can finally move my toes inside my shoes.

"This way," Ursula whispers, taking me down a dark alley across from the school grounds. A few ramshackle row homes appear. They aren't my coven's cottages, but they look almost as old. "I think he lives in one of these."

We traverse the slippery brick streets, peering at names on mailboxes. My gaze zings this way and that, hoping to find a certain mystical bat hanging from a spindly tree branch. If only. Then I wouldn't even have to bother tracking down Martha.

"So about the book you're looking for," Ursula says, as if reading my mind. "If the ball was right about Dr. Novis, maybe the clue it gave you about the book is right, too."

I cluck my tongue. "Doubt it. That clue was to a location that doesn't exist anymore."

"Are you sure?" Ursula checks another nameplate on a door, but it's for someone named Arthur Crossfield. "Salem has changed, but not that much. Maybe you're missing something. What was the clue, anyway?"

"The ball showed this family's house from 1691. A young girl in our coven was friends with the daughter. They had this cellar—that's where I found the bat the first time—but it doesn't exist anymore."

"And you're sure it's not another old cellar that's here in modern times?"

"It definitely looked . . ."

Then I stop. In front of me is yet another tired-looking row home, its porch cluttered with weedy potted plants and a few of the window shutters hanging crookedly off their hinges. I don't even need to look at the nameplate on the building to know this is Dr. Novis's place. I can tell by the flashes in the upper window. *Eerie* flashes, like someone is casting a spell.

A shiver goes through me. "He's here. *She's* here."

I square my shoulders. This is my chance. With Martha distracted, I can catch her off guard. My only hope is that my magic is strong enough to subdue her.

We creep to the front door. It's locked, naturally, but I cast a quick and easy spell to turn the dead bolt. As I pull on the handle, I glance at Ursula. "You've gotten me this far. I don't know what I'd do without you. But you don't want to come in."

Ursula looks worried. "What if you get hurt?"

"I won't." At least I hope not. "You have to trust me."

A flash of panic crosses Ursula's face. "But will I ever see you again?"

My heart twists. Will she? What if something terrible happens? But I can't think that way. "I'm just making sure Martha isn't a problem. I still need to find the Darkhold."

"Please let me at least walk up with you. At least up the stairs. Then I'll go. I promise."

I hate the idea of Ursula setting foot in this vile witch's house, but she insists. And so, we creep inside together. The foyer smells a little musty, but it's very tidy. To our left is a dark, eerie sitting room with stuffy antique furniture and an old-fashioned hearth and mantel, though it's warm and dry. It's not unlike the way some of the living rooms looked in Salem in the 1690s, to be honest, which makes me wonder if this building was built around that time. Ahead of us is an old wooden staircase, the finish chipping a little.

"This is a real blast from the past," I mutter.

"Does it remind you of that family's house you were talking about?" Ursula whispers.

I nod. "Actually, pretty similar."

Thunder sounds from the upstairs, and we both jump. Nevertheless, I grip the banister hard and start up the stairs. Ursula follows behind me, though the color has drained from her face.

I insist, again, that she leave. "Things might get dangerous. I don't want anything to happen to you."

"I know. I'm okay."

Our footsteps creak on the risers. Another *bang* sounds from the second floor. The landing has a crack in the wall that's so massive a raccoon could fit inside. All the upstairs doors are closed, but it's obvious which room Dr. Novis is in—we just have to look at the lightning flickering beneath the frame. I creep along the wall until I'm right next to the door in question. Ursula stands beside me, practically shivering with fear.

*"Go,"* I tell her again, more sternly this time. "Wait outside. Seriously."

She nods and turns back for the stairs. But then she pivots and looks over her shoulder. "I have to know, though. What was the family's name?"

"What family?"

"The one with the cellar. Where you found the bat."

*She's worried about this* now? "The Parrises," I say, exasperated. "They had a young daughter, Betty Parris. My friend Prudence knew her."

Ursula's eyes widen. "*The* Betty Parris?"

"Huh?"

"The famous Betty Parris from the museum?"

"The—?" I start. But then another loud *boom* sounds from behind the door. I turn back, my hand on the knob, my wrist twisting it to open. And . . . it *does* open.

The bright light hurts my eyes. I shield my face from the painful heat. Dr. Novis stands in the center of the room, eyes closed in concentration, hands outstretched. Mystical light floats off his palms and forms a fuzzy V above his head. The whole room is aglow with it, the energy enough to power the sun.

My jaw drops. This is definitely magic. Here is Martha, finally. I've found her. I've *done* it.

I'm shoved hard from behind. I stumble forward,

startled, crashing into the room and onto the dusty wood floor. I push myself up quickly, puzzled by what just happened. Did I trip? Was it the forceful energy in here?

At the same time, Dr. Novis looks up and sees me on the ground. An expression of terror and confusion crosses his features. *"Alice?"*

All the light dies away. That's when I see he's holding an orb and a long staff that would be a wand. But without the ethereal light, it's just a plain old room.

"Wh-what is all this?" I demand.

He places the orb and wand on a table and walks toward me. "Something I've been working on. I'm trying to harness energy, all in hopes of combating the weather issues. Once Evan was trapped in that ice—I knew that what we were working with wouldn't obey the laws of science. But what are you doing here? How did you find me?" Now he seems angry. "Don't you know it's dangerous to be out? If you're found, you'll be killed!"

"I saw the flashes. Aren't you . . . ?" But something isn't right in my mind. This isn't the picture I thought I'd see. And his concern is puzzling. Why isn't he flying toward me, ready to battle? Isn't *he* the one who wants to kill me?

Dr. Novis lowers his shoulders and then says, as if he can read my mind, "Alice, I'm not the one you should fear. It's *her*. I've been trying to tell you."

My thoughts grind to a halt. This makes no sense. "Her . . . who?" I stammer. "What do you mean?"

Dr. Novis takes a few more steps toward me. His mouth is moving, but I'm too overwhelmed to hear the words. But something behind me makes him stop short. His face goes slack with panic. At the same time, I'm also still hearing his words in my mind, especially what he said about Evan's block of ice—*it wouldn't obey the laws of science.*

A new idea forms, and something crystallizes. It's the thing that's been bugging me. The thing I couldn't put my finger on when I was talking to Ursula. In the woods just now, she said something about Evan. *He was stuck in ice that heat can't melt,* she said.

But how did she know that? In the normal world, ice is always ice, and heat is always heat. It's basic chemistry that applying heat to ice melts it—there's never such a thing as *ice that heat can't melt*. Unless, of course, it's *magic ice*—like the ice Evan was stuck in.

But how would Ursula know that? Mortals aren't aware of magic ice. It's not a thing. And she seemed so assured about it, like she'd come in contact with magic ice before.

Something trips in my brain.

"Wait," I say, time slowing down. And then I see the crystal ball's prophesy one more time: my face in the mirror, my school schedule in my hands, the rest of the dorm room behind me. But the reflection showed someone else, too. There was someone else in that picture, in that room—the person who held the camera.

My roommate.

I twist around, all at once understanding what I've missed. I'm just in time to see Ursula in the doorway, her hand on the knob. She sees me staring and breaks into a devilish grin.

"Thank you, Agatha," she crows. "You've told me everything I need to know. The Darkhold is mine."

She slams the door hard. And locks us in.

# *Twenty*

For a few moments, all I hear is the sound of Ursula's footsteps as she clomps back down the stairs. I hurl myself at the door and twist the knob to unlock it. Nothing happens. It's a magic lock. Magic . . . because Ursula can *do* magic. And Ursula can do magic . . . because Ursula is Martha.

"I've been trying to warn you about her," Dr. Novis says again, behind me.

I swing around. "*Excuse* me?"

"I had a feeling there was something off about Ursula. About you as well—but not in the same way. I can sense energy, you see. I don't have strong powers like you do, but I came here because of a big energy disturbance. Hunting disrupters of energy is my passion. The weather swings, the tornadoes—I knew they weren't natural, but I also didn't know who or what was behind them. I didn't know Ursula from before her friend went missing, but I received enough reports that she hasn't been her normal self since. Almost, as someone said, like someone *took over her body*. Of course, mere mortals don't believe that's real, but both you and I know that it is."

I stare at him, full of questions, most of them I can't ask right now. "Could you have not *told* me that before she shut us in here?"

"I tried to. At the dance. But there was only so much I could say, and then there was the issue with Evan. I didn't have time, Alice."

"My name is Agatha," I answer wearily.

Dr. Novis pauses for a moment. "Fine. Agatha. My apologies."

I twist the knob again. It still doesn't budge. The only spell I can think to use is one that will melt metal, though it takes some time. Still, I cup my hands around the knob and start the process, feeling the heat start to build.

"So you're telling me that my enemy . . . *usurped* Ursula's body when she came to the academy?" I mutter.

"And she planted herself as my roommate? So, wait, did she know it was me all along?"

"I'm not sure," Dr. Novis says.

But I think Martha did know my identity all along. Maybe, somehow, Martha arrived at Conant Academy ahead of me—months ahead. Portals can be glitchy: You and your enemy can fly through them at nearly the same instant but wind up at different points on the space-time continuum. If Martha came first, she might have had some time to carry out a plan: find an unsuspecting body at school. Take it over. Get rid of her host body's roommate so that *I* could be her host body's new roommate and she could keep close tabs on me.

At first glance, it seems ridiculous, a huge risk. What if I'd walked out of the academy and refused to be a student? Then again, the moment I told Headmistress Peabody that Conant Academy wasn't for me, she cast that tornado spell—almost like she could *hear* me. She knew I'd change my mind and stay, knowing she was near.

But why not kill me off immediately? Wasn't her end goal to destroy me forever?

Only, maybe Martha couldn't kill me right away. Maybe . . . she *needed* me. *I* have the power to find the Darkhold, not her. Oh, Martha tried to find it on her own—trying to unearth it with all those weather stunts—but they didn't work. Weather is her only power. She can't cast spells like I can—her magic is very limited. So she went with plan B: waiting for me to gather clues and figure it out myself.

In the meantime, she pretended to be friends with me. Made sure my guard was down. Created more drama with enemies than there needed to be. Yes, Campbell is a bully and seems to have something against the coven, but Ursula definitely used that to her advantage. Pushing me toward suspecting Campbell while actually imprisoning Evan in that ice block herself was a deft touch. Of course I blew up at Campbell at the dance. I showed my hand, exposed who I was, acted erratically, and turned all of Conant Academy against me. Martha knew I'd have to run away to hide. But when she found me in the woods as Ursula, I trusted her because, well, Ursula and I were friends. By then, I even had my clue about the Darkhold, and she milked it out of me. She was one step ahead of me this whole time.

Only, why lead me to Dr. Novis? What role does he play in all of this?

"I witnessed her working her magic," Dr. Novis says when I voice this question. "It was at the dance, shortly after the costume contest was announced. As I said, I'm sensitive to energy disruptions. I could tell something was happening at the back of the building, and naturally, because of all the weather problems before, I wanted to nip the problem in the bud."

"Why didn't you stop her then?" I ask.

"Because I was taken aback by it happening." He shakes his head disappointedly. "I also had no idea who she was—her back was to me, and she was surrounded by a cloud. I ran inside to warn people of what was coming and then rushed here to gather my wits so I could stop her." He gestures to all of his wires. "But it was too late. The storm hit immediately. And then there was all that destruction—I had to go and save your classmates before the roof caved in."

I keep waving my hands over the knob. Whatever spell Martha has cast on the thing, it's a doozy. "So how did you realize it was Ursula?"

"It was a guess. I watched as you came in and started accusing Campbell of creating an ice storm. It could have been a diversion tactic, but when we were leaving, I asked West if it was true that you two had been on the playing fields when the storm started. He told me that you had. He'd been around you the whole time, he said. And, well, I trusted that West was telling the truth."

"West vouched for me?" I feel a lump in my throat.

Novis nods. "Yes, and Ursula was right there when we spoke. I saw her watching us. And as I already said, I'd sensed energy differences in her, too. It had to be her.

"I think she could instantly tell what I'd deduced," Novis continues. "I came back here to see if my magic could battle her, but"—he sighs and looks up at the ceiling—"I'm not sure I can."

I sigh. "It's pointless, anyway, since we're both locked up. Score even more points for old Martha, eh?"

"What's this witch trying to gain with all of this mischief?" Dr. Novis asks. "You mentioned some sort of object you're both searching for—is it that?"

I lean heavily against the locked door. There is part of me that really, *really* doesn't want to go through this again. When I tell him about the Darkhold, he nods sagely—he's heard of it. "It's very dangerous, though," he says. "In the wrong hands, it could do terrible things."

As if I don't know that already? "Yeah, well, it looks like I've led her right to it." I fill him in on the crystal ball, the clue, the family's cellar. As I'm talking, the knob finally starts to jiggle. "She perked up when I said the family's name—like it meant something. Then again, I guess if she's Martha, she remembers that family from the past, too. They were pretty prominent."

He hurries over to me as I finally get the door to turn. We wrench it open together, and I've never been so happy to see an ugly set of stairs in my life.

"What was their name?" Novis asks as we barrel to the first floor and out onto the street.

"The Parrises."

He stops short. "As in *Betty* Parris?"

I frown, annoyed. "Is she famous or something?"

"Sort of. She basically started the witch trials."

A ripple of terror goes through me. Dr. Novis doesn't look like he's kidding.

Then he adds, "And I think I know how Martha cracked your clue. It's true, their cellar doesn't exist anymore—but a version of it does."

*"Where?"*

"In the Witch Dungeon Museum. There's a . . . a *display*, a replica of the Parrises' cellar. Witches were imprisoned there. They used one of the original beams from the dungeon."

It feels like my head is going to explode. "There's a whole *museum* about the Parris family?"

"Yes, and . . ." But then Dr. Novis trails off and looks past me, and his shoulders straighten. "Oh no."

I whirl around, spotting lights shining at the end of the streets. There are voices, too, and footsteps coming closer. The search party.

Dr. Novis grabs my hand hard and pulls me into an alley. "We have to act fast," he says. "I know another way there."

We hurtle through back alleys, ducking behind cars when the angry mob gets close. Now that they know I'm a witch and there's no worry of exposing myself to Martha, I throw every magical trick I can at them. Force fields. Time-stopping spells. Magically opening a gate to a chicken coop so that all the chickens emerge en masse, blocking their way. Each spell only works for a few seconds to minutes at best.

It buys us enough time to get to the museum lawn unscathed. I stare up at the facade. It looks like a church, sort of, with arched windows and a tall ceiling, and has jaunty words that read *Witch Dungeon Museum* across the front. There are a few stocks lined up for people to take photos in, as well as a little barred basement area where, if I'm to understand correctly, the townspeople imprisoned the witches.

I can't believe the Darkhold has been in a *museum* all along. I mean, really, bat! What if a tourist came along and found you?

"Come on," Dr. Novis says, grabbing my hand.

Predictably, the front door is locked tight. I wave my hand at the bolt, but nothing happens. I run to the side door, but it doesn't budge, either.

Voices drift from behind me, and when I turn, the mob is rounding the corner. There are four cops on motorcycles now. Tons of search dogs. Squad cars. They're so close. We have maybe a minute, tops.

I look at Dr. Novis. "I'm trying to use an unlocking spell, but it's not working. You're free to go if you want! Get out while you still can!"

"And let a power-hungry witch harness all the bad energy in the universe? No thank you." Dr. Novis pushes me aside and yanks at the knocker himself, like that's going to do any good.

The mob moves closer. When Headmistress Peabody sees that Dr. Novis is with me, she starts to shriek. "She's taken Dr. Novis hostage now! They're both enchanted by the devil!"

A policeman revs his motorcycle and yells through a megaphone: "Alice Harvey, stop and put your hands up!"

I throw one more force field at them to buy us a minute. A blurry wall rises between us and the group, suspending them on the other side. I look at the face of this strange little dungeon museum again. I can feel Martha inside the walls, her icy, dangerous power oozing and blazing. But the building is a fortress. She's barricaded herself inside.

"Can't you explode the building or something?" Dr. Novis asks.

"I'm not exploding anything," I snap. "There's history inside. The only information about people's lives. People I *knew*, maybe." Also, I need Martha to be the bad guy, not me. The less I can destroy, the better.

The force field is starting to warp, a clear sign the

spell is wearing off. Dr. Novis yanks at the knob some more, but to no avail. "Fire? Astral projection? How about you create a portal to take you inside?"

I groan. "Stone doesn't burn. Astral projection means it's just my soul, not my body, and not my magic. And portals—they're not very reliable."

"Well, then how are we going to get in? What if she's already *got* the Darkhold?"

*Psst!* comes a voice. *I know a way!*

I startle to attention. "Did you hear that?" I ask.

He stares at me like I've lost my mind. "Do I hear the angry mob? Do I hear the sounds of certain death? Be specific, Agatha!"

But then I hear it again. A voice. *Over here! Quickly!*

I squint in the darkness. Whoever is talking is on the back side of the building. I run to follow the sound.

"Agatha?" Novis whispers. "Where are you going?"

"Come on," I say over my shoulder. "Just go with it."

Novis hurries after me. I run all the way to the grass, but there's no one there. The only being is a small crow standing at a set of stairs that leads to a basement door. I try to shoo him away, but he doesn't move. He stares at me sort of pointedly, actually.

"You?" I snap. I know this crow. It's *the* crow. But I'm frustrated with him. He told me that he was certain Martha didn't know my identity. Had he deliberately lied?

"Go away," I snap. "For all I know, you're a double-crosser. You're probably working with Martha. Did she tell you to say she had no idea I was the witch? Are you in on her evil plot?"

*I'm not,* the crow tells me. *I had bad information when we spoke before, that's all. Now I realize how wrong I was. I want to help.*

Then I notice something shiny in his beak: Ursula's earring, the one I gave him the day I landed here through the portal. It's not surprising—I've known lots of crows who carry their shiny prizes from place to place. But he's holding it like a tool.

*I used this to pick the lock,* the crow says, flipping the earring over in its beak. *Come through here. Door's open.*

I turn back to Dr. Novis. He seems puzzled, and I realize how this must look—the crow and I are just *staring* at each other, it communicating through thoughts, me muttering words.

"Uh, this is the same crow who screwed me over a while ago," I explain. I look back at the bird, still not sure whether I should believe him. "Why do you care so much about making it up to me?" I know plenty of crows who wouldn't care if they lied to a witch.

*Because,* he answers. *A goat vouched for you. Janice?*

I bark out a laugh. "You know *Janice*?"

"What's happening?" Dr. Novis asks. "Who's Janice?"

"Never mind," I say. I hurry down the steps and

try the knob. True to his word, the crow has actually unlocked it. Well, well, well. I guess all can be forgiven.

The basement is dusty, crumbling cinder block and so dark I can't see my hand in front of my face. I manage to conjure up a small light spell, but even that only provides enough light to make sure we aren't tripping over things as we walk.

A light snaps on, red and ghoulish. Mere feet in front of us, a garish witch imprisoned under a series of rocks appears. I let out a shriek, stretch out my fingers, and blast it with flames. Only once I smell burning wax do I realize it's not Martha.

"It's just a figure," Novis tells me. "A display."

I stare, goggle-eyed, at the dummy on fire. A woman in a bonnet has an imploring expression as she tries to unearth herself from the rocks. A lump forms in my throat—she looks like Prudence. What kind of museum *is* this?

Another light flashes on, illuminating the entire cellar for a moment. That's when I see Ursula . . . *Martha* . . . in the corner, lurking covertly, staring at us with wide, frantic eyes. She's standing next to what looks like a stone hearth—a wooden beam halfway up the wall, with stone above it—her smile snaggle-toothed and giddy. My gaze drops to her hands. There, lying in her arms, is the Darkhold bat. Sleeping. Subdued. She grips it tightly, like she's ready to suffocate it.

"Too late, Harkness," Martha giggles. "I got here first!"

But it isn't Martha talking. It's Ursula. It's painful to see the words coming out of Ursula's mouth. Painful to think that Ursula, whom I trusted, whom I thought of as a friend, was always just . . . *this.*

I try to put it out of my mind, though, as I stride toward her. I can't go even a few steps, though, before Martha raises a hand and freezes me in my tracks. I stare down at my immobile feet, feeling a rise of terror.

Martha giggles. "You think you can come in here and just take it away? That's not how it works."

I pry my dry, frozen lips apart, desperate to talk. "Give it up." My voice is a husk. "You'll never be able to understand its powers."

"Like you will?"

I square my shoulders. "You couldn't even find it on your own. You had to rely on me. You had to pull every trick out of your arsenal to make all of this work."

"So what? I succeeded." She cradles the bat. "I tricked you, Agatha. *Again.* Just deal with it."

It stings. Of course it does. But I push the humiliation aside. "At what cost, though? What did you do to Sylvie and Mr. Haverford? It was you who got rid of them, right?"

She shrugs. "I had to. They were asking too many questions once I occupied the human host. *Why are you acting so strangely, Ursula? Why don't you seem to know me, Ursula?* I did what I had to do."

I wince.

She snorts. "Since when are you so high and mighty? You're just as evil as I am! What were you going to do with the Darkhold, use it for good?" She tips her head back and cackles.

I stiffen. "I was going to use its powers for better things than you will."

"That's what you think. I have big plans for the Darkhold. I'm using its powers to start a coven—only the most powerful witches in the world will be in it, and we'll all benefit from the spells. We'll challenge the likes of Wanda Maximoff. You hate her, don't you? I can tell. Always so jealous. Though, sorry, Agatha"—she pouts—"*you* aren't getting an invite."

I scoff. "I don't *want* an invite. Whatever plans you have for the Darkhold, I want no part of it."

"You're no better than I am. You're the same Agatha who literally couldn't care less about the coven in Salem. You haven't changed."

"I have."

"No, you haven't." Her smile is so eerie. "You know how I know? Because in the world you just came from, a few years later, you're going to say *this*."

Lightning shoots from her fingers, projecting an

image into the atmosphere. It's the same vision I saw where I floated through city streets, zooming in on Old Agatha as she peers out the window of a shack. But I have no idea how Martha has access to this vision, too.

Martha looks over me to Dr. Novis. "You picked the wrong horse to bet on, Doctor. Your friend here? She isn't the hero you think she is."

I start to argue, but she cuts me off. "Don't say anything until you watch it all. Just wait."

The vision rolls forward like a movie. I stare up at the scenes I've already witnessed: Old Agatha waiting, that fiery-haired mutant woman, Firestar, knocking at her door, Agatha opening it after some hesitation, and Firestar begging Agatha to return to Salem. But then a part I haven't seen yet unfolds.

"Please," Firestar implores. "You're our only hope. You must come with us to help stop the trials. They're dying right and left. People are accusing women for the most trifling of infractions. They killed a dog because it gave them the evil eye! They've lost their minds! Although the townspeople don't believe or understand it, I don't possess magic of my own—but you do. With your magic, you can set things right. I know you can."

She's on her knees now, begging before Old Agatha. But the old woman looks at her with disdain, curling her lip over her teeth. Finally, Old Agatha shakes her head. "I'm sorry, but I won't do it."

*"Won't do it?"* I say, right in time with the fire woman in the vision. *"Why?"*

"Keep watching," Martha says through gnashed teeth.

Old Agatha looks into the middle distance, a thoughtful expression on her face. "I've had a lot of time to think about the trials, and after a lot of reflection, I support them. I think they were the right move. Those who didn't make it weren't strong. It was a useful culling of our ranks, witches and mutants both, weeding out those who were dragging the rest of us down. The townsfolk–as misguided as they were, are actually doing us a favor."

*"What?"* How was I saying this? Did I have a flesh-eating worm in my brain?

Firestar presses Old Agatha again and again, but she won't budge. Finally, Firestar leaves empty-handed.

The vision fades. I can feel Dr. Novis shifting behind me, probably as uncomfortable as I am. Martha, meanwhile, is still cackling.

"You're no better than the townspeople who hated the witches. I always knew you had that in you, though—intolerance. *Hatred.* Know why you really didn't want to look at any information in the Witch Museum? Don't give me a sob story about not wanting to see your coven's names on that commemorative wall. No, you didn't want to see your *own* name there—as one of the *accusers*. Agatha Harkness, traitor."

"That's not true!" I shout.

She smiles. "It is. You turn on your coven, Agatha. You accuse them one by one, all to throw shade on them so no one suspects *you* of being the true witch."

I back up, my heart fluttering fast. "I wouldn't do that!"

"No? Look inside yourself. You know you would. Your heart is black."

I gaze imploringly at Dr. Novis, but all he gives me is an uneasy stare. "It's not . . ." I start. "I didn't . . ."

But doubt creeps in. What *would* I do if the townspeople figured out I was the true witch and captured me in a way I couldn't escape from? Maybe I would give names. Maybe I'd give up the whole coven if I had to. That's always been my modus operandi, hasn't it? Agatha Harkness looks out for herself. Agatha Harkness goes it alone.

What if the name I was afraid to see on that list in the Witch Museum was my own? Maybe this has been inside me all along?

My knees buckle. My voice dries up. I stare at the person I thought was my friend, feeling so weak and small.

But then, from somewhere inside me, a little voice starts to protest. *They're just words. She's trying to wear you down.* I'm not sure whose voice it is. Maybe my own. Maybe someone else's.

It gives me a tiny lift. I have to remember that she's trying to manipulate me. She wants me to feel disappointed in myself. She wants to win.

I can't let her.

"That's one version of me," I whisper to myself. "But it isn't the only version. It doesn't have to be. I'm in control of my future. Not her."

I feel strength build in my chest. I straighten up and send a levitating spell at Martha with surprising force. Not only does it lift her off the ground, but she's so caught off guard that the bat slips from her hands. I send a second bolt to freeze it in place. It flaps inside a bubble, suspended. Good. It can stay there until I figure out what to do with it.

Martha stretches her arms and snaps free of my spell. She drops to the ground with the lightness of a cat and springs toward me, sending a similar bubble of energy my way. Twisted vines coil around my arms and legs. My gaze swings to Dr. Novis—she's got him bound up, too. Martha turns to the bat and pops its protective bubble; the thing plops back into her arms.

I squeeze my eyes tightly and undo the spell, sending the vines cascading to the floor. But just like how things unfolded in old Salem, Martha is escaping toward the cellar stairs. I send a glowing lariat to drag her back, but she breaks free of it instantly, as though the rope were made of dental floss. I scramble over the cellar's awkward cobblestones toward her, grabbing her hard by the shoulder and whirling her around. But when she does, her face has been transformed into a nuclear, radiating sun.

I recoil. Flames dance across my skin. Martha's features lurk beneath the roiling balls of fire, and she tilts her head back in another laugh. It's hard for me to stand this close to her for too long. Another weather-witch trick, and I fell for it.

Water douses our heads, and I wheel back. It extinguishes Martha's heat instantly, and she drops to the ground, spluttering. Dr. Novis stands behind me, staring at the empty bucket levitating near his hands.

"Good thinking," I tell him.

Martha wipes water from her eyes and gives me a furious glare. Letting out a guttural groan, she sends another zigzag of energy straight at us, binding us both together in chains. I try to fight against the force, but she overpowers me, sucking me downward to the floor. My knee hits hard against the rocky ground. When I look to my left, a wax dummy of a witch imprisoned under the rocks stares at me, empty-eyed. A scratching sound fills the air, and when I look up, a thick wall of hay forms around Dr. Novis and me. Martha is sealing us inside the prison with the wax dummies.

I aim my hands at the lattice of hay, but it doesn't budge. Dr. Novis starts to claw at it, too, but not even a single straw is disrupted. On the other side of the prison, Martha sighs like she's bored.

"You're not going to win, Agatha," she drones. "Why are you even bothering?"

Biting my lip, I swing around the tiny space, looking for something that might help us—a torch, maybe, or some kind of cutting tool. There's nothing. I trip over a raised cobblestone and go sprawling onto my chest.

Martha's footsteps echo noisily on the cellar floor. There's a *thwop-thwop* of the bat's fluttering wings. It lets out an eardrum-piercing screech.

"What's she doing?" Dr. Novis asks, his face a mask of fear.

I wobble to stand. "Probably trying to enchant the bat into the Darkhold form. Then she'll get rid of us for good."

But I can't have that.

The terror reenergizes both of us. I throw my body against the hay wall again and again. Dr. Novis hefts up one of the dummies and uses it as a battering ram. Finally, the hay starts to splinter and break. I manage to send a strong enough beam of energy to make a hole big enough to climb through. I hurtle out of the hole and tackle Martha from behind, knocking the bat to the floor. The bat flutters free—Martha has not been able to enchant it back to book form yet—and Dr. Novis leaps up and catches it around its torso. He looks horrified as the creature writhes in his hands.

"Hold on to it tight!" I scream at him. "Don't let it go!"

Martha tosses me off, her face a knot of rage. Then she throws everything she's got at me—wind, rain, rumbling ground, bolts of lightning, radiating heat, and punishing cold. Items fall off the walls. The foundation starts to crumble. I am soaked and freezing and burning up and steps from being electrocuted.

Martha looks positively elated as I fend off each weather disaster. Dr. Novis covers himself from a constant onslaught of hail, working hard to keep hold of the bat. He glares at me in helpless frustration. "Is there nothing you can do? Why are you just standing there?"

It is true I'm just standing here, my feet planted, my body still. But something has occurred to me. In many ways, Martha is stronger than I am. I haven't figured out a normal way to defeat her with my magic. I hate admitting this. I *hate* not being the strongest witch in the room.

But it doesn't mean she's smarter than I am.

No witch's magic can go on forever—not without the Darkhold, and that's still in bat form. Fighting the wind, I make my way over to Dr. Novis and murmur that to him, hopefully in a voice low enough so Martha won't hear.

"We'll be able to outlast her," I tell him. "We just need to hold on."

He shakes his head, beads of sweat now rolling down his face—the room has warmed considerably, and it feels like we're sitting on the surface of the sun. "I can't."

I don't know if I can, either. My insides feel broiled. My skin is starting to burn. But when I look at Martha, I notice that her fingers are starting to tremble. She's weakening. Her magic stores are growing depleted. I have to time my next move carefully.

As the light in her eyes dims just a little, I can sense Martha's energy flagging—this battle is taking a lot out of her. It's the right moment for me to strike. I muster up all my strength to charm a portal into being. The glowing door shivers at the end of the room. Martha whips around and stares at it, then looks back at me, her face a twisted mask of disgust.

"You're not going anywhere. Your life ends *here*."

I glower at her. "That portal isn't for me. It's for you."

I raise my hands to send enough energy to shove her through the glowing door. It *should* work, but to my surprise, Martha pushes back with surprising force, her magic creating a wall that mine can't penetrate. She walks closer and closer to me, and I walk closer and closer to her, and it's like we're in an arm-wrestling contest with our forces, each pushing equally against the other. We're both dangerously close to the portal, so close that I can hear its low electric hum. Either of us could tumble through at any moment.

Martha grins at me from the other side of her force field. Her gaze darts to the left, and I can feel her magic pushing me toward the portal. I feel its magnetic pull, too, sucking me closer. I try to plant my feet, but my legs start to give out. Dr. Novis struggles to hold me from behind, but I can feel his fingers slipping around my waist.

I stare at the glowing door. In mere seconds I'm going to be sucked through, and all of this will be for nothing. I close my eyes, cursing myself. I muster up all my strength to push back against her, but her magic edges out mine just slightly. But then I notice something behind Martha. The cellar door is now open. A few people stand on the stairs, watching. Jamira, Ivy, Francie, and West are behind Martha's wall of magic, meaning they're unaffected—and she doesn't see them.

What happens next seems to move in slow motion. All four of them barrel down the stairs at once and storm Martha from behind before she has a chance to even notice them. They're already on her by the time she sees them; she has no time to focus her magic on them instead of me. I watch in terror and awe as, collectively, they shove her through the portal like they've done it a million times.

Martha screams. The portal snaps and crackles, and there's the telltale magnetic *suck* sound as the forces pull her in. But then I realize something. The portal doesn't discriminate. It won't just pull Martha through—it'll pull Martha's host body along for the ride. *Ursula*.

I raise my hands to start a spell. This isn't Ursula's fault. She doesn't deserve any of this. Quickly, I recite a spell I pray will work to separate Martha's spirit from her host. It's not a spell I've ever done on people before—only on an owl I thought was possessed, and only *once*. I stumble over the magic words—"*Separatum symposum morexa*"—hoping I have them right. But maybe I do, because Martha turns and glares at me, seemingly understanding what I'm trying to do. She wraps her arms around her waist—Ursula's waist—as if to say, *I'm not letting this body go.*

But I shout the words again, more confidently this time. And slowly, I watch as Martha's essence peels away from Ursula's body just as cleanly as that evil spirit left the owl. And *there* she is, the Martha I remember, wearing her long dress and her furious expression, shimmering translucently a few feet in the air. Ursula's body drops limply to the ground, boneless.

I gesture toward Martha's apparition and guide it toward the portal. In ghost form, Martha is weakened—it's not even hard. First, her head goes through, then her body, then her feet, her aura turning bright violet, then blue, then black. Her scream echoes loud and long through the cellar: *"I'll kill you for this, Harkness!"*

And then it's silent.

Dead silent.

The portal is gone.

And Martha's spirit with it.

## *Twenty-One*

The portal leaves no trace in the cellar. The light from Martha's powers has died out, and it's just damp and dark again. All the hail and snow and wind damage and other weather effects have disappeared, too. Martha is gone, and her magic has left with her.

I lean over my legs, still breathing hard. "Put that in a box or something," I gasp to Dr. Novis, gesturing to the wriggling bat he's still holding. He roots around behind him and manages to find an old trunk. The metal locks click noisily as he secures the bat inside.

Then I turn to Ivy, Francie, Jamira, and West. "Do

you people have a death wish? You could have gotten killed!"

Ivy frowns. "Um, a *thank you* would be nice."

"We thought you might need us," Francie says at the same time. "We pooled our strength. I had no idea we were that strong together."

"I felt like I tapped into her spirit," Jamira said. "And knew exactly where her weakness was."

"And I could feel her dark, terrible aura—and I fought against it," Francie boasts.

Ivy shrugged. "I just shoved as hard as I could."

"But . . ." I blink hard. "I thought you . . . I didn't think . . . Did you see what was *happening*? That was deadly magic!"

"We're a coven," Ivy says simply. "We can handle it. Evan wishes he could have been here, too."

Jamira walks toward me. "We're sorry about our reaction at the dance. We were shocked, but soon enough we knew you were trying to help us—especially once we found out that Ursula was the one who told Peabody and Dr. Novis that we were meeting in the cave."

I blink. "She . . . did?"

Ivy nods. "She gave Peabody and Dr. Novis specific directions straight to the cave. Even said we were performing devil-worshipping rituals. Isn't that right, Dr. Novis?"

Dr. Novis shrugs. "Headmistress just relayed the tip to me, but yes, that's essentially what she said."

I'm baffled. Why would Ursula send them after me? Didn't she realize I'd get in trouble and that would hinder me from moving freely around school to find the Darkhold? Only, maybe it wasn't about me getting in trouble at all. Maybe it was about the coven more. I think of the little comments Ursula made about how the coven really liked me—had she actually been jealous? Perhaps she worried about exactly this happening—the coven taking my side. She certainly didn't bank on me conjuring a secret tunnel for our escape. It actually surprises me that she didn't choose to use her magic to cover up the tunnel . . . then again, a weather witch doesn't have endless skills and powers. But she definitely conjured that rainstorm on the other side in hopes of washing the coven away.

But none of it worked. Not really.

I look up at the group. "How did you figure out it was Ursula who told? Wasn't the tip anonymous?"

West clears his throat. "I saw Ursula go into Peabody's office a few days ago. I was in that hallway talking to another teacher, and I heard her say something about a cave. I didn't really put things together until tonight, though. I was about to tell you that on the soccer field, actually—but then that storm hit."

"Someone asked Peabody tonight, just to make sure," Jamira says. "And she confirmed it."

"Who?" I ask.

Jamira looks conflicted. "Campbell, actually. Peabody was kind of shaken up and her guard was down, so she was honest. She said Ursula was the one who talked about the students meeting at the caves. And then Campbell came over and told us immediately. Said that maybe Ursula was double-crossing us for some reason."

I flinch. Campbell . . . did something *useful*?

"We didn't want to believe Ursula was the traitor," Ivy says again. "It wasn't like her—we've all known her for years. But we realized something was really wrong—and that you were innocent and might need help."

"It wasn't the real Ursula who betrayed you," I explain. "It was a witch who took over her body. I wish I'd seen it earlier. She was right in front of me this whole time."

"Well, good thing you have us," Ivy says primly. "Don't you think, Alice?"

"My name's Agatha." I roll my eyes. "And yes . . . *thank you*. Thank you for finding me, and thank you for shoving Martha into that portal. I couldn't do it without you."

"You're *welcome*," Ivy simpers. She looks kind of smug. Unfazed. Maybe she really *is* a witch.

Then Jamira looks down at the limp body in the shadows where the portal once was. "Ursula?"

She shines her flashlight there. Ursula lies on her side, her eyes closed. She isn't moving.

We all run over. Francie leans down and places her hand on Ursula's forehead. I watch as she mutters something under her breath. Maybe I'm mistaken, but I swear it's an old healing spell—though I have no clue how Francie would know it.

A few moments later, though, Ursula lets out a cough. Everyone sighs with relief. When Ursula sees us standing over her, her mouth makes an O, and she tries to sit up.

"Ivy?" Her voice comes out like a croak. "Jamira?" Her gaze focuses on all of us in turn. It seems like she recognizes everyone—well, except for me and Dr. Novis. She squints at both of us like she's trying to place who we are.

"What's going on?" she asks.

"It's a long story." Jamira kneels down. "Are you all right? You feeling okay? You want some water?"

Ursula looks around. "Are we . . . in the Witch Dungeon Museum in town?"

"Yes. It's a long story." Ivy leans down too. "Evan would have wanted to be here, too, but he . . . he had a small accident. No big deal."

Ursula nods slowly. "I sort of . . . *remember.* Bits and pieces . . . was there a horrible winter storm? Was Evan . . . *trapped*?" But then she looks afraid. "It's blank after that."

"That makes sense that she sort of remembers but sort of doesn't," I tell the group. "There were times when the real Ursula seemed to . . . poke through. Like I could tell she was trying to tell me something, break through Martha's spell, but Martha wouldn't let her."

Ursula turns to me and nods. "Right." I can tell she half recognizes me . . . but also doesn't at all. It hurts. Martha tricked me. I still can't believe I let it happen.

We help Ursula to her feet just as a loud crash sounds from the upper level. Heavy boots *thunk* against the floorboards, and someone calls out, "Nobody move! Stay where you are!"

The cellar door whips open, and heavy black boots thunder down the stairs. It's a few police officers and Headmistress Peabody. When they spy us, they stiffen, on alert, but we all raise our hands in surrender—even me, even Dr. Novis.

"We're not the ones you want," Dr. Novis pleads. "We took care of the real witch."

"You have to believe us," Francie says.

Peabody's chest heaves up and down as she tries to take this all in. She still looks out for blood—maybe all of ours. I wonder if explaining ourselves isn't going to do the trick this time.

But then something occurs to me. I've been so used to suppressing my magic that I keep forgetting I can use it freely now. I don't need to hide from Martha anymore. I can enchant these people all I want.

So that's exactly what I do.

I shut my eyes, and just like that, the police and the headmistress disappear. So does the angry mob at the gates. Dr. Novis is gone, too. I enchant them straight to bed, which will buy me some time.

Over the next few hours of the night, I'll work hard to undo the rest of the damage. I'll thaw the frozen ground at school. I'll restore the skylight and the roof of the main building. I'll fix the water-damaged floors, the wrecked Halloween decorations, and I'll dry out the carpets and couches and shelves of waterlogged books.

It will take a while, but I'll erase it all from happening. I'll even erase it from people's minds. And I'll heal Evan from the inside out and, after some effort, beam his body so that he'll be back with us in the dorms by morning. But that's the other thing: While I'll erase it from most people's minds, I'll spare Francie, Ivy, Jamira, Evan, and West. They can handle what happened. They can handle *me*. All the fear is gone. It's only trust now—and even a big flash of respect.

But for now, still in the dungeon, I can only send the

police away. The mist that surrounded me as I cast the spell gently burns off. Everyone left in the cellar is staring at me knowingly—except Ursula, who gawks at me.

"I'm sorry, what exactly is happening?" she asks. "Is anyone going to fill me in?"

The next morning, I conjure a spell to drag my friends out of bed and gather them on the green. They seem groggy but not that confused, like they know it's my magic at work—and that it's important.

"I just wanted to show you what I've been up all night doing," I announce.

I wave my hand around in *ta-da!* No icicles hang from the trees. There are no downed limbs or power lines from the wind. We can spot other academy buildings in the distance—my magic has restored them, too. All that ice damage in the main building never happened. The roof is still there. Even the mild tornado damage from the day I arrived has been repaired.

"Looks good," Jamira says.

"Looks better than good," Evan admits. "Looks perfect. Like nothing ever happened."

A crisp wind whips around the corners, kicking up dried leaves. Bare tree branches rub together. Carved Halloween pumpkins grin at us from doorsteps. West gives us space as Jamira, Francie, Ivy, and Evan put their arms around Ursula to help her walk. She's had a lot of questions. "*I* destroyed the school?" I heard her ask Francie as we walked to the dorms last night. "No, no, not you—someone who took over your body," Francie said gently. And then Ursula made a frightened little whimper. *"How?"*

But this morning, no one says much. It's a comfortable silence. The silence of a coven that understands one another. A coven who's been through a lot together.

I care for these people, I've realized. But now that I have the bat in my possession—it bangs noisily against the old trunk I'm holding—I know what I must do next. Maybe it's especially because I saw that unpleasant vision of my older self, refusing to help fight the witch trials—I don't want to turn into her. Or maybe it's because we're in Salem with all this doomed history around us—I know I can try to change some of that. Or maybe it's because something about Ursula—the real Ursula—reminds me of Prudence, and how Prudence still needs to be saved.

Then I clear my throat and turn to face everyone.

"Ursula," I say quietly, "do you mind if I stop in your room to collect my things? I left a cape and awful leather shoes in there, and I'll be needing them where I'm going."

Ursula shrugs and says that's fine. But the others

shift, the weight of what I've said slowly sinking in. Jamira's chin trembles. Francie cocks her head. Evan lets out a little whimper, and Ivy looks like she's going to burst into tears.

"I was hoping . . ." Jamira says, but then she stops and shakes her head.

"Are you *sure* you have to leave?" Ivy blurts. "Like, forever?"

I nod. "I'm sure. But . . . *forever* is a harsh word."

"But the coven needs you *now*," Francie says.

"We have so many other wrongs to right," Evan adds. "We've barely gotten started."

"You guys will be okay without me. You're more powerful than you think." And I really believe that. I think of all the ways that the coven helped me defeat Martha. I think they have some magic in them after all.

Ivy steps forward and wraps me in a big, fierce hug. I place the trunk on the ground to hug her back, feeling something stirring inside me as she presses her body close.

"Thanks for being a sparring partner," I whisper in her ear.

"Thanks for being a know-it-all," she shoots back.

Jamira is next. There are tears in her eyes. "I don't want this to be goodbye."

I stare at the ground. I don't want it to, either. As

much as I want to promise that I'll come back, I don't want to make promises I can't keep.

Francie unwinds a knitted scarf from her neck and drapes it around my shoulders. "I hope this can travel through portals."

"It will." I press the scarf to my nose and breathe in Francie's flowery perfume.

And then Evan wraps his arms around me. "Thanks for, you know—busting me out of that ice. It's such a good story, but I'm guessing I can only tell it among this group, huh?"

"That would probably be the smartest, considering to everyone else here, this never happened," I say, laughing.

After a few more tearful goodbyes, everyone trails off, back to their beds. It's really early, after all.

The only person who remains is West. I duck my head, suddenly bashful. I haven't talked to him since the ice storm. We didn't even get to process our kiss. It feels like it was three centuries ago.

"So, *Agatha*. You got anything to tell me?" he says jokingly.

"Don't say I didn't warn you. You should always believe what a woman says."

"I absolutely will from now on."

*From now on.* I feel a pang. His *now on* will be without me. West flinches, like he gets that, too.

I pick up the trunk again as we walk toward my dorm. For me, it'll be the last time I ever go in. Then I let out a breath and glance at him. "Thank you for vouching for me with Dr. Novis. And thank you for coming to help me with the others. I still think it was ridiculously dangerous and you people are crazy, though."

"We are, but I wasn't going to miss a battle between two witches. I mean, how many times do you get to see something like that?"

"Probably a once-in-a-lifetime experience."

West bites his lip. "And that's what you meant at the soccer field, when you said you didn't want to leave."

I nod.

"No one's forcing you to. You cast a spell for everyone to forget, right? It's not like you're in trouble anymore."

"But I have to. There's someone where I came from who needs my help. She's going to be persecuted in the witch trials, and I can't let that happen."

"Can't you just, I don't know, do a spell on her from afar?" He snaps his fingers. "Done and done?"

"You really want to keep me here, huh?"

"Well, yeah," West says bashfully. "It would be nice."

"You do realize I'm a witch, right?"

West rolls his eyes. "*Yes.* I've figured that out by now, thank you."

He grabs my hand. For a moment, we face each other, looking into each other's eyes. My nose starts to twitch.

My eyes start to sting with something salty and wet. *Tears?*

He pulls me into a strong hug. I shift the trunk to my hip and rest my head on his shoulder, promising myself that I'll remember this moment. Then I pull away. "I can't stay," I say softly. "For this spell, I have to actually be there. Besides, it isn't just Prudence. There's a whole group that needs warning. Maybe I can get some of them to a safer place."

"That's really noble of you."

"Yeah, well, maybe someone cast a spell on me, because I'm not normally like this."

He squeezes my hand hard. "I think you are. You just don't want to admit it."

I walk up the dorm steps. Before I can use my key card one last time, I hear a strange little bleat. I whirl around, confused.

"Well, if it isn't my rescuer," I murmur. "How'd you get out?"

The goat trots up to us. This time, I don't shoo her away, instead petting her between her crooked horns. I look at West. "This pesky girl saved me tonight. She made sure this crow that I know unlocked a few doors. Who knew a goat and crow were buddies?"

West shakes his head. "That sentence *shouldn't* make sense. But somehow, it does."

I look at the dorm's front door again. There's a lump

the size of a golf ball in my throat. Part of me wishes I could just continue being an academy student. Pretend none of this happened. Meet with the coven. Be with West. Even take classes—though still cheating with magic, of course.

I want it so much it kind of hurts.

West is choked when he speaks. "Is this where I leave you?"

I nod, but I can't look him in the eye. Will I ever feel this way about someone again? Will I *want* to?

We step closer together. West's breath is soft on my cheek. He brushes hair off my face. When I close my eyes, I feel West's lips lightly touch mine.

I only let the kiss last a few seconds, though. After that, I whip around, swipe my ID on the pad at the door and rush inside without saying goodbye. It's easier that way. *You won't cry,* I tell myself. *You won't cry.*

I clomp up the stairs to my room for the last time. The dorms are quiet and still. No alarms go off, and Jenna the RA doesn't wake. At the window on the landing, I peer out to the woods, but all I see is darkness.

My dorm room door creaks open. Inside, Ursula is sitting at the edge of her bed. I'm surprised to see she's still awake. She looks calm, though—even happy. She looks up and frowns a little at me, but she doesn't seem particularly surprised that I'm here.

Then I open the door wider. There's another girl on my side of the room. A girl I've only seen in pictures and as a glowing, shimmering specter in the woods. I know I shouldn't be startled to see her, but I am. Glee surges through me. Through the night, I'd cast this spell, too, but I wasn't sure if it had actually worked.

"Sylvie?" I gasp. "It's you, right?"

Sylvie, Ursula's roommate, wrinkles her brow. "Wait. Why do I know you?"

I glance at the nightstand drawer. It's ajar, and I can just make out the little *Darkness is among us* message inscribed on the inside. It's practically the only thing left that proves this actually happened and that Martha was here. Sylvie knew it, too. She might not remember it now, but she knew something was wrong, and she was smart enough to send up a warning flare—something that Martha hadn't been able to catch before I saw it. That's a little bit of magic in itself.

"You don't," I tell her, grabbing my cloak from the closet. "But believe me when I say that you kind of saved all of us."

# *Twenty-Two*

I've been sitting against the iron fence for about an hour now, trying to collect my thoughts, watching as the sun slowly peeks over the rooftops. I'm in front of the Witch Museum, its gloomy facade looming before me. It felt only fitting that I'd stand in front of a museum commemorating the time period I plan to return to.

It's still pretty early in the morning. I'm in my old cloak, long dress, and tight shoes again, but it feels so uncomfortable after weeks of modern clothes. I've also decided to keep the costume-shop cape—at least I'll have something warm and nice to bring with me. I didn't want to stick Ursula with the bill, so I may or may not have cast a small spell to empty out all the change in the soda machine in the dorm's lobby. I hated to leave forty bucks in quarters on Ursula's doorstep, but, well, I don't know any spells that can turn coins into paper money.

Soon enough, modern Salem proper will wake up and start its day. Conant Academy students will go to class. I'd say they'll celebrate Sylvie's return, but the memory spell I've cast is so all-encompassing that the narrative of her going missing has been undone in everyone's minds. I'm pretty sure Mr. Haverford is back, too, once again teaching his classes and coaching field hockey. No one will know anything was ever different except for my coven and West.

And Dr. Novis, it seems. Because about a half an hour ago, as I sat at the base of the Roger Conant statue, I heard footsteps, and there he was. I was surprised to see him at first, and I jumped up in alarm.

"Hello, Agatha," he said.

"You're not supposed to know who I am."

He smirked. "Memory spells don't work on me. Sorry."

I felt prickly. He wasn't supposed to know what memory spells were. "Wh-why not?"

Dr. Novis smiled sneakily. I got it then. Dr. Novis might not be like me, but he wasn't like everyone else, either. Martha-as-Ursula was right in suspecting him of mischief.

"So you *can* do magic," I said. It's the question I've wanted to ask since, well, maybe I arrived here. Maybe I've always had a sense. "Why didn't you help me more in the dungeon?"

"I'm sorry about my limited abilities, though I did help with that water bucket." He trained his gaze on the Witch Museum across the street. "My real name is Doctor Strange. I'm guessing you've heard of me?"

I blink. *Have I?* The name seems familiar.

"We have a lot in common. But my magic isn't like yours. Yes, what you saw in my home was real magic. But as I said, it wasn't ready to defeat Martha. I still need to work with it more and harness what it can do. So technically, I *was* powerless with Martha. But you didn't need me."

I snorted. "You just knew that? Thanks for the confidence, I guess."

He smiled mysteriously. "I'm glad *you* finally realized it, too." Then he shifted his weight. "Do you think it was the right choice, sparing your friends from the memory spell? What happened was quite traumatic . . . and abnormal."

"I think they can handle it," I answered. "And I didn't think they'd want to forget the experience. They're more like me than I thought."

"And what about what you did to Campbell?"

"I didn't do anything to Campbell." When he doesn't

answer, I sat up straighter. "What are you talking about?"

"I saw a light on in her dorm room through the trees on my way here. Her room—and only her room—was still encased in ice."

"That wasn't me! Honest!"

Novis—Strange?—was quiet for a moment, pondering this. "Sometimes, with certain energies, there are other forces at play. Perhaps it's karma. Maybe the universe is trying to teach her a lesson."

I wasn't sure about that. "None of this was her fault, though. *She* wasn't Martha."

"True, but she isn't a very nice person, is she?"

I thought about Campbell's little barbs and prickly intolerance, how she was certainly the one to spread the rumors that we were causing the weather disturbances. I never really understood why she hated the group so much, but maybe she really was just like the Puritans—judgmental and nasty toward people they don't understand.

"Don't worry," he added. "It's more inconvenient than anything else. I'm sure she isn't even sleeping in the room—it's more just that all her things are ice cubes. But maybe she learned something from it."

"Maybe," I say uncertainly. While I can't help but feel a little bit satisfied at the thought of Campbell bemoaning how frigid her room is and how all her books and clothes are unusable at the moment, I have no idea if it's going to make her change her ways.

Then Dr. Strange slid down the fence and sat next to me. "Any reason you're sitting here still? I thought you were going back from whence you came."

I pulled my cloak around me. "Just trying to collect myself."

"Ah." He nodded. "Same here." He eyed me with a smirk. "It seems I'm out of a job."

He taught Dr. Haverford's classes, I realized. He must be back, too. "Oh. Sorry about that."

He waved his hand. "No matter. I came because of the disruption in energy—your enemy. Had you not arrived, too, all her vile weather conditions would have remained. She might have kept disrupting the climate until something even worse happened." Then he pulled a cape around his shoulders. It was a cape I hadn't seen before, red with gold trim and beautiful embroidery. It made him look otherworldly. "I don't mind moving on. I'm sure there are other places that need me."

My gaze slid to the trunk at my feet. The bat had given up its incessant thumping, but every so often I heard it hiss and squeak. "So you're not after *this*?"

He shook his head. "No, Agatha. I'm not."

But that confused me. Why wouldn't he be? Doesn't everyone want the Darkhold?

Before I could ask, though, the strange doctor rose again and stretched. "I said this when I met you for the first time here, Agatha, but I hope you find what you're looking for." And then he gave me a long, solemn nod and walked away into the night.

I watched him disappear into the darkness. And I've been staring at the street where he disappeared for what seems like hours now.

I peer at the Witch Museum. In a few hours, the museums will open. Tourists will come and learn about the witch trials. Academy students will act as tour guides. People will study the names of accusers and victims on the wall. Right now, some of those names might be ones I know. Right now, maybe *my* name is even there—as a victim, as an accuser, it's hard to tell.

But it won't be forever. I don't know who I'll be able to save, but I have to at least try and protect Prudence. I'll search high and low for her. But as for the others? As for the trials themselves? How can I, as one witch, stop history from unfolding? I've seen enough history to know that sometimes people can't abide strong, outspoken, independent women. It scares them. It threatens them. Even if I rounded up my entire coven and took them to a safe place, who's to say the people of Salem won't find other women to blame? Is *that* why Old Agatha refused to help? Because she knew, deep down, that things were inevitable?

I have to go back and see. I have to make my own fate. I have to try.

Speaking of the Darkhold . . .

I look down at the battered leather trunk in my lap, finally feeling ready. Gingerly, I undo the latches and lift the lid. The bat glares up at me. It immediately starts to flap away, but I grab it with both hands and hold it steady. I stare into its beady little eyes, feeling a rush of satisfaction. All the effort I've put into finding this thing. I've nearly died. I've nearly gotten other people killed. I was dragged into this strange future time where . . . well, where things weren't so terrible.

But now I'm here. Now I'm holding the Darkhold in my hands. Something not even Martha could enchant back into its powerful form. It gives me a whoosh of pride: Maybe I *am* more powerful than she is. Maybe I always have been.

My hands shake as I recite the ancient words. I say them low, into the bat's ear, its fangs dangerously close to my neck. I feel the creature shifting and transforming in my hands, changing from its enchanted shape into something square and hard and heavy. A book lands in my lap with a satisfying *slap*. I've done it, I realize. I've transformed the bat. I'm holding the Darkhold.

Except something doesn't look right.

I stare at the leather cover. It's appropriately dusty, like it hasn't seen the light for hundreds of years, but I've envisioned the Darkhold for long enough that I know that its cover is a weathered brown, not a beat-up black. Also, the pages should be gilded, not deckle-edged. When I open up the book, the pages are blank. The moment the pages hit the light, they start to disintegrate. Within a few moments, I'm holding only ash.

The book is a fake.

I'm so numb I can't think. It's been a fake all along. Could Doctor Strange have known this? Maybe *that's* why he had no interest in taking it from me—because he knew it wasn't real? Still, I can't process this. Martha and I have both been following a false lead. The Darkhold isn't here. I have no idea who enchanted the bat and tricked me—not Firestar, since she isn't a witch, but maybe she had something to do with it?

And now I have to start all over.

I sit back against the bench and stare blankly at the statue of Roger Conant. His flowing robes, his large hat, standing atop a boulder. I never actually had to go to Salem in the first place. The Darkhold was never there. All of this agony . . . *for nothing.*

But then I start laughing. It's just so ridiculous. And also fitting, in a way—*of course* at the end of all this, I don't even get my prize. The only upshot is that Martha didn't get it, either. And when I really think about it, I don't have regrets. Maybe everything does happen for a reason. In some ways, going to 1691 Salem was a waste of time—the Darkhold wasn't even there. But it also brought me here. Which, if I'm being totally honest, wasn't a waste at all.

I dump the ashes of the fake book next to the statue. Maybe someone will find it and turn it in to one of the witch shops—I can only imagine the ridiculous spells and rituals they'll create with it for the tourists. Back to shake down my ancient sources, then, about where the Darkhold actually is. I'm not stopping my search. First, though, back to my Salem. I made a promise, even if half of those witches will be too stubborn to follow me. I have to at least try. And I certainly don't need the Darkhold to conjure up a portal. With my magic returned, I can do it myself.

I look over my shoulder at the sound of a car door slamming. People are starting their mornings. If I'm going to do this, I need to do it now. Summoning my strength, I conjure the portal in the small square of grass at Roger Conant's feet. If I've done this spell correctly, it will land me a few days before Prudence goes missing—I won't even have to rescue her from the Parrises' cellar. I've pictured talking to the coven, too. Warning them of what's to come. Some of them might not believe me, but maybe some will. I should probably give them a chance. You never know—I could find a few decent witches in there, as companionable as Jamira, Ivy, Francie, and Evan. It wouldn't *kill* me to be a little bit compassionate.

The portal vibrates. It takes all my magic to conjure,

and I can't linger too long, or it will close up. Suddenly, I hear rustling behind me, a noisy clank of a bell. Janice nudges against my hip. I burst out laughing.

"How did you get out of the gates?"

She bleats. *I wanted to find you.*

I groan. "Well, I'm actually leaving. Sorry."

*Can I come?*

The goat stares at me with her weird, rectangular pupils. While I want to groan and nudge her away, I can't. The stupid creature has weaseled her way into my heart.

An idea warms me then. Where I'm going, I can't take any friends . . . but I could certainly take a familiar. Janice will live just as well in 1691 as she does in 2025.

"Are you sure?" I ask, petting her neck. "It'll be a bumpy ride. And you absolutely *cannot* sleep in my cottage with me."

*Who are you kidding?* she says. *You know you'll let me.*

I roll my eyes. This goat totally has my number.

Janice eyes the portal, seemingly unafraid. I take the rope around her neck and guide her forward. I can feel its magnetic suck. But just before I dive in, I take one more look at this strange, modern Salem. The Witch Museum. The Witch Dungeon Museum. Conant Academy's spire in the distance. I shut my eyes, hoping I'm making the right choice.

"Let's get this over with, Janice," I mutter, taking the rope around her neck. And then we both step through.

The End